Aesop's Fables
Illustrated

Aesop's Fables Illustrated

Introduction by Ken Mondschein, PhD

Canterbury Classics
San Diego

Canterbury Classics
An imprint of Printers Row Publishing Group
9717 Pacific Heights Blvd, San Diego, CA 92121
www.canterburyclassicsbooks.com • mail@canterburyclassicsbooks.com

Publisher: Peter Norton
Associate Publisher: Ana Parker
Art Director: Charles McStravick
Senior Developmental Editor: April Graham
Editor: Angela Garcia
Production Team: Beno Chan, Julie Greene

Cover design: Linda Lee Mauri
Interior design: Linda Lee Mauri

Image credits: iStock/Getty/Sveta_Aho

Library of Congress Cataloging-in-Publication Data

Names: Aesop.
Title: Aesop's fables illustrated / Aesop.
Description: San Diego : Printers Row Publishing Group, 2023. | Summary: An illustrated collection of Aesop fables.
Identifiers: LCCN 2022040777 | ISBN 9781667201368 | ISBN 9781667204802 (ebook)
Subjects: LCSH: Fables, Greek--Translations into English. | CYAC: Fables. | Animals--Folklore. | LCGFT: Fables.
Classification: LCC PZ8.2 .A254 2023 | DDC 398.24/52--dc23/eng/20230210
LC record available at https://lccn.loc.gov/2022040777

Printed in China
27 26 25 24 23   1 2 3 4 5

Editor's Note: These works have been published in their original form to preserve the authors' intent and style.

CONTENTS

INTRODUCTION

AESOP'S FABLES

Dating back to Greek antiquity, Aesop's fables are the prototype of the "talking animal story"—a figure we can see everywhere from Geoffrey Chaucer's "The Nun's Priest's Tale" to Disney cartoons to Beatrix Potter's *Peter Rabbit*, Richard Adams's *Watership Down*, and George Orwell's *Animal Farm*. And, just as Aesop's fables have become the template for much of Western literature and media, so, too, has Aesop himself become a sort of archetype. Though dividing the historical Aesop, if he ever lived, from the long tradition of invented and elaborated biographies is a nigh-impossible task, these "fictional" biographies can tell us much about the impact of Aesop's fables, their millennia of reception, and the effect they have had on Western culture. Though we tend to think of Aesop as part of "classical" Greek literature claimed as patrimony by centuries of Europeans and inhabitants of the lands settled by Europeans, the fables also have a surprising connection to Africa and to the African diaspora.

WHAT IS A FABLE?

Before delving into Aesop's biography (if we can call it that), we should first look at the idea of what a *fable* is. Simply put, it is a story: the word *fable* ultimately derives from the Latin *fari*, "to speak." And, as anyone with even a cursory familiarity with Aesop's fables knows, they are teaching stories, meant to illustrate moral lessons, provide wisdom, or serve as examples. They usually, but not always, involve anthropomorphized animals. *Anthropomorphized*, here, does not necessarily mean animals who wear clothes and stand upright in the manner of a Disney cartoon, but rather animals endowed with human reason, speech, and intelligence. These animals, including their behaviors and their foibles, stand in for human beings as sorts of stock "types": the trickster, the innocent, the avaricious. Fables often contain humor, or at least an unexpected irony or reversal of fortune, which is related to their teaching purpose. Finally, they are usually simple and have a short plot with a single conflict. Characterization is similarly simple, with animals becoming types and symbols: saying "there was a wolf" is easier than establishing a character's amorality and rapaciousness. In short, they tell a truth through a clearly invented story.

Thus, "The Fox and the Grapes" tells us that we often despise that which we cannot get, while "The Goose That Laid the Golden Eggs" warns us not to spend our capital. "The Lion and the Mouse" shows the advantages of treating those we see as weaker or less powerful than we with kindness, "The Fox and the Stork" makes it clear that we need do unto others as we would have done unto us, and "The Wolf in Sheep's Clothing" is an admonition that our schemes may rebound upon us. These, of course, are only some of the best-known tales; many others are contained in this volume. However, they are illustrative of how fables can serve to demonstrate rhetorical points.

Fables are different from, but blend into, fairy tales. Fairy tales usually involve conflict between human beings or between human beings and supernatural creatures—even if the people or "fairies" may turn into animals. Furthermore, while fairy tales usually have a supernatural element, the fable's plot elements are usually naturalistic. In other words, in a fable, animals behave in a way that they would in nature and have understandable motivations such as hunger; they are stand-ins for human beings, not supernatural agents. Despite this, the human world is often present: even if human beings don't always appear, the animals in the fable may make use of human technology such as houses, dishes, and cups, and they are often domesticated animals, such as sheep or dogs. Just as predator versus prey (or weak versus strong) can be one axis of tension, so, too, can the contrast between the human domestic sphere and that of wild nature. Still, the distinctions are not hard and fast, and such authors as the Grimm Brothers include stories that we would recognize as fables (such as "Cat and Mouse in Partnership" and "The Death of the Little Hen") alongside more traditional fairy tales with supernatural elements (such as "Hansel and Gretel" and "Cinderella").

Today, we think of fables as suitable for children, but in the past, they were serious business. Aristotle discusses fables in the twentieth chapter of the second book of his *Rhetoric* as a sort of example that could be used in public speaking. Such speeches could be high stakes, indeed, such as criminal trials where the death penalty was possible, or political cases where the well-being of the city was at risk. Aristotle concludes his discourse on the use of fables by saying that the morals and points shown by fables or other fictional stories are easier to understand, but those taken from history are more intellectually satisfying. Fables, then, are a sort of philosophy, but an immediate sort that appeals to the intuitive, rather than the contemplative, mind.

THE LIFE AND AFTERLIFE OF AESOP

I f a real Aesop ever actually lived, he would have been born in the sixth or seventh century BC— well before the "classical" era of ancient Greece, and centuries before the earliest written record of his tales. Our source for Aesop's lifespan is Diodorus of Sicily, who lived in the first century BC and wrote that Aesop lived around the time of the Seven Sages of Greece, in the 600s BC—that is, 500 years before Diodorus's own time. Similarly, the earliest written collection of the *Fables* that we know of (if only by later references, since no manuscript survives) was written by Demetrius of Phalerum at least 300 years after Aesop's purported death. Any "historical" detail about his life therefore has more hearsay about it than fact.

More likely, rather than having any single authorship, the *Fables*—like the *Iliad* and the *Odyssey*— are a collection of folk tales and oral traditions gathered through the centuries. Indeed, we can read the prototypes of Aesop's fables on clay tablets dating back to ancient Mesopotamia, and similar stories exist in the Jewish Talmud, in classical Arabic literature, and in other Greek oral traditions, such as the narrative poetry attributed to Hesiod. Yet, just as there may have never been a historical Homer or Hesiod, the biography of Aesop that the Greeks and their inheritors shared is itself instructive because it tells us about the sort of person they thought *would* have written these stories.

So, who was the pseudohistorical Aesop? Passing references to him are peppered throughout the canon of classical Greek texts. Eugeon of Samos, who wrote around 500 BC and whose work survives only in fragments, says that he came from Thrace, the lands around the Black Sea northeast of Greece. Herodotus (c. 485–425 BC), in his *Histories*, relates that Aesop was enslaved to a man named Iadmon of Samos and won his freedom by telling stories; his fellow slave, Rhodopis, won her freedom by her beauty and became a famous courtesan. In his dialogue the *Phaedo*, Plato (c. 420s–340s BC) mentions Socrates as turning Aesop's fables into verse while in prison and, as we saw above, Plato's student Aristotle (384–322 BC) examines the use of fables such as Aesop's in public speaking. The playwright Aristophanes (c. 446–386 BC) has characters cite Aesop in this context, as well as in more comedic ways, in three of his comedies. Since such plays were meant for a broad audience, this shows that even common people of classical Athens were expected to be familiar with the *Fables* and their tropes.

Herodotus also alludes to Aesop meeting some sort of unnatural end in the Greek city of Delphi, and later writers fill in the details. The Greek writer Plutarch (AD 46–119) says that Aesop was in Delphi on a mission for the legendary King Croesus of Lydia (in what is now western Turkey), but the Delphians were insulted by his wit, so he was pushed off a cliff after being framed for stealing from the Temple of Apollo.

Perhaps most influential of all the ancient sources on the fabulist is the *Life of Aesop*, also called the Aesop Romance. This anonymous biography was apparently first written in the second century AD, though the first surviving copies are medieval. The *Life of Aesop* was perhaps partially based on earlier, now-lost texts, but more likely is almost wholly fanciful. It survives in numerous differing versions, with later copyists adding or taking away as they saw fit. Of all these versions, perhaps the best known is by the medieval scholar Maximus Planudes (c. 1260–1305), who lived in the declining years of the Byzantine Empire, the remnant of the Roman Empire that survived in the Greek-speaking eastern Mediterranean. Planudes's *Life*, which added elements of the biblical tale of Joseph, was soon translated into Latin, English, French, and German, and was widely circulated in western Europe by the fifteenth century.

All the differing versions of the *Life of Aesop* lay down the same broad strokes: He was born a slave—perhaps in Phrygia, in what is now central Turkey, or perhaps in Samos, an island in the northern Aegean Sea between Greece and Turkey. He was remarkably ugly—so much so that he scarcely seemed human—and incapable of speech. In other words, Aesop begins as the opposite of everything a Greek should be: enslaved rather than free, ugly as opposed to handsome, animalistic as opposed to eloquent—and, of course, a foreigner.

Despite his muteness, Aesop is highly intelligent and resourceful: he escapes an accusation of having stolen some figs by making himself vomit, showing he had not eaten them, and then causing his fellow slaves to vomit until the culprit is found. He also has a good heart: one day, he helps a priestess of Isis who has become lost. As a reward, the goddess grants him the abilities to speak eloquently and to invent stories. His overseer, fearing his newfound powers of speech, sells Aesop to a passing slave dealer, but, on account of Aesop's ugliness, the slave dealer can hardly give him away at the market. Aesop's new master, Xanthus, buys him cheaply. Xanthus claims to be a learned philosopher, but is, in reality, a vainglorious blowhard. Through a number of incidents, Aesop repeatedly shows himself to be both more clever and more virtuous than his master, and wins his freedom when Xanthus is called before the city assembly to interpret an omen. Xanthus, of course, cannot—though Aesop can. Since it is not fitting for a slave to address free men, Xanthus must free Aesop, who quickly interprets the future for the assembly and is rewarded.

After being freed, Aesop travels the world and wins fame and fortune as an advisor to kings, including the fantastically rich Croesus of Phrygia. Similarly, the king of Babylon is so grateful that he raises a golden statue of Aesop. The people of Delphi, however, refuse to pay Aesop for his wisdom, so he mocks them as worthless, since their ancestors were slaves—thus embodying the classical trope of *hubris*, or pride, since Aesop himself was once a slave. The Delphians' vengeance echoes Plutarch's account: they hide a golden cup taken from the Temple of Apollo in Aesop's luggage to frame him for theft and blasphemy. Sentenced to die by being pushed off a cliff, Aesop instead chooses to jump of his own volition.

Aesop as African?

Though our earliest sources have Aesop originating from Thrace, and later ones suggest Phrygia or Samos, there is also a medieval tradition of his originally hailing from Africa. For instance, the *Life of Aesop* says that he is "black-skinned." Building on this, Maximus Planudes claims that Aesop was "Ethiopian," and that his name was, in fact, a shortened version of that country's name. Of course, "Ethiopian," at the time, could mean anyone of African descent, no matter whether from East or West Africa. This perhaps points to a European cognizance of the long tradition of talking-animal morality stories in many African cultures. (Along with being attributed to Aesop, fables were also called "Libyan stories" by writers of antiquity—the Mediterranean coast of Libya becoming a metonym for all of Africa.) There was also an active market for enslaved Africans in the medieval eastern Mediterranean; so, it would have seemed natural to Planudes for Aesop to have come from there, whereas Samos, Phrygia, and Thrace had all long since been Christianized and were at least nominally part of the Byzantine Empire. Since it was forbidden for a Christian to enslave a Christian, a medieval writer would have needed to locate Aesop's origin elsewhere. (Today, of course, Samos, Phrygia, and Thrace are all part of Turkey, Greece, or Bulgaria; the Ottoman Turks ended the Byzantine Empire when they sacked Constantinople—modern Istanbul—in 1453.)

The idea of Aesop's African origins was both passed down and debated through the following centuries. The British illustrator Francis Barlow, in his 1666 edition of the *Fables*, agreed: he has Aesop identify himself as "a Negro," while Robert Dodsley, in his edition of the 1760s, says Aesop "was of a black complexion (whence some call him an Ethiopian) with thick lips, and splay feet," but nonetheless believed

Aesop was Phrygian. Dodsley's rendition of the *Fables* and his attribution of Aesop to Phrygia was, in turn, republished by the illustrator Thomas Bewick, together with new illustrations, in 1818.

Graphic depictions of Aesop also continued the African tradition. In the mid-1700s, the Chelsea porcelain factory in England produced porcelain figures of Aesop and his fables that showed him as distinctly African. Similarly, the intellectual William Godwin, father of Mary Shelley, published *Fables Ancient and Modern* in 1805. The frontispiece illustration has an African Aesop telling stories to young children. The Italian painter Roberto Fontana's 1876 painting *Aesop Narrates His Fables to the Handmaids of Xanthus* has him as indisputably African. In more modern times, Bill Cosby played Aesop in a 1971 TV production. (The illustrations in this edition are by Walter Crane and Arthur Rackham, whose lives are discussed below.)

The idea of Aesop's African-ness has also had a long afterlife—notably, in a book of tales attributed to another formerly enslaved storyteller of African descent; tales that had begun as an oral tradition but were appropriated by literati. Uncle Remus made his first appearance in print in Joel Chandler Harris's newspaper columns in the late nineteenth century, before they were collected in book form in 1881. Chandler Harris was likely familiar with the history of Aesop in creating his version of the character, but Uncle Remus's best-known incarnation is in Walt Disney's infamous 1946 adaptation, *Song of the South*, where he was played by James Franklin Baskett. Numerous critics have noted that in the details of his fictional biography, as well as his penchant for telling educational animal stories to children, Uncle Remus bears a striking resemblance to the African version of Aesop. This offers good grounds to claim Aesop as a cultural patrimony for Africa and African Americans. (One of the original *Fables*, however, entitled "The Ethiopian," has strong racial connotations and is not included in this volume.)

In the end, it is not important whether the historical figure, if he even existed, was Phrygian or African; it is that Aesop was thought to be moral, clever, and wise, and told entertaining stories that have survived centuries.

PUBLICATION HISTORY OF THE *FABLES*

The talking-animal story has had a long afterlife, and the body of *Fables* called "Aesop's" has been added to and elaborated on over the years. This is only natural: human beings understand the world through narrative, and encoding wisdom into simple stories that have been passed on for millennia helps us to transmit these lessons to the next generation. Some of the fables clearly predate Aesop and are found in the Talmud or even as far east as India; some are present only in the Latin sources; and some have been modified or added by later redactors. With careful analysis, however, the fables can be sorted by probable date; the American classicist Ben Edwin Perry (1892–1968) listed them by language and age, sorting out later additions and inventions. His *Index* is still used by scholars.

It was through Latin that Aesop's fables were introduced to medieval Europe. Although numerous

Latin translations were made throughout the era of the Roman Empire, perhaps the most important and widespread was by a pseudonymous "Romulus." This was the version most found in medieval scriptoria and used for the instruction of students, and the one from which most medieval redactions and translations into vernacular languages such as French and English were made. Many of these translations changed the material considerably, often by Christianizing it. The Renaissance rediscovered Greek learning, and scholars copied, published, and made numerous translations of the original Greek *Fables* as they had survived in Byzantine manuscripts. Aesop's fables, in both prose and verse, in the original Greek and in translations into French, German, English, and other European languages, were some of the earliest printed books; in fact, the first printed Aesop in English was published by John Caxton in 1484. Portuguese missionaries brought Aesop to Japan in the sixteenth century, and even after the Tokugawa Shogunate expelled European influence from the islands, the stories of *Esopo* continued to be printed.

This edition owes much to Dodsley and Bewick's versions from the eighteenth and early nineteenth centuries. However, just as Dodsley owed much to the seventeenth-century French translation produced by the mathematician, poet, and classical scholar Claude Gaspar Bachet de Méziriac, the editors of this volume have taken the stories from a variety of sources.

ABOUT THE ILLUSTRATIONS

This volume includes illustrations by Walter Crane (1845–1915), which have been reproduced in black-and-white, and by Arthur Rackham (1867–1939). Crane was a prolific and renowned English illustrator of children's books, and fully participated in the Victorian idealization of childhood as a special, protected time of life. His moralistic illustrations and poetic surmises of the fables participate in this: they are teaching stories to impart morality to the next generation. The anachronistic classicism of his art also bespeaks his time: he was influenced by both the Arts and Crafts Movement and the Pre-Raphaelites; later, he was also influenced by Japanese woodblock printing. His illustrations for *Baby's Own Aesop* were first published in 1887 in New York by George Routledge & Sons.

Arthur Rackham was another prolific and influential Victorian children's book illustrator, though he worked primarily in ink. He began his career as a newspaper reporter and illustrator but became a full-time book illustrator at the age of 27. Rackham specialized in fantasy art and was noted for his masterful use of line and evocative imagery. His illustrations for *Aesop's Fables* were published in London by William Heinemann in 1912.

Ken Mondschein, PhD
Northampton, Massachusetts
2023

The Fables

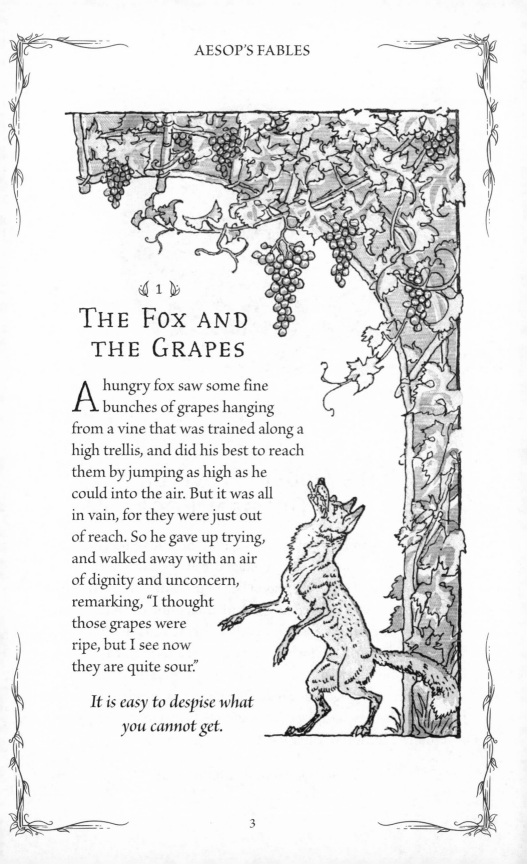

☙ 1 ❧
THE FOX AND THE GRAPES

A hungry fox saw some fine bunches of grapes hanging from a vine that was trained along a high trellis, and did his best to reach them by jumping as high as he could into the air. But it was all in vain, for they were just out of reach. So he gave up trying, and walked away with an air of dignity and unconcern, remarking, "I thought those grapes were ripe, but I see now they are quite sour."

It is easy to despise what you cannot get.

❧ 2 ❧

THE GOOSE THAT LAID
THE GOLDEN EGGS

A man and his wife had the good fortune to possess a goose which laid a golden egg every day. Lucky though they were, they soon began to think they were not getting rich fast enough, and, imagining the bird must be made of gold inside, they decided to kill it in order to secure the whole store of precious metal at once. But when they cut it open they found it was just like any other goose. Thus, they neither got rich all at once, as they had hoped, nor enjoyed any longer the daily addition to their wealth.

Much wants more and loses all.

THE CAT AND THE MICE

There was once a house that was overrun with mice. A cat heard of this, and said to herself, "That's the place for me," and off she went and took up her quarters in the house, and caught the mice one by one and ate them. At last the mice could stand it no longer, and they determined to take to their holes and stay there. "That's awkward," said the cat to herself. "The only thing to do is to coax them out by a trick." So she considered a while, and then climbed up the wall and let herself hang down by her hind legs from a peg, and pretended to be dead. By and by a mouse peeped out and saw the cat hanging there. "Aha!" it cried, "you're very clever, madam, no doubt; but you may turn yourself into a bag of meal hanging there, if you like, yet you won't catch us coming anywhere near you."

If you are wise you won't be deceived
by the innocent airs of those whom you
have once found to be dangerous.

THE MISCHIEVOUS DOG

There was once a dog who used to snap at people and bite them without any provocation, and who was a great nuisance to everyone who came to his

master's house. So his master fastened a bell around his neck to warn people of his presence. The dog was very proud of the bell, and strutted about tinkling it with immense satisfaction. But an old dog came up to him and said, "The fewer airs you give yourself the better, my friend. You don't think, do you, that your bell was given you as a reward of merit? On the contrary, it is a badge of disgrace."

Notoriety is often mistaken for fame.

⚜ 5 ⚜
THE CHARCOAL BURNER AND THE FULLER

There was once a charcoal burner who lived and worked by himself. A fuller, however, happened to come and settle in the same neighborhood; and the charcoal burner, having made his acquaintance and finding he was an agreeable sort of fellow, asked him if he would come and share his house: "We shall get to know one another better that way," he said, "and, beside, our household expenses will be diminished." The fuller thanked him, but replied, "I couldn't think of it, sir: why, everything I take such pains to whiten would be blackened in no time by your charcoal."

Like will draw like.

❦ 6 ❧
THE WOLF AND THE SHEPHERDS

A Wolf, chancing to pass a Shepherd's hut, saw some Shepherds making merry over a joint of mutton. "A pretty row," quoth he, "would these Men have raised if they had caught me at such a supper."

Men are apt to condemn in others the very thing they themselves practice.

❦ 7 ❧
THE BULL AND THE GOAT

A Bull, being pursued by a Lion, spied a cave and fled towards it, meaning to take shelter there. A Goat came to the mouth of the cave, and, menacing the Bull with his horns, disputed the passage. The Bull, having no time to lose, was obliged to make off again without delay, but not before saying to the Goat, "Were it not for the Lion that is behind me, I would soon let you know the difference between a Bull and a Goat."

Valor does not always show itself in blows.

THE LAMB AND THE WOLF

A Flock of Sheep were feeding in a meadow while their Dogs were asleep, and their Shepherd at a distance, playing on his pipe beneath the shade of a spreading elm. A young, inexperienced Lamb, observing a half-starved Wolf peering through the pales of the enclosure, entered into conversation with him. "Pray, what are you seeking for here?" said the Lamb. "I am looking," replied the Wolf, "for some tender grass; for nothing, you know, is more pleasant than to feed in a fresh pasture, and to slake one's thirst at a crystal stream, both of which I perceive you enjoy here. Happy creature," continued he, "how much I envy your lot, who are in full possession of the utmost I desire; for philosophy has long taught me to be satisfied with a little!" "It seems, then," returned the Lamb, "that those who say you feed on flesh accuse you falsely, since a little grass will easily content you. If this be true, let us for the future live like brethren, and feed together." So saying, the simple Lamb crept through the fence, and at once became a prey to the pretended philosopher, and a sacrifice to his own inexperience and credulity.

Experience is a dear school, but
fools will learn in no other.

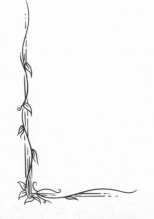

THE MICE IN COUNCIL

Once upon a time all the mice met together in council, and discussed the best means of securing themselves against the attacks of the cat. After several suggestions had been debated, a mouse of some standing and experience got up and said, "I think I have hit upon a plan which will ensure our safety in the future, provided you approve and carry it out. It is that we should fasten a bell around the neck of our enemy the cat, which will by its tinkling warn us of her approach." This proposal was warmly applauded, and

it had been already decided to adopt it, when an old mouse got upon his feet and said, "I agree with you all that the plan before us is an admirable one. But may I ask who is going to bell the cat?"

⚜ 10 ⚜
AESOP AND THE POULTRY

The populace of the neighborhood in which Aesop was a slave, one day observed him attentively overlooking some Poultry in an enclosed fence that was near the roadside; and those speculative wits, who spend more time prying into other people's concerns, to no purpose than in adjusting their own, were moved with curiosity to know why this philosopher should bestow his attention on those animals. "I am struck," replied Aesop, "to see how mankind so readily imitate this foolish animal." "In what?" asked the neighbors. "Why, in crowing well and scraping so ill," replied Aesop.

It is far more easy to talk boldly than to act nobly.

⚜ 11 ⚜
THE BEE AND THE CUCKOO

A Bee, flying out of his hive, said to a Cuckoo, who was chanting on a bush hard by, "Peace! Why do you not leave off your harsh monotonous pipe? There never was a bird who had such a tiresome unvaried song as you have: Cuckoo, cuckoo, cuckoo, and cuckoo again and again."—"Oh," cries the Cuckoo, "I wonder you find fault with my note, which is at least as much varied as your labors; for if you had a hundred hives to fill, you would make them all exactly alike: if I invent nothing new, surely everything you do is as old as the creation of the world." To which the Bee replied: "I allow it; but in useful arts the want of variety is never an objection. But in works of taste and amusement, monotony is of all things to be avoided."

Those who do not have the capacity to judge works of art and taste expose themselves to ridicule when they assume the critic.

⁕ 12 ⁕

THE WIDOW AND HER SHEEP

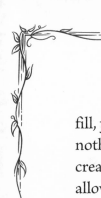A certain poor Widow had one solitary Sheep. At shearing time, wishing to take his fleece, and to avoid expense, she sheared him herself, but used the shears so unskillfully that with the fleece she sheared the flesh. The Sheep, writhing with pain, said: "Why do you hurt me so, Mistress? What weight can my blood add to the wool? If you want my flesh, there is the butcher, who will kill me in a trice; but if you want my fleece and wool, there is the shearer, who will shear and not hurt me."

The least outlay is not always the greatest gain.

❧ 13 ❧

THE BAT AND THE WEASELS

A bat fell to the ground and was caught by a weasel, and was just going to be killed and eaten when it begged to be let go. The weasel said he couldn't do that because he was an enemy of all birds on principle. "Oh, but," said the bat, "I'm not a bird at all. I'm a mouse." "So you are," said the weasel, "now I come to look at you." And he let it go. Some time after this the bat was caught in just the same way by another weasel, and, as before, begged for its life. "No," said the weasel, "I never let a mouse go by any chance." "But I'm not a mouse," said the bat. "I'm a bird." "Why, so you are," said the weasel; and he too let the bat go.

*Look and see which way the wind blows
before you commit yourself.*

❧ 14 ❧

THE DOG AND THE SOW

A dog and a sow were arguing and each claimed that its own young ones were finer than those of any other animal. "Well," said the sow at last, "mine can see, at any rate, when they come into the world; but yours are born blind."

⚜ 15 ⚜
THE WOLF
AND THE
LAMB

A wolf came upon a lamb straying from the flock, and felt some compunction about taking the life of so helpless a creature without some plausible excuse; so he cast about for a grievance and said at last, "Last year, sirrah, you grossly insulted me." "That is impossible, sir," bleated the lamb, "for I wasn't born then." "Well," retorted the wolf, "you feed in my pastures." "That cannot be," replied the lamb, "for I have never yet tasted grass." "You drink from my spring, then," continued the wolf. "Indeed, sir," said the poor lamb, "I have never yet drunk anything but my mother's milk." "Well, anyhow," said the wolf, "I'm not going without my dinner." And he sprang upon the lamb and devoured it without more ado.

Any excuse will serve a tyrant.

❧ 16 ❧

THE PASSENGER
AND THE PILOT

It had blown a violent storm at sea, and the whole crew of a vessel were in imminent danger of shipwreck. After the rolling of the waves was somewhat abated, a certain Passenger, who had never been to sea before, observing the Pilot to have appeared wholly unconcerned, even in their greatest danger, had the curiosity to ask him what death his father died, "What death?" said the Pilot; "why, he perished at sea, as my grandfather did before him." "And are you not afraid of trusting yourself to an element that has proved thus fatal to your family?" "Afraid? by no means; why, we must all die: is not your father dead?" "Yes, but he died in his bed." "And, why, then, are you not afraid of trusting yourself in your bed?" "Because I am there perfectly secure." "It may be so," replied the Pilot; "but if the hand of Providence is equally extended over all places, there is no more reason for me to be afraid of going to sea than for you to be afraid of going to bed."

Faith is not a relative matter.

◊ 17 ◊

THE SPARROW AND THE HARE

A Hare, being seized by an Eagle, cried out in a piteous manner. A Sparrow sitting on a tree close by, so far from pitying the poor animal, made merry at his expense. "Why did you stay there to be taken?" said he. "Could not so swift a creature as you have easily escaped from an Eagle?" Just then a Hawk swooped down and carried off the Sparrow, who, when he felt the Hawk's talons in his sides, cried still more loudly than the Hare. The Hare, in the agonies of death, received comfort from the fact that the fate of the mocking Sparrow was no better than his own.

When calamity overtakes the hard-hearted they receive no sympathy.

◊ 18 ◊

AESOP AND HIS FELLOW SERVANTS

A Merchant, who was at one time Aesop's master, ordered all things to be got ready for an intended journey. When the burdens were being shared among the Servants, Aesop requested that he might have the lightest. He was told to choose for himself, and he took up the basket of bread. The other Servants laughed, for that was the largest and heaviest of all. When dinnertime came, Aesop, who had with some difficulty sustained his load, was told to distribute an equal share of bread all round. He did so, and this lightened his burden one-half; and when suppertime arrived he got rid of the rest. For the remainder of the journey he had nothing but the empty basket to carry, and the other Servants, whose loads seemed to get heavier and heavier at every step, could not but applaud his ingenuity.

Ingenuity lightens labor.

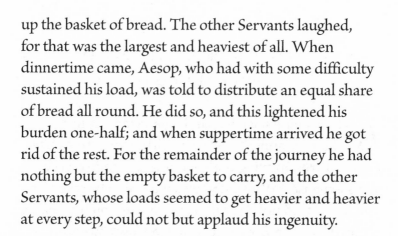

⚜ 19 ⚜

THE MAN AND THE STONE

Aesop was sent one day by his master Xanthus to see what company were at the public bath. He saw that many who came stumbled, both going in and coming out, over a large Stone that lay at the entrance to the bath, and that only one person had the good sense to remove it. He returned and told his master that there was only one Man at the bath. Xanthus accordingly went, and finding it full of people, demanded of Aesop why he had told him falsely. Aesop replied that only he who had removed the Stone could be considered a Man, and that the rest were not worthy the name.

A man is judged by his deeds.

⟨ 20 ⟩

THE HARE WITH MANY FRIENDS

A Hare was very popular with the other beasts, who all claimed to be her friends. But one day she heard the hounds approaching and hoped to escape them by the aid of her many Friends. So she went to the horse, and asked him to carry her away from the hounds on his back. But he declined, stating that he had important work to do for his master. He felt sure, he said, that all her other friends would come to her assistance. She then applied to the bull, and hoped that he would repel the hounds with his horns. The bull replied: I am very sorry, but I have an appointment with a lady; but I feel sure that our friend the goat will do what you want. The goat, however, feared that his back might do her some harm if he took her upon it. The ram, he felt sure, was the proper friend to apply to. So she went to the ram and told him the case. The ram replied: Another time, my dear friend. I do not like to interfere on the present occasion, as hounds have been known to eat sheep as well as hares. The Hare then applied, as a last hope, to the calf, who regretted that he was unable to help her, as he did not like to take the responsibility upon himself, as so many persons older than himself had declined the task. By this time the hounds were quite near, and the Hare took to her heels and luckily escaped.

He that has many friends, has no friends.

21

THE FOX AND THE CROW

A crow was sitting on a branch of a tree with a piece of cheese in her beak when a fox observed her and set his wits to work to discover some way of getting the cheese. Coming and standing under the tree he looked up and said, "What a noble bird I see above me! Her beauty is without equal, the hue of her plumage exquisite. If only her voice is as sweet as her looks are fair, she ought without doubt to be queen of the birds." The crow was hugely flattered by this, and just to show the fox that she could sing she gave a loud caw. Down came the cheese, of course, and the fox, snatching it up, said, "You have a voice, madam, I see. What you want is wits."

Do not trust flatterers.

The Fox and the Crow

❧ 22 ❧

THE COCK AND THE FOX

One bright spring morning a Cock, perched among the branches of a lofty tree, crowed loud and long. The shrillness of his voice echoed through the wood, and the well-known note brought a Fox, who was prowling in quest of prey, to the spot. Reynard, seeing that the Cock was at a great height, set his wits to work to find some way of bringing him down. He saluted the Bird in his mildest voice, and said, "Have you not heard, cousin, of the proclamation of peace and harmony among all kinds of Beasts and Birds? We are no longer to prey upon and devour one another, but love and friendship are to be the order of the day. Do come down, and we will talk over this great news at our leisure." The Cock, who knew that the Fox was only at his old tricks, pretended to be watching something in the distance. Finally the Fox asked him what it was he looked at so earnestly. "Why," said the Cock, "I think I see a pack of Hounds yonder." "Oh, then," said the Fox, "your humble servant; I must be gone." "Nay, cousin," said the Cock; "pray do not go: I am just coming down. You are surely not afraid of Dogs in these peaceable times!" "No, no," said the Fox; "but ten to one they have not heard of the proclamation yet."

'Tis a poor rule that will not work both ways.

❧ 23 ❧
GENIUS, VIRTUE, AND REPUTATION

Genius, Virtue, and Reputation, three great friends, agreed to travel over the island of Great Britain, to see whatever might be worthy of observation. But as some misfortune, said they, may happen to separate us, let us consider before we set out, by what means we may find each other again. Should it be my ill fate, said Genius, to be severed from my friends, which heaven forbid! you may find me kneeling in devotion before the tomb of Shakespeare; or rapt in some grove where Milton talked with angels; or musing in the grotto where Pope caught inspiration. Virtue, with a sigh, acknowledged, that her friends were not very numerous; but were I to lose you, she cried, with whom I am at present so happily united, I should choose to take sanctuary in the temples of religion, in the palaces of royalty, or in the stately domes of ministers of state; but as it may be my ill fortune to be there denied admittance, inquire for some cottage where contentment has a bower, and there you will certainly find me. Ah, my dear friends, said Reputation very earnestly, you, I perceive, when missing, may possibly be recovered; but take care, I entreat you, always to keep sight of me, for if I am once lost, I am never to be retrieved.

There are few things which can be so
irreparably lost as reputation.

✥ 24 ✥

THE HORSE AND
THE GROOM

There was once a groom who used to spend long hours clipping and combing the horse of which he had charge, but who daily stole a portion of his allowance of oats, and sold it for his own profit. The horse gradually got into worse and worse condition, and at last cried to the groom, "If you really want me to look sleek and well, you must comb me less and feed me more."

A man may smile yet be a villain.

✥ 25 ✥

THE PEACOCK AND
THE CRANE

A peacock taunted a crane with the dullness of her plumage. "Look at my brilliant colors," said she, "and see how much finer they are than your poor feathers." "I am not denying," replied the crane, "that yours are far gayer than mine; but when it comes to flying I can soar into the clouds, whereas you are confined to the earth like any dunghill cock."

Fine feathers don't make fine birds.

⟨ 26 ⟩

THE CAT AND THE BIRDS

A cat heard that the birds in an aviary were ailing. So he got himself up as a doctor, and, taking with him a set of the instruments proper to his profession, presented himself at the door, and inquired after the health of the birds. "We shall do very well," they replied, without letting him in, "when we've seen the last of you."

A villain may disguise himself, but
he will not deceive the wise.

⟨ 27 ⟩

THE SPECTACLES

Jupiter one day, enjoying himself over a bowl of nectar, and in a merry humor, determined to make mankind a present. Momus was appointed to convey it to them; who mounted on a rapid car, was presently on earth. Come hither, says he, ye happy mortals, great Jupiter has opened for your benefit his all-gracious hands. It is true, he made you somewhat short-sighted, but to remedy that inconvenience, behold how he has favored you! So saying, he unloosed his portmanteau; an infinite number of spectacles tumbled out, and mankind picked them up with great eagerness. There was enough for all, every man had his pair. But it was soon found that these spectacles did not represent objects to all mankind alike, for one pair was purple, another blue; one was white, and another black; some of the glasses were red, some green, and some yellow. In short, there were all manner of colors, and every shade of color. However, notwithstanding this diversity, every man was charmed with his own, as believing it the best, and enjoyed in opinion, all the satisfaction of truth.

Our opinions of things are altogether as various as though each saw them through a different medium; our attachments to these opinions as fixed and firm are as though all saw them through the medium of truth.

28

THE MOCKING BIRD

There is a certain Bird in America which has the faculty of mimicking the notes of every other songster, without being able himself to add any original strains to the concert. As one of these Mocking Birds was displaying his talent of ridicule among the branches of a venerable wood, " 'Tis very well," said a little warbler, speaking in the name of all the rest; "we grant you that our music is not without its faults; but why will you not favor us with a strain of your own?"

Many ridicule the things that they themselves cannot do.

29

THE TWO SCYTHES

It so happened that a couple of mower's Scythes were placed together in the same barn: one of them was without its proper handle, and therefore remained useless and rusty; the other was complete, bright, and in good order, and was frequently made use of in the hands of the mowers. "My good neighbor," said the rusty one, "I much pity you, who labor so much for the good of others, and withal so constantly are fretted with that odious whetstone, that scours you till you strike fire, whilst I repose in perfect ease and quiet." — "Give me leave," replied the bright one, "to explain to you, neighbor, the difference of our conditions: I must own that I labor, but then I am well rewarded in consideration that it is for the benefit of multitudes; and this gives me all my importance: it is true also that I am renovated by a harsh whetstone, but this still increases my capability to become useful in a more powerful degree: whilst you remain the insignificant and helpless victim of your pride and idleness, and in the end fall a prey to a devouring rust, useless, unpitied, and unknown."

Idleness in every station in life is attended by a portion of misery.

⚜ 30 ⚜
THE YOUNG MOUSE, THE COCK, AND THE CAT

A Young Mouse, on his return to his hole after leaving it for the first time, thus recounted his adventures to his Mother. "Mother," said he, "quitting this narrow place where you have brought me up, I rambled about today like a Mouse of spirit, who wished to see and to be seen, when two such notable creatures came in my way! One was so gracious, so gentle and benign! The other, who was just as noisy and forbidding, had on his head and under his chin, pieces of raw meat, which shook at every step he took; and then, all at once, beating his sides with the utmost fury, he uttered such a harsh and piercing cry that I fled in terror; and this, too, just as I was about to introduce myself to the other stranger, who was covered with fur like our own, only richer-looking and much more beautiful, and who seemed so modest and benevolent that it did my heart good to look at her." "Ah, my son," replied the Old Mouse, "learn while you live to distrust appearances. The first strange creature was nothing but a Fowl, that will ere long be killed, and off his bones, when put on a dish in the pantry, we may make a delicious supper; while the other was a nasty, sly, and bloodthirsty hypocrite of a Cat, to whom no food is so welcome as a young and juicy little Mouse like yourself."

Do not trust appearances.

◁ 31 ▷
THE ASS AND THE FROGS

An Ass, carrying a load of wood, passed through a pond. As he was crossing through the water he lost his footing, and stumbled and fell, and not being able to rise on account of his load, he groaned heavily. Some Frogs frequenting the pool heard his lamentation, and said, "What would you do if you had to live here always as we do, when you make such a fuss about a mere fall into the water?"

Men often bear little grievances with less
courage than they do large misfortunes.

⚜ 32 ⚜
THE SPENDTHRIFT
AND THE SWALLOW

A spendthrift, who had wasted his fortune, and had nothing left but the clothes in which he stood, saw a swallow one fine day in early spring. Thinking that summer had come, and that he could now do without his coat, he went and sold it for what it would fetch. A change, however, took place in the weather, and there came a sharp frost which killed the unfortunate swallow. When the spendthrift saw its dead body he cried, "miserable bird! Thanks to you I am perishing of cold myself."

One swallow does not make summer.

⚜ 33 ⚜
THE MOON AND
HER MOTHER

The moon once begged her mother to make her a gown. "How can I?" replied she; "there's no fitting your figure. At one time you're a new moon, and at another you're a full moon; and between whiles you're neither one nor the other."

The Moon and Her Mother

❦ 34 ❦
THE OLD WOMAN
AND THE DOCTOR

An old woman became almost totally blind from a disease of the eyes, and, after consulting a doctor, made an agreement with him in the presence of witnesses that she should pay him a high fee if he cured her, while if he failed he was to receive nothing. The doctor accordingly prescribed a course of treatment, and every time he paid her a visit he took away with him some article out of the house, until at last, when he visited her for the last time, and the cure was complete, there was nothing left. When the old woman saw that the house was empty she refused to pay him his fee; and, after repeated refusals on her part, he sued her before the magistrates for payment of her debt. On being brought into court she was ready with her defense. "The claimant," said she, "has stated the facts about our agreement correctly. I undertook to pay him a fee if he cured me, and he, on his part, promised to charge nothing if he failed. Now, he says I am cured; but I say that I am blinder than ever, and I can prove what I say. When my eyes were bad I could at any rate see well enough to be aware that my house contained a certain amount of furniture and other things; but now, when according to him I am cured, I am entirely unable to see anything there at all."

He who plays a trick must be prepared to take a joke.

35

MERCURY AND THE WOODMAN

A woodman was felling a tree on the bank of a river, when his ax, glancing off the trunk, flew out of his hands and fell into the water. As he stood by the water's edge lamenting his loss, Mercury appeared and asked him the reason for his grief; and on learning what had happened, out of pity for his distress he dived into the river and, bringing up a golden ax, asked him if that was the one he had lost. The woodman replied that it was not, and Mercury then dived a second time, and, bringing up a silver ax, asked if that was his. "No, that is not mine either," said the woodman. Once more Mercury dived into the river, and brought up the missing ax. The woodman was overjoyed at recovering his property, and thanked his benefactor warmly; and the latter was so pleased with his honesty that he made him a present of the other two axes. When the woodman told the story to his companions, one of these was filled with envy of his good fortune and determined to try his luck for himself. So he went and began to fell a tree at the edge of the river, and presently contrived to let his ax drop into the water. Mercury appeared as before, and, on learning that his ax had fallen in, he dived and brought up a golden ax, as he had done on the previous occasion. Without waiting to be asked whether it was his or not the fellow cried, "That's mine, that's mine," and stretched out his hand eagerly for the prize. But Mercury was so disgusted at

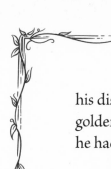

his dishonesty that he not only declined to give him the golden ax, but also refused to recover for him the one he had let fall into the stream.

Honesty is the best policy.

⚜ 36 ⚜
THE ASS, THE FOX, AND THE LION

An ass and a fox went into partnership and sallied out to forage for food together. They hadn't gone far before they saw a lion coming their way, at which they were both dreadfully frightened. But the fox thought he saw a way of saving his own skin, and went boldly up to the lion and whispered in his ear, "I'll manage that you shall get hold of the ass without the trouble of stalking him, if you'll promise to let me go free." The lion agreed to this, and the fox then rejoined his companion and contrived before long to lead him by a hidden pit, which some hunter had dug as a trap for wild animals, and into which he fell. When the lion saw that the ass was safely caught and couldn't get away, it was to the fox that he first turned his attention, and he soon finished him off, and then at his leisure proceeded to feast upon the ass.

Betray a friend, and you'll often find
you have ruined yourself.

❧ 37 ❧
THE LION AND THE MOUSE

A lion asleep in his lair was waked up by a mouse running over his face. Losing his temper he seized it with his paw and was about to kill it. The mouse, terrified, piteously entreated him to spare its life. "Please let me go," it cried, "and one day I will repay you for your kindness." The idea of so insignificant a creature ever being able to do anything for him amused the lion so much that he laughed aloud, and good-humoredly let it go. But the mouse's chance came, after all. One day the lion got entangled in a net which had been spread for game by some hunters, and the mouse heard and recognized his roars of anger and ran to the spot. Without more ado it set to work to gnaw the ropes with its teeth, and succeeded before long in setting the lion free. "There!" said the mouse, "you laughed at me when I promised I would repay you: but now you see, even a mouse can help a lion."

No act of kindness, no matter how small, is ever wasted.

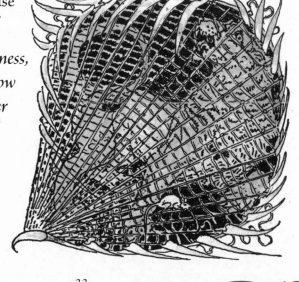

⚜ 38 ⚜
THE FATAL COURTSHIP

The freed Lion, spoken of in the last Fable, was so grateful to the Mouse, that he told him to name what he most desired, and he should have his wish. The Mouse, fired with ambition, said, "I desire the hand of your daughter in marriage." This the Lion good-naturedly gave him, and called the young Lioness to come that way. She did so; and rushed up so heedlessly that she did not see her small suitor, but placed her paw on him and crushed him to death.

Bad wishing makes bad getting.

❧ 39 ❧

THE FOX AND THE SICK LION

It was reported that the Lion was sick and confined to his den, where he would be happy to see any of his subjects who might come to pay the homage that was due to him. Many accordingly went in, and fell an easy prey to the old Lion, who devoured them at his leisure. But it was observed that the Fox very carefully kept away. The Lion noticed his absence, and sent one of his Jackals to express a hope that he would show he was not insensible to motives of respect and charity, by coming and paying his duty like the rest. The Fox told the Jackal to offer his sincerest reverence to his master, and to say that he had more than once been on the point of coming to see him. "But the truth of the matter," he observed dryly, "is that all the footprints I see go into the cave, but none come out again. So for the present my health demands that I stay away."

It is wise to see our way out before we venture in.

❧ 40 ❧

THE THIEF AND THE BOY

A Boy sat weeping upon the side of a well. A Thief happening to come by just at the same time, asked him why he wept. The Boy, sighing and sobbing,

showed a bit of cord, and said that a silver tankard had come off from it, and was now at the bottom of the well. The Thief pulled off his clothes and went down into the well, meaning to keep the tankard for himself. Having groped about for some time without finding it, he came up again and found not only the Boy gone, but his own clothes also, the dissembling rogue having made off with them.

It takes a thief to catch a thief.

41

THE MOUSE AND THE WEASEL

A lean and hungry Mouse once pushed his way, not without some trouble, through a small hole into a corn-crib, and there fed for some time so busily, that when he would have returned by the same way he entered, he found himself too plump to get through the hole, push as hard as he might. A Weasel, who had great fun in watching the vain struggles of his fat friend, called to him, and said, "Listen to me, my good Mouse. There is but one way to get out, and that is to wait till you have become as lean as when you first got in."

The remedy is often as bad as the disease.

◁ 42 ▷
THE CROW AND
THE PITCHER

A thirsty crow found a pitcher with some water in it, but so little was there that, try as she might, she could not reach it with her beak, and it seemed as though she would die of thirst within sight of the remedy. At last she hit upon a clever plan. She began dropping pebbles into the pitcher, and with each pebble the water rose a little higher until at last it reached the brim, and the knowing bird was enabled to quench her thirst.

Necessity is the mother of invention.

❧ 43 ❧
THE HOUNDS IN COUPLES

A Huntsman was leading forth his Hounds one morning to the chase, and had linked several of the young dogs in couples, to prevent them from following every scent, and hunting disorderly, as their own inclinations and fancy should direct them. Among others, it was the fate of Jowler and Vixen to be thus yoked together. Jowler and Vixen were both young and inexperienced, but had for some time been constant companions, and seemed to have entertained a great fondness for each other. They used to be perpetually playing together; and in any quarrel that happened, always took one another's part. It might have been expected, therefore, that it would not have been disagreeable to them to be still more closely united. However, in fact it proved otherwise; they had not been long joined together before both parties were observed to express uneasiness at their present situation. Different inclinations and opposite wills began to discover and to exert themselves. If one chose to go this way, the other was as eager to take the contrary; if one was pressing forward, the other was sure to lag behind; Vixen pulled back Jowler, and Jowler dragged along Vixen; Jowler growled at Vixen, and Vixen snapped at Jowler; till at last it came to a downright quarrel between them, and Jowler treated Vixen in a very rough and ungenerous manner, without any regard to the inferiority of her strength or the tenderness of her sex. As they were thus continually

vexing and tormenting each other, an old hound, who had observed all that had passed, came up to them and thus reproved them: "What a couple of silly puppies you are, to be perpetually worrying yourselves at this rate! What hinders your going on peaceably and quietly together? Can't you compromise the matter between you by each consulting the other's inclination a little? When I was in the same circumstances with you, I soon found that thwarting my companion was only tormenting myself; and my yoke-fellow happily came into the same way of thinking."

Mutual compliances are necessary
to matrimonial happiness.

⚜ 44 ⚜
THE LION AND THE EAGLE

An Eagle stayed his flight, and entreated a Lion to make an alliance with him to their mutual advantage. The Lion replied, "I have no objection, but you must excuse me for requiring you to find surety for your good faith; for how can I trust any one as a friend, who is able to fly away from his bargain whenever he pleases?"

Try before you trust.

❦ 45 ❧
THE BOYS AND THE FROGS

Some mischievous boys were playing on the edge of a pond, and, catching sight of some frogs swimming about in the shallow water, they began to amuse themselves by pelting them with stones, and they killed several of them. At last one of the frogs put his head out of the water and said, "Oh, stop! Stop! I beg of you. What is sport to you is death to us."

One man's pleasure is another man's pain.

❦ 46 ❧
THE NORTH WIND
AND THE SUN

A dispute arose between the north wind and the sun, each claiming that he was stronger than the other. At last they agreed to try their powers upon a traveler, to see which could soonest strip him of his cloak. The north wind had the first try; and, gathering up all his force for the attack, he came whirling furiously down upon the man, and caught up his cloak as though he would wrest it from him by one single effort. But the harder he blew, the more closely the man wrapped it around himself. Then came the turn of the sun. At first he beamed gently upon the traveler, who soon unclasped his cloak and walked on with it hanging loosely about his shoulders. Then he shone forth in his full strength, and the man, before he had gone many steps, was glad to throw his cloak right off and complete his journey more lightly clad.

Persuasion is better than force.

The North Wind and the Sun

❧ 47 ❧
THE MISTRESS AND
HER SERVANTS

A widow, thrifty and industrious, had two servants, whom she kept pretty hard at work. They were not allowed to lie long abed in the mornings, but the old lady had them up and doing as soon as the cock crew. They disliked intensely having to get up at such an hour, especially in wintertime: and they thought that if it were not for the cock waking up their mistress so horribly early, they could sleep longer. So they caught it and wrung its neck. But they weren't prepared for the consequences. For what happened was that their mistress, not hearing the cock crow as usual, waked them up earlier than ever, and set them to work in the middle of the night.

❧ 48 ❧
THE GOODS AND THE ILLS

There was a time in the youth of the world when goods and ills entered equally into the concerns of men, so that the goods did not prevail to make them altogether blessed, nor the ills to make them wholly miserable. But owing to the foolishness of mankind the ills multiplied greatly in number and increased in strength, until it seemed as though they would deprive the goods of all share in human affairs, and banish them from the earth. The latter, therefore, betook themselves to heaven and complained to Jupiter of the treatment they had received, at the same time praying him to grant them protection from the ills, and to advise them concerning the manner of their intercourse with men. Jupiter granted their request for protection, and decreed that for the future they should not go among men openly in a body, and so be liable to attack from the hostile ills, but singly and unobserved, and at infrequent and unexpected intervals. Hence it is that the earth is full of ills, for they come and go as they please and are never far away; while goods, alas, come one by one only, and have to travel all the way from heaven, so that they are very seldom seen.

⪦ 49 ⪧

THE HARES AND THE FROGS

The hares once gathered together and lamented the unhappiness of their lot, exposed as they were to dangers on all sides and lacking the strength and the courage to hold their own. Men, dogs, birds, and beasts of prey were all their enemies, and killed and devoured them daily; and sooner than endure such persecution any longer, they one and all determined to end their miserable lives. Thus resolved and desperate, they rushed in a body toward a neighboring pool, intending to drown themselves. On the bank were sitting a

number of frogs, who, when they heard the noise of the hares as they ran, with one accord leaped into the water and hid themselves in the depths. Then one of the older hares who was wiser than the rest cried out to his companions, "Stop, my friends, take heart; don't let us destroy ourselves after all. See, here are creatures who are afraid of us, and who must, therefore, be still more timid than ourselves."

There is always someone worse off than yourself.

◁ 50 ▷

THE ASS EATING THISTLES

An Ass laden with very choice provisions, which he was carrying in harvest-time to the field for his master and the reapers, stopped by the way to eat a large and strong Thistle that grew by the roadside. "Many people would wonder," said he, "that with such delicate viands within reach, I do not touch them; but to me this bitter and prickly Thistle is more savory and relishing than anything else in the world."

What is one man's meat is another man's poison.

◁ 51 ▷

THE APE AND THE CARPENTER

An Ape sat looking at a Carpenter who was cleaving a piece of wood with two wedges, which he put into the cleft one after another as the split opened. The Carpenter leaving his work half done, the Ape must needs try his hand at log-splitting, and coming to the piece of wood, pulled out the wedge that was in it without knocking in the other. The wood closing again held the poor Monkey by his fore paws so fast that he was not able to get away. The surly Carpenter, when he returned, knocked the prisoner's brains out for meddling with his work.

It is easier to get into mischief than to get out again.

༒ 52 ༒
THE THREE VASES

By a lifetime of scraping, a Miser once hoarded up a large quantity of gold, which he placed in three Vases and buried. When at length, being on his deathbed, he called his three sons to him, and informed them of the treasure he had left them, and of the spot in which it lay hid, in three separate Vases—one for each of them—he could not finish all he had to say; a fainting fit seized him, and he expired. Now, as the young men had never seen these Vases, they concluded that in all probability they would differ in size and value; and as their father died before he could assign to each his particular Vase, that business must be settled by themselves. Thus, on the division of their wealth they entered into warm dispute, each laying claim to the largest Vase—one because he was the eldest; the second son because he had no property in lands to support him; and the youngest because he was the favorite of his father, and therefore was sure the largest share would have been bequeathed to him, had his dying parent been but able to finish his last speech. Words at length ran very high, and quickly came to blows, from which none of them escaped unhurt; when, after all this wrangle, ill-blood, and mischief done, it was discovered, on digging up the three Vases, that they were exactly equal in size and value.

Be sure of your cause before you quarrel.

THE FOX AND THE STORK

A fox invited a stork to dinner, at which the only fare provided was a large flat dish of soup. The fox lapped it up with great relish, but the stork with her long bill tried in vain to partake of the savory broth. Her evident distress caused the sly fox much amusement. But not long after the stork invited him in turn, and set before him a pitcher with a long and narrow neck, into which she could get her bill with ease. Thus, while she enjoyed her dinner, the fox sat by hungry and helpless, for it was impossible for him to reach the tempting contents of the vessel.

One bad turn deserves another.

❧ 54 ☙

THE WOLF IN SHEEP'S CLOTHING

A wolf resolved to disguise himself in order that he might prey upon a flock of sheep without fear of detection. So he clothed himself in a sheepskin, and slipped among the sheep when they were out at pasture. He completely deceived the shepherd, and when the flock was penned for the night he was shut in with the rest. But that very night as it happened, the shepherd, requiring a supply of mutton for the table, laid hands on the wolf in mistake for a sheep, and killed him with his knife on the spot.

Appearances are deceptive.

❧ 55 ☙

THE STAG IN THE OX STALL

A stag, chased from his lair by the hounds, took refuge in a farmyard, and, entering a stable where a number of oxen were stalled, thrust himself under a pile of hay in a vacant stall, where he lay concealed, all but the tips of his horns. Presently one of the oxen said to him, "What has induced you to come in here? Aren't you aware of the risk you are running of being captured by the herdsmen?" To which he replied, "Pray let me stay for the present. When night comes I shall easily escape under cover of the dark." In the course of the afternoon more than one of the farmhands came in, to attend to the wants of the cattle, but not one of them noticed the presence of the stag, who accordingly began to congratulate himself on his escape and to express his gratitude to the oxen. "We wish you well," said the one who had spoken before, "but you are not out of danger yet. If the master comes, you will certainly be found out, for nothing ever escapes his keen eyes." Presently, sure enough, in he came, and made a great to-do about the way the oxen were kept. "The beasts are starving," he cried; "here, give them more hay, and put plenty of litter under them." As he spoke, he seized an armful himself from the pile where the stag lay concealed, and at once detected him. Calling his men, he had him seized at once and killed for the table.

There is no eye like the master's.

❧ 56 ❧
THE MILKMAID AND HER PAIL

A farmer's daughter had been out to milk the cows, and was returning to the dairy carrying her pail of milk upon her head. As she walked along, she fell a-musing after this fashion: "The milk in this pail will provide me with cream, which I will make into butter and take to market to sell. With the money I will buy a number of eggs, and these, when hatched, will produce chickens, and by and by I shall have quite a large poultry yard. Then I shall sell some of my fowls, and with the money which they will bring in I will buy myself a new gown, which I shall wear when I go to the fair; and all the young fellows will admire it, and come and make love to me, but I shall toss my head and have nothing to say to them." Forgetting all about the pail, and suiting the action to the word, she tossed her head. Down went the pail, all the milk was spilled, and all her fine castles in the air vanished in a moment!

Do not count your chickens before they hatch.

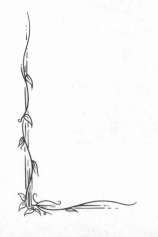
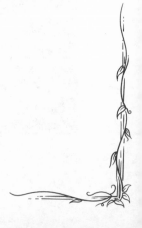

❧ 57 ❧

THE DOLPHINS, THE WHALES, AND THE SPRAT

The dolphins quarreled with the whales, and before very long they began fighting with one another. The battle was very fierce, and had lasted some time without any sign of coming to an end, when a sprat thought that perhaps he could stop it; so he stepped in and tried to persuade them to give up fighting and make friends. But one of the dolphins said to him contemptuously, "We would rather go on fighting till we're all killed than be reconciled by a sprat like you!"

❧ 58 ❧

THE FOX AND THE MONKEY

A fox and a monkey were on the road together, and fell into a dispute as to which of the two was the better born. They kept it up for some time, till they came to a place where the road passed through a cemetery full of monuments, when the monkey stopped and looked about him and gave a great sigh. "Why do you sigh?" said the fox. The monkey pointed to the tombs and replied, "All the monuments that you see here were put up in honor of my forefathers, who in their day were eminent men." The fox was speechless for a moment, but quickly recovering he said, "Oh!

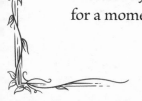

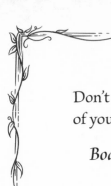

Don't stop at any lie, sir; you're quite safe. I'm sure none of your ancestors will rise up and expose you."

Boasters brag most when they cannot be detected.

❧ 59 ❧

THE ASS AND THE LAPDOG

There was once a man who had an ass and a lapdog. The ass was housed in the stable with plenty of oats and hay to eat and was as well off as an ass could be. The little dog was made a great pet of by his master, who fondled him and often let him lie in his lap; and if he went out to dinner, he would bring back a tidbit or two to give him when he ran to meet him on his return. The ass had, it is true, a good deal of work to do, carting or grinding the corn, or carrying the burdens of the farm; and ere long he became very jealous, contrasting his own life of labor with the ease and idleness of the lapdog. At last one day he broke his halter, and frisking into the house just as his master sat down to dinner, he pranced and capered about, mimicking the frolics of the little favorite, upsetting the table and smashing the crockery with his clumsy efforts. Not content with that, he even tried to jump on his master's lap, as he had so often seen the dog allowed to do. At that the servants, seeing the danger their master was in, belabored the silly ass with sticks and cudgels, and drove him back to his stable half dead with his beating. "Alas!" he cried, "all this I have brought on myself. Why could I not be satisfied with my natural and honorable position, without wishing to imitate the ridiculous antics of that useless little lapdog?"

To be satisfied with one's lot is better than to desire something which one is not fit to receive.

⚜ 60 ⚜
THE HAWK AND THE FARMER

A Hawk, pursuing a Pigeon with great eagerness, was caught in a net which had been set in a cornfield for the Crows. The Farmer, seeing the Hawk fluttering in the net, came and took him. The Hawk besought the Man to let him go, saying piteously that he had done him no harm. "And pray what harm had the poor Pigeon you followed done to you?" replied the Farmer. Without more ado he wrung off his head.

Do unto others as you would have them do to you.

⚜ 61 ⚜
THE TWO RABBITS

A Rabbit, who was about to have a family, entreated another Rabbit to lend her her hutch until she was able to move about again, and assured her that she should then have it without fail. The other very readily consented, and, with a great deal of civility, resigned it to her immediately. However, when the time was up, she came and paid her a visit, and very modestly intimated that now she was up and well she hoped she might have her hutch again, for it was really inconvenient for her to be without it any longer; she must, therefore, be so free as to desire her to provide herself with other lodgings as soon as she could. The other replied that truly she was ashamed of having kept her so long out of her own house, but it was not upon her own account (for, indeed, she was well enough to go anywhere) so much as that of her young, who were yet so weak that she was afraid they would not be able to follow her; and if she would be so good as to let her stay a fortnight longer she would take it for the greatest obligation in the world. The second Rabbit was so good-natured and compassionate as to comply with this request, too, but at the end of the term came and told her positively that she must turn out, for she could not possibly let her be there a day longer. "Must turn out!" says the other; "we will see about that; for I promise you unless you can beat me and my whole litter of young, you are never likely to have anything more to do here."

Majorities promote tyranny.

THE BLIND SHEEP

A certain poor Sheep was so unfortunate as some years before his death to become blind, when the Owl, who had assumed to himself the profession of Oculist to his Majesty the Eagle, undertook to cure him. On the morning when the operation was to have been performed, the Sheep placed himself in the seat, and asked the Oculist if all things were ready for cure. The Oculist answered, "Yes, his instruments and plasters were all prepared, and nothing wanting." "Ay," said the Sheep; "the things you have mentioned are of least importance toward giving me that satisfaction I desire by the recovery of my sight; tell me, how goes the world?" "Why, even just as it did," said the Owl, "when you fell blind." "Sayest thou so, friend?" replied the Sheep. "Then, prithee, hold thy hand and proceed no further, for I would not give a blade of grass to recover my sight if I must again be punished in beholding enormities so odious in the eyes of all innocent creatures on earth."

Improvements are not always help.

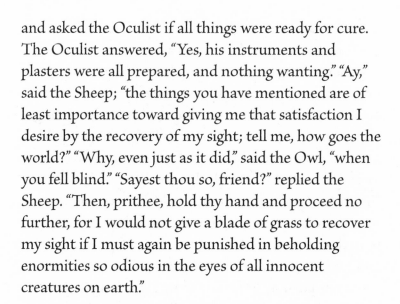

◁ 63 ▷

THE ASS, THE DOG, AND THE WOLF

A laden Ass was jogging along, followed by his tired master, at whose heels came a hungry Dog. Their path lay across a meadow, and the Man stretched himself out on the turf and went to sleep. The Ass fed on the pasture, and was in no hurry at all to move. The Dog alone, being gnawed by the pangs of hunger, found that the time passed heavily. "Pray, dear companion," said he to the Ass, "stoop down, that I may take my dinner from the pannier." The Ass turned a deaf ear,

and went on cropping away the green and tender grass. The Dog persisted, and at last the Ass replied, "Wait, can't you, till our master wakes. He will give you your usual portion, without fail." Just then a famished Wolf appeared upon the scene, and sprang at the throat of the Ass. "Help, help, dear Towzer!" cried the Ass; but the Dog would not budge. "Wait till our master wakes," said he; "he will come to your help, without fail." The words were no sooner spoken, than the Ass lay strangled upon the sod.

Favors beget favors.

❦ 64 ❦

THE GENEROUS LION

A Lion having slain a Bullock, stood over it, lashing his sides with his tail. A Robber who was passing by stopped and impudently demanded half shares. "You are always too ready to take what does not belong to you," answered the Lion; "go your way, I have nothing to say to you." The Thief saw that the Lion was not to be trifled with, and went off. Just then a Traveler came up, and seeing the Lion, modestly withdrew. The generous Beast, with a courteous air, called him forward, and, dividing the Bullock in halves, told the Man to take one, and in order that the latter might be under no restraint, carried his own portion away into the forest.

Modesty gains favor in a king's eyes.

◁ 65 ▷

THE FIR TREE AND
THE BRAMBLE

A fir tree was boasting to a bramble, and said,
somewhat contemptuously, "You poor creature,
you are of no use whatever. Now, look at me. I am
useful for all sorts of things, particularly when men
build houses; they can't do without me then." But the
bramble replied, "Ah, that's all very well, but you wait
till they come with axes and saws to cut you down, and
then you'll wish you were a bramble and not a fir."

*Better poverty without a care than
wealth with its many obligations.*

THE FROGS' COMPLAINT AGAINST THE SUN

Once upon a time the sun was about to take to himself a wife. The frogs in terror all raised their voices to the skies, and Jupiter, disturbed by the noise, asked them what they were croaking about. They replied, "The sun is bad enough even while he is single, drying up our marshes with his heat as he does. But what will become of us if he marries and begets other suns?"

THE DOG, THE COCK, AND THE FOX

A dog and a cock became great friends, and agreed to travel together. At nightfall the cock flew up into the branches of a tree to roost, while the dog curled himself up inside the trunk, which was hollow. At break of day the cock woke up and crew, as usual. A fox heard, and, wishing to make a breakfast of him, came and stood under the tree and begged him to come down. "I should so like," said he, "to make the acquaintance of one who has such a beautiful voice." The cock replied, "Would you just wake my porter who sleeps at the foot of the tree? He'll open the door and let you in." The fox accordingly rapped on the trunk, when out rushed the dog and tore him in pieces.

❧ 68 ☙

TWO TRAVELERS OF DIFFERING HUMORS

There were two Men together upon a journey, of very different humors. One went despondingly on, with a thousand cares and troubles in his head, exclaiming every now and then, "Whatever shall I do to live!" The other jogged merrily along, determined to keep a good heart, to do his best, and leave the issue to Fortune. "How can you be so merry?" said the Sorrowful plodder. "As I am a sinner, my heart is ready to break, for fear I should want bread." "Tut, Man!" said the other, "there's enough bread and to spare for all of us." Presently the Grumbler had another heavy thought which made him groan aloud. "What a dreadful thing it would be if I were struck blind!" said he, and he must needs walk on ahead with his eyes shut, to try how it would seem if that misfortune should befall him. His Fellow-traveler, coming after him, picked up a purse of gold which the other, having his eyes shut, had not perceived; and thus was he punished for his mistrust, for the purse had been his, if he had not first willingly put it out of his power to see it.

Fortune helps those who help themselves.

❦ 69 ❦

THE GARDENER AND HIS MASTER

In the midst of a beautiful flower garden there was a large pond filled with carp, tench, perch, and other fresh-water fish; it was also intended to water the garden. The foolish Gardener, being particularly careful in attending to his flowers, so emptied the pond of its water, that there scarcely remained sufficient to preserve the fish in existence. His Master coming down to walk in the garden, and seeing this mismanagement, reprimanded the Gardener, saying, "Though I am very fond of flowers, I am also very fond of regaling myself with fish." The Gardener, being a coarse ignorant peasant, obeyed his Master so punctually, that he gave no water to the flowers, in order that the fish might be abundantly supplied. Some time after the Master again visited his garden, and, to his great mortification, saw the flowers, which so greatly ornamented it, all dead or drooping. "You blockhead," he cries, "in future remember not to devote so much of the water of the pond to the flowers, as to leave me without fish, nor yet be so liberal to the fish as to kill my beauteous blossoms."

Whoever wishes to attain excellence
must always avoid extremes.

❧ 70 ☙

THE GNAT AND THE BULL

A gnat alighted on one of the horns of a bull, and remained sitting there for a considerable time. When it had rested sufficiently and was about to fly away, it said to the bull, "Do you mind if I go now?" The bull merely raised his eyes and remarked, without interest, "It's all one to me; I didn't notice when you came, and I shan't know when you go away."

Some men are of more consequence in their
own eyes than in the eyes of their neighbors.

⸭ 71 ⸭
THE BEAR AND THE TRAVELERS

Two travelers were on the road together, when a bear suddenly appeared on the scene. Before he observed them, one made for a tree at the side of the road, and climbed up into the branches and hid there. The other was not so nimble as his companion; and, as he could not escape, he threw himself on the ground and pretended to be dead. The bear came up and sniffed all around him, but he kept perfectly still and held his breath: for they say that a bear will not touch a dead body. The bear took him for a corpse, and went away. When the coast was clear, the traveler in the tree came down, and asked the other what it was the bear had whispered to him when he put his mouth to his ear. The other replied, "He told me never again to travel with a friend who deserts you at the first sign of danger."

Misfortune tests the sincerity of friendship.

⸭ 72 ⸭
THE SLAVE AND THE LION

A slave ran away from his master, by whom he had been most cruelly treated, and, in order to avoid capture, betook himself into the desert. As he wandered about in search of food and shelter, he came to a cave,

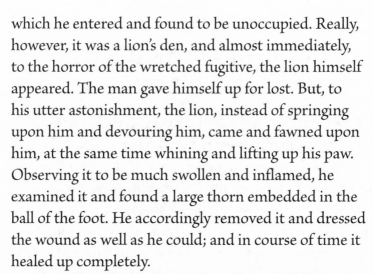

which he entered and found to be unoccupied. Really, however, it was a lion's den, and almost immediately, to the horror of the wretched fugitive, the lion himself appeared. The man gave himself up for lost. But, to his utter astonishment, the lion, instead of springing upon him and devouring him, came and fawned upon him, at the same time whining and lifting up his paw. Observing it to be much swollen and inflamed, he examined it and found a large thorn embedded in the ball of the foot. He accordingly removed it and dressed the wound as well as he could; and in course of time it healed up completely.

The lion's gratitude was unbounded; he looked upon the man as his friend, and they shared the cave for some time together. A day came, however, when the slave began to long for the society of his fellowmen, and he bade farewell to the lion and returned to the town. Here he was presently recognized and carried off in chains to his former master, who resolved to make an example of him, and ordered that he should be thrown to the beasts at the next public spectacle in the theater.

On the fatal day the beasts were loosed into the arena, and among the rest a lion of huge bulk and ferocious aspect. And then the wretched slave was cast in among them. What was the amazement of the spectators, when the lion after one glance bounded up to him and lay down at his feet with every expression of affection and delight! It was his old friend of the cave! The audience clamored that the slave's life should be spared; and the governor of the town, marveling at such gratitude and fidelity in a beast, decreed that both should receive their liberty.

❧ 73 ❧
THE FLEA AND THE MAN

A flea bit a man, and bit him again, and again, till he could stand it no longer, but made a thorough search for it, and at last succeeded in catching it. Holding it between his finger and thumb, he said—or rather shouted, so angry was he—"Who are you, pray, you wretched little creature, that you make so free with my person?" The flea, terrified, whimpered in a weak little voice, "Oh, sir! Pray let me go; don't kill me! I am such a little thing that I can't do you much harm." But the man laughed and said, "I am going to kill you now, at once. Whatever is bad has got to be destroyed, no matter how slight the harm it does."

Do not waste your pity on a scamp.

❧ 74 ❧
THE BEE AND JUPITER

A queen bee from Hymettus flew up to Olympus with some fresh honey from the hive as a present to Jupiter, who was so pleased with the gift that he promised to give her anything she liked to ask for. She said she would be very grateful if he would give stings to the bees, to kill people who robbed them of their honey. Jupiter was greatly displeased with this request, for he loved mankind. But he had given his word, so he said that stings they should have. The stings he gave them, however, were of such a kind that whenever a bee stings a man the sting is left in the wound, and the bee dies.

Evil wishes, like chickens, come home to roost.

❧ 75 ❧
THE OAK AND THE REEDS

An oak that grew on the bank of a river was uprooted by a severe gale of wind, and thrown across the stream. It fell among some reeds growing by the water, and said to them, "How is it that you, who are so frail and slender, have managed to weather the storm, whereas I, with all my strength, have been torn up by the roots and hurled into the river?" "You were stubborn," came the reply, "and fought against the storm, which proved stronger than you. But we bow and yield to every breeze, and thus the gale passed harmlessly over our heads."

Stoop to conquer.

The Oak and the Reeds

❦ 76 ❦

THE BLIND MAN AND THE CUB

There was once a blind man who had so fine a sense of touch that, when any animal was put into his hands, he could tell what it was merely by the feel of it. One day the cub of a wolf was put into his hands, and he was asked what it was. He felt it for some time, and then said, "Indeed, I am not sure whether it is a wolf's cub or a fox's: but this I know—it would never do to trust it in a sheepfold."

Evil tendencies are shown in early life.

❦ 77 ❦

THE BOY AND THE SNAILS

A farmer's boy went looking for snails, and, when he had picked up both his hands full, he set about making a fire at which to roast them; for he meant to eat them. When it got well alight and the snails began to feel the heat, they gradually withdrew more and more into their shells with the hissing noise they always make when they do so. When the boy heard it, he said, "You abandoned creatures, how can you find heart to whistle when your houses are burning?"

◁ 78 ▷

THE APES AND THE TWO TRAVELERS

Two men were traveling together, one of whom never spoke the truth, whereas the other never told a lie; and they came in the course of their travels to the land of apes. The king of the apes, hearing of their arrival, ordered them to be brought before him; and by way of impressing them with his magnificence, he received them sitting on a throne, while the apes, his subjects, were ranged in long rows on either side of him. When the travelers came into his presence he asked them what they thought of him as a king. The lying traveler said, "Sire, everyone must see that you are a most noble and mighty monarch." "And what do you think of my subjects?" continued the king. "They," said the traveler, "are in every way worthy of their royal master." The ape was so delighted with his answer that he gave him a very handsome present.

The other traveler thought that if his companion was rewarded so splendidly for telling a lie, he himself would certainly receive a still greater reward for telling the truth; so, when the ape turned to him and said, "And what, sir, is your opinion?" he replied, "I think you are a very fine ape, and all your subjects are fine apes too." The king of the apes was so enraged at his reply that he ordered him to be taken away and clawed to death.

❧ 79 ❧

THE ASS AND HIS BURDENS

A pedlar who owned an ass one day bought a quantity of salt, and loaded up his beast with as much as he could bear. On the way home the ass stumbled as he was crossing a stream and fell into the water. The salt got thoroughly wetted and much of it melted and drained away, so that, when he got on his legs again, the ass found his load had become much less heavy. His master, however, drove him back to town and bought more salt, which he added to what remained in the panniers, and started out again. No sooner had they reached a stream than the ass lay down in it, and rose, as before, with a much lighter load. But his master detected the trick, and turning back once more, bought a large number of sponges, and piled them on the back of the ass. When they came to the stream the ass again lay down. But this time, as the sponges soaked up large quantities of water, he found, when he got up on his legs, that he had a bigger burden to carry than ever.

You may play a good card once too often.

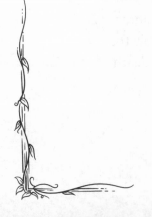

80

THE SHEPHERD'S BOY AND THE WOLF

A shepherd's boy was tending his flock near a village, and thought it would be great fun to hoax the villagers by pretending that a wolf was attacking the sheep; so he shouted out, "Wolf! Wolf!" And when the people came running up, he laughed at them for their pains. He did this more than once, and every time the villagers found they had been hoaxed, for there was no wolf at all. At last a wolf really did come, and the boy cried, "Wolf! Wolf!" as loud as he could. But the people were so used to hearing him call that they took no notice of his cries for help. And so the wolf had it all his own way, and killed off sheep after sheep at his leisure.

You cannot believe a liar even when
he tells the truth.

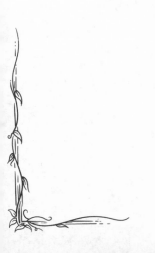

⚘ 81 ⚘

THE FOX AND THE GOAT

A fox fell into a well and was unable to get out again. By and by a thirsty goat came by, and seeing the fox in the well asked him if the water was good. "Good?" said the fox, "it's the best water I ever tasted in all my life. Come down and try it yourself." The goat thought of nothing but the prospect of quenching his thirst, and jumped in at once. When he had had enough to drink, he looked about, like the fox, for some way of getting out, but could find none. Presently the fox said, "I have an idea. You stand on your hind legs, and plant your forelegs firmly against the side of the well, and then I'll climb on to your back, and, from there, by stepping on your horns, I can get out. And when I'm out, I'll help you out too." The goat did as he was requested, and the fox climbed on to his back and so out of the well; and then he coolly walked away. The goat called loudly after him and reminded him of his promise to help him out. But the fox merely turned and said, "If you had as much sense in your head as you have hair in your beard you wouldn't have got into the well without making certain that you could get out again."

Look before you leap.

⊲ 82 ⊳

THE FISHERMAN
AND THE SPRAT

A fisherman cast his net into the sea, and when he drew it up again it contained nothing but a single sprat that begged to be put back into the water. "I'm only a little fish now," it said, "but I shall grow big one day, and then if you come and catch me again I shall be of some use to you." But the fisherman replied, "Oh, no, I shall keep you now I've got you. If I put you back, should I ever see you again? Not likely!"

A little thing in hand is worth more
than a great thing in prospect.

⚜ 83 ⚜
THE HUNTED BEAVER

The tail of the Beaver was once thought to be of use in medicine, and the animal was often hunted on that account. A shrewd old fellow of the race, being hard pressed by the Dogs, and knowing well why they were after him, had the resolution and the presence of mind to bite off his tail, and leave it behind him, and thus escaped with his life.

The skin is nearer than the cloak.

⚜ 84 ⚜
THE BOAR AND THE ASS

A little scamp of an Ass, meeting in a forest with a Boar, came up to him and hailed him with impudent familiarity. The Boar was about to resent the insult by ripping up the Ass's flank, but, wisely keeping his temper, he contented himself with saying: "Go, you sorry beast; I could easily teach you manners, but I do not care to foul my tusks with the blood of so base a creature."

Scoffs are best paid with disdain.

THE WILD AND THE TAME GEESE

Two Geese strayed from a farmyard, and swam down a stream to a large swamp, which afforded them an extensive range and plenty of food. A flock of Wild Geese frequently resorted to the same place; and though they were at first so shy as not to suffer the Tame ones to join them, by degrees they became well acquainted and associated freely together. One evening their cackling reached the ears of a Fox that was prowling at no great distance from the swamp. The artful plunderer directed his course through a wood on the borders of it, and was within a few yards of his prey before any of the Geese perceived him. But the alarm was given just as he was springing upon them, and the whole flock instantly ascended into the air, with loud and dissonant cries. "The Fox! the Fox!" the Wild Geese called as they rose swiftly out of his clutches; and they winged their flight into higher regions and were seen no more. "The Fox! the Fox!" replied the two Tame Geese, rising after them; but being heavy, clumsy, and unused to using their wings, they soon dropped down, and became the victims of the Fox.

Those who aspire to a higher station should be able to maintain their position.

❦ 86 ❦
THE BOASTING TRAVELER

A man once went abroad on his travels, and when he came home he had wonderful tales to tell of the things he had done in foreign countries. Among other things, he said he had taken part in a jumping match at Rhodes, and had done a wonderful jump which no one could beat. "Just go to Rhodes and ask them," he said; "everyone will tell you it's true." But one of those who was listening said, "If you can jump as well as all that, we needn't go to Rhodes to prove it. Let's just imagine this is Rhodes for a minute; and now—jump!"

Deeds, not words.

⊰ 87 ⊱

THE SHEEP-BITER

A certain Shepherd had a Dog in whom he placed such great trust, that he would often leave the flock to his sole care. As soon, however, as his Master's back was turned, the Cur, although well fed and kindly treated, used to worry the Sheep, and would sometimes kill one and devour a portion. The Man at last found out how much his confidence had been abused, and resolved to hang the Dog without mercy. When the rope was put around his neck, he pleaded hard for his life, and begged his Master rather to hang the Wolf, who had done ten times as much harm to the flock as he had. "That may be," replied the Man sternly; "but you are ten times the greater villain for all that. Nothing shall save you from the fate which your treachery deserves."

The most dangerous enemy is that one within.

⊰ 88 ⊱

THE PRINCE AND THE PAINTED LION

A certain King had an only son, of whom he was dotingly fond. The Prince delighted in hunting, and went every day into the forest, in chase of wild beasts. His father believed firmly in dreams, omens, and the like, and dreaming one night that his son was killed by a Lion, resolved that he should not go to the forest any more. He therefore built a spacious tower, and kept the Prince there closely confined. That his captivity might be less tedious to bear, he surrounded him with books, music, and pictures; and on the walls of the tower were painted in life-size all the beasts of the chase, and among the rest a Lion. The Prince stood one day gazing for a long time at this picture, and, in his rage at being imprisoned, he struck the painted Lion a violent blow with his fist, saying, "Thou, cruel beast, art the cause of all my grief! Had it not been for the lying dream of thee which came to my father, I should now be free." The point of a nail in the wainscot under the canvas entered his hand through the force of his blow; the wound became inflamed, and the youth died from its effects.

Fancied dangers lead to real ones.

◁ 89 ▷

THE VILLAGE QUACK

A waggish idle fellow, in a country town, being desirous of playing a trick on the simplicity of his neighbors, and at the same time to put a little money in his pocket at their cost, advertised that he would on a certain day show a wheel-carriage that should be so contrived as to go without horses. By silly curiosity the rustics were taken in; and each succeeding group who came out from the show were ashamed to confess to their neighbors that they had seen nothing but a wheelbarrow.

It is mortifying to see by what artful knavery one half of the world would impose upon the folly of the other.

◁ 90 ▷

THE PEACH, THE APPLE, AND THE BLACKBERRY

A dispute arose once between a Peach and an Apple as to which was the fairer fruit of the two. They were so loud in their wrangling that a Blackberry from the next hedge overheard them. "Come," said the Blackberry, who thought herself quite fine, also, "we are all friends, and all fair. Pray let us have no quarrels among ourselves."

Know thyself.

✤ 91 ✤

THE HUNTER, THE FOX, AND THE TIGER

A certain Hunter saw in the middle of a field a Fox, whose skin was so beautiful that he wished to take him alive. Having this in view, he found out his hole, and just before the entrance to it he dug a large and deep pit, covered it with slender twigs and straw, and placed a piece of horseflesh on the middle of the covering. When he had done this he went and hid himself in a corner out of sight, and the Fox, returning to his hole and smelling the flesh, ran up to see what dainty morsel it was. When he came to the pit he would fain have tasted the meat, but fearing some trick he refrained from doing so, and retreated into his hole. Presently up came a hungry Tiger, who, being tempted by the smell and appearance of the horseflesh, sprang in haste to seize it, and tumbled into the pit. The Hunter, hearing the noise made by the Tiger in falling, ran up and jumped into the pit without looking into it, never doubting that it was the Fox that had fallen in. But there, to his surprise, he found the Tiger, which quickly tore him in pieces and devoured him.

Look before you leap.

◁ 92 ▷
THE CRAB AND HIS MOTHER

An old crab said to her son, "Why do you walk sideways like that, my son? You ought to walk straight." The young crab replied, "Show me how, dear mother, and I'll follow your example." The old crab tried, but tried in vain, and then saw how foolish she had been to find fault with her child.

Example is more powerful than principle.

❧ 93 ❧
THE ASS AND HIS SHADOW

A certain man hired an ass for a journey in summertime, and started out with the owner following behind to drive the beast. By and by, in the heat of the day, they stopped to rest, and the traveler wanted to lie down in the ass's shadow; but the owner, who himself wished to be out of the sun, wouldn't let him do that; for he said he had hired the ass only, and not his shadow. The other maintained that his bargain secured him complete control of the ass for the time being. From words they came to blows; and while they were belaboring each other the ass took to his heels and was soon out of sight.

*In quarreling about the shadow we
often lose the substance.*

❧ 94 ❧
THE FARMER AND HIS SONS

A farmer, being at death's door, and desiring to impart to his sons a secret of much moment, called them around him and said, "My sons, I am shortly about to die; I would have you know, therefore, that in my vineyard there lies a hidden treasure. Dig, and you will find it." As soon as their father was dead, the sons took spade and fork and turned up the soil of the vineyard over and over again, in their search for the treasure which they supposed to lie buried there. They found none, however; but the vines, after so thorough a digging, produced a crop such as had never before been seen.

Industry sometimes pays unexpected dividends.

৬ 95 ৬

THE DOG AND THE COOK

A rich man once invited a number of his friends and acquaintances to a banquet. His dog thought it would be a good opportunity to invite another dog, a friend of his; so he went to him and said, "My master is giving a feast. There'll be a fine spread, so come and dine with me tonight." The dog thus invited came, and when he saw the preparations being made in the kitchen he said to himself, "My word, I'm in luck. I'll take care to eat enough tonight to last me two or three days." At the same time he wagged his tail briskly, by way of showing his friend how delighted he was to have been asked.

But just then the cook caught sight of him, and, in his annoyance at seeing a strange dog in the kitchen, caught him up by the hind legs and threw him out of the window. He had a nasty fall, and limped away as quickly as he could, howling dismally. Presently some other dogs met him, and said, "Well, what sort of a dinner did you get?" To which he replied, "I had a splendid time. The wine was so good, and I drank so much of it, that I really don't remember how I got out of the house!"

Be shy of favors bestowed at the expense of others.

◁ 96 ▷
THE MONKEY AS KING

At a gathering of all the animals the monkey danced and delighted them so much that they made him their king. The fox, however, was very much disgusted at the promotion of the monkey. So having one day found a trap with a piece of meat in it, he took the monkey there and said to him, "Here is a dainty morsel I have found, sire; I did not take it myself, because I thought it ought to be reserved for you, our king. Will you be pleased to accept it?" The monkey made at once for the meat and got caught in the trap. Then he bitterly reproached the fox for leading him into danger; but the fox only laughed and said, "O monkey, you call yourself king of the beasts and haven't more sense than to be taken in like that!"

◁ 97 ▷

THE THIEVES AND THE COCK

S ome thieves broke into a house, and found nothing worth taking except a cock, which they seized and carried off with them. When they were preparing their supper, one of them caught up the cock, and was

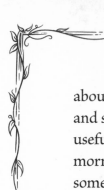

about to wring his neck, when he cried out for mercy and said, "Pray do not kill me. You will find me a most useful bird, for I rouse honest men to their work in the morning by my crowing." But the thief replied with some heat, "Yes, I know you do, making it still harder for us to get a livelihood. Into the pot you go!"

The safeguards of virtue are hateful
to those with evil intentions.

⚜ 98 ⚜
THE FARMER AND FORTUNE

A farmer was plowing one day on his farm when he turned up a pot of golden coins with his plow. He was overjoyed at his discovery, and from that time forth made an offering daily at the shrine of the Goddess of the Earth. Fortune was displeased at this, and came to him and said, "My man, why do you give Earth the credit for the gift which I bestowed upon you? You never thought of thanking me for your good luck; but should you be unlucky enough to lose what you have gained I know very well that I, Fortune, should then come in for all the blame."

Show gratitude where gratitude is due.

❧ 99 ❧

JUPITER AND THE MONKEY

Jupiter issued a proclamation to all the beasts, and offered a prize to the one who, in his judgment, produced the most beautiful offspring. Among the rest came the monkey, carrying a baby monkey in her arms, a hairless, flat-nosed little fright. When they saw it, the gods all burst into peal on peal of laughter; but the monkey hugged her little one to her, and said, "Jupiter may give the prize to whomsoever he likes, but I shall always think my baby the most beautiful of them all."

❧ 100 ❧

THE LAMP

A lamp, well filled with oil, burned with a clear and steady light, and began to swell with pride and boast that it shone more brightly than the sun himself. Just then a puff of wind came and blew it out. Someone struck a match and lit it again, and said, "You just keep alight, and never mind the sun. Why, even the stars never need to be relit as you had to be just now."

☙ 101 ❧

FATHER AND SONS

A certain man had several sons who were always quarreling with one another, and, try as he might, he could not get them to live together in harmony. So he determined to convince them of their folly by the following means. Bidding them fetch a bundle of sticks, he invited each in turn to break it across his knee. All tried and all failed. And then he undid the bundle, and handed them the sticks one by one, when they had no difficulty at all in breaking them. "There, my boys," said he, "united you will be more than a match for your enemies. But if you quarrel and separate, your weakness will put you at the mercy of those who attack you."

Union is strength.

✤ 102 ✤

The Frog and the Fox

A Frog came out of his native marsh, and, hopping to the top of a mound of earth, gave out to all the Beasts around that he was a great physician, and could heal all manner of diseases. The Fox demanded why, if he was so clever, he did not mend his own blotched and spotted body, his stare eyes, and his lantern jaws.

Physician, heal thyself.

✤ 103 ✤

The Cat and the Bat

A Cat having devoured a favorite Bullfinch of her master's, overheard him threatening to put her to death the moment he could find her. In this distress she preferred a prayer to Jupiter, vowing, if he would deliver her from her present danger, that never while she lived would she eat another bird. Not long afterwards a Bat most invitingly flew into the room where Puss was purring in the window. The question was, how to act upon so tempting an occasion? Her appetite pressed hard on one side, and her vow threw some scruples in her way on the other. At length she hit upon a most convenient distinction to remove all difficulties, by determining that as a bird indeed it was an unlawful prize, but as a mouse she might very

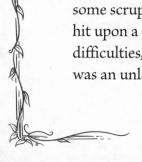

conscientiously eat it, and accordingly without further debate fell to the repast. Thus it is that men are apt to impose upon themselves by vain and groundless distinctions, when conscience and principle are at variance with interest and inclination.

Inclination seems to have got the start of duty, when we seek to find it in books of casuistry.

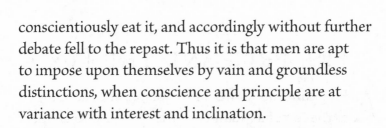

104

THE SILKWORM AND THE SPIDER

A Silkworm was one day working at her shroud: the Spider, her neighbor, weaving her web with the greatest swiftness, looked down with contempt on the slow, although beautiful, labors of the Silkworm. "What do you think of my web, my lady?" she cried; "see how large it is! I began it only this morning, and here it is half finished. Look and acknowledge that I work much quicker than you." "Yes," said the Silkworm, "but your webs, which are at first designed only as base traps to ensnare the harmless, are destroyed as soon as they are seen, and swept away as dirt and worse than useless; while mine are preserved with the greatest care, and in time become ornaments for princes." So saying, my Lady Silkworm took up her thread again, and continued to weave her beautiful fabric with even greater care.

Not how much but how well.

ᦙ 105 ᦚ

THE ASS IN THE LION'S SKIN

An ass found a lion's skin, and dressed himself up in it. Then he went about frightening everyone he met, for they all took him to be a lion, men and beasts alike, and took to their heels when they saw him coming. Elated by the success of his trick, he loudly brayed in triumph. The fox heard him, and recognized him at once for the ass he was, and said to him, "Oho, my friend, it's you, is it? I, too, should have been afraid if I hadn't heard your voice."

Clothes may disguise a fool, but his
words will give him away.

❧ 106 ☙

THE GOOSE AND THE SWANS

A Goose, affected, empty, vain, the shrillest of the
cackling train, with proud and elevated crest,
precedence claimed above the rest. Says she, "I laugh at
human race, who say Geese hobble in their pace; look
here—the slander base detect; not haughty man is so
erect. That Peacock yonder, see how vain the creature's
of his gaudy train. If both were stripped, I'd pledge my
word a Goose would be the finer bird. Nature, to hide
her own defects, her bungled work with finery decks.
Were Geese set off with half that show, would men
admire the Peacock? No!" Thus vaunting, 'cross the
mead she stalks, the cackling breed attend her walks;
the sun shot down his noontide beams, the Swans
were sporting in the streams. Their snowy plumes and
stately pride provoked her spleen. "Why, there," she
cried, "again, what arrogance we see! Those creatures,
how they mimic me! Shall every fowl the waters skim,
because we Geese are known to swim? Humility they
soon shall learn, and their own emptiness discern." So
saying, with extended wings, lightly upon the wave
she springs; her bosom swells, she spreads her plumes,
and the Swan's stately crest assumes. Contempt and
mockery ensued, and bursts of laughter shook the
flood. A Swan, superior to the rest, sprung forth,
and thus the fool addressed: "Conceited thing, elate
with pride, thy affectation all deride; these airs thy
awkwardness impart, and show thee plainly as thou
art. Among thy equals of the flock, thou hadst escaped

the public mock; and, as thy parts to good conduce, been deemed an honest, hobbling Goose." Learn hence to study wisdom's rules; know, foppery's the pride of fools: and, striving Nature to conceal, you only her defects reveal.

Bragging merely reveals one's faults.

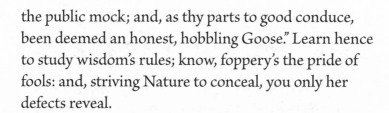

⚜ 107 ⚜
THE FROG AND THE HEN

Dear me!" said the Frog to himself one day as he heard a Hen cackling near his bog; "what a very noisy creature that Hen is to be sure! Mrs. Hen," he called out, "do be quiet; you'll alarm the whole neighborhood. Really, one would think you had made a grand discovery. What is the cause or the meaning of all this uproar?" "My dear sir, have patience with me; I've laid an egg." "Upon my word you make a great fuss over one egg." "Well, well, I am sorry to see you so ill-tempered at my little song of joy, when I've endured without a murmur your croaking all day and night long. But I claim to have done some good, though that may be small. You, on the contrary, should hold your tongue, for you certainly do no good whatever."

Croakers seldom become doers.

⟨ 108 ⟩

THE OWL AND THE BIRDS

The owl is a very wise bird; and once, long ago, when the first oak sprouted in the forest, she called all the other birds together and said to them, "You see this tiny tree? If you take my advice, you will destroy it now when it is small; for when it grows big, the mistletoe will appear upon it, from which birdlime will be prepared for your destruction." Again, when the first flax was sown, she said to them, "Go and eat up that seed, for it is the seed of the flax, out of which men will one day make nets to catch you." Once more, when she saw the first archer, she warned the birds that he was their deadly enemy, who would wing his arrows with their own feathers and shoot them.

But they took no notice of what she said. In fact, they thought she was rather mad, and laughed at her. When, however, everything turned out as she had foretold, they changed their minds and conceived a great respect for her wisdom. Hence, whenever she appears, the birds attend upon her in the hope of hearing something that may be for their good. She, however, gives them advice no longer, but sits moping and pondering on the folly of her kind.

The Owl and the Birds

✦ 109 ✦

THE SHE-GOATS AND THEIR BEARDS

Jupiter granted beards to the she-goats at their own request, much to the disgust of the he-goats, who considered this to be an unwarrantable invasion of their rights and dignities. So they sent a deputation to him to protest against his action. He, however, advised them not to raise any objections. "What's in a tuft of hair?" said he. "Let them have it if they want it. They can never be a match for you in strength."

It matters little if those who are inferior to us in merit should be like us in outside appearances.

✦ 110 ✦

THE OLD LION

A lion, enfeebled by age and no longer able to procure food for himself by force, determined to do so by cunning. Betaking himself to a cave, he lay down inside and feigned to be sick; and whenever any of the other animals entered to inquire after his health, he sprang upon them and devoured them. Many lost their lives in this way, till one day a fox called at the cave, and, having a suspicion of the truth, addressed the lion from outside instead of going in, and asked him how he did. He replied that he was in a very bad way.

"But," said he, "why do you stand outside? Pray come in."
"I should have done so," answered the fox, "if I hadn't
noticed that all the footprints point towards the cave
and none the other way."

❧ 111 ☙

THE BOY BATHING

A boy was bathing in a river and got out of his depth,
and was in great danger of being drowned. A man
who was passing along a road heard his cries for help,
and went to the riverside and began to scold him for
being so careless as to get into deep water, but made no
attempt to help him. "Oh, sir," cried the boy, "please help
me first and scold me afterward."

Give assistance, not advice, in a crisis.

The Quack Frog

⚜ 112 ⚜

THE QUACK FROG

Once upon a time a frog came forth from his home in the marshes and proclaimed to all the world that he was a learned physician, skilled in drugs and able to cure all diseases. Among the crowd was a fox, who called out, "You a doctor! Why, how can you set up to heal others when you cannot even cure your own lame legs and blotched and wrinkled skin?"

Physician, heal thyself.

⚜ 113 ⚜

THE SWOLLEN FOX

A hungry fox found in a hollow tree a quantity of bread and meat, which some shepherds had placed there against their return. Delighted with his find he slipped in through the narrow aperture and greedily devoured it all. But when he tried to get out again he found himself so swollen after his big meal that he could not squeeze through the hole, and fell to whining and groaning over his misfortune. Another fox, happening to pass that way, came and asked him what the matter was; and, on learning the state of the case, said, "Well, my friend, I see nothing for it but for you to stay where you are till you shrink to your former size; you'll get out then easily enough."

❦ 114 ❧

THE MOUSE, THE FROG, AND THE HAWK

A mouse and a frog struck up a friendship; they were not well mated, for the mouse lived entirely on land, while the frog was equally at home on land or in the water. In order that they might never be separated, the frog tied himself and the mouse together by the leg with a piece of thread. As long as they kept on dry land all went fairly well; but, coming to the edge of a pool, the frog jumped in, taking the mouse with him, and began swimming about and croaking with pleasure. The unhappy mouse, however, was soon drowned, and floated about on the surface in the wake of the frog. There he was spied by a hawk, who pounced down on him and seized him in his talons. The frog was unable to loose the knot which bound him to the mouse, and thus was carried off along with him and eaten by the hawk.

Harm hatch, harm catch.

❦ 115 ❧

THE BOY AND THE NETTLES

A boy was gathering berries from a hedge when his hand was stung by a nettle. Smarting with the pain, he ran to tell his mother, and said to her between his sobs, "I only touched it ever so lightly, mother." "That's just why you got stung, my son," she said; "if you had grasped it firmly, it wouldn't have hurt you in the least."

Whatever you do, do with all of your might.

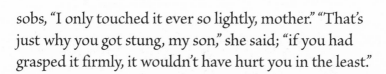

116

THE PEASANT AND THE APPLE TREE

A peasant had an apple tree growing in his garden, which bore no fruit, but merely served to provide a shelter from the heat for the sparrows and grasshoppers which sat and chirped in its branches. Disappointed at its barrenness he determined to cut it down, and went and fetched his ax for the purpose. But when the sparrows and the grasshoppers saw what he was about to do, they begged him to spare it, and said to him, "If you destroy the tree we shall have to seek shelter elsewhere, and you will no longer have our merry chirping to enliven your work in the garden." He, however, refused to listen to them, and set to work with a will to cut through the trunk. A few strokes showed that it was hollow inside and contained a swarm of bees and a large store of honey. Delighted with his find he threw down his ax, saying, "The old tree is worth keeping after all."

Utility is most men's test of worth.

⊰ 117 ⊱
THE JACKDAW AND THE PIGEONS

A jackdaw, watching some pigeons in a farmyard, was filled with envy when he saw how well they were fed, and determined to disguise himself as one of them, in order to secure a share of the good things they enjoyed. So he painted himself white from head to foot and joined the flock; and, so long as he was silent, they never suspected that he was not a pigeon like themselves. But one day he was unwise enough to start chattering, when they at once saw through his disguise and pecked him so unmercifully that he was glad to escape and join his own kind again. But the other jackdaws did not recognize him in his white dress, and would not let him feed with them, but drove him away: and so he became a homeless wanderer for his pains.

⊰ 118 ⊱
JUPITER AND THE TORTOISE

Jupiter was about to marry a wife, and determined to celebrate the event by inviting all the animals to a banquet. They all came except the tortoise, who did not put in an appearance, much to Jupiter's surprise. So when he next saw the tortoise he asked him why he had not been at the banquet. "I don't care for going out," said the tortoise; "there's no place like home." Jupiter was so much annoyed by this reply that he decreed that from that time forth the tortoise should carry his house upon his back, and never be able to get away from home even if he wished to.

ৠ 119 ৡ

THE DOG IN THE MANGER

A dog was lying in a manger on the hay which had been put there for the cattle, and when they came and tried to eat, he growled and snapped at them and wouldn't let them get at their food. "What a selfish beast," said one of them to his companions; "he can't eat himself and yet he won't let those eat who can."

People often begrudge others what
they cannot enjoy themselves.

❧ 120 ❧

THE TWO BAGS

Every man carries two bags about with him, one in front and one behind, and both are packed full of faults. The bag in front contains his neighbors' faults, the one behind his own. Hence it is that men do not see their own faults, but never fail to see those of others.

❧ 121 ❧

THE OXEN AND THE AXLETREES

A pair of oxen were drawing a heavily loaded wagon along the highway, and, as they tugged and strained at the yoke, the axletrees creaked and groaned terribly. This was too much for the oxen, who turned around indignantly and said, "Hullo, you there! Why do you make such a noise when we do all the work?"

They complain most who suffer least.

❧ 122 ❧

THE BOY AND THE HAZELNUTS

A boy put his hand into a jar of hazelnuts and grasped as many as his fist could possibly hold. But when he tried to pull it out again, he found he couldn't do so, for the neck of the jar was too small to allow the passage of so large a handful. Unwilling to lose his nuts but unable to withdraw his hand, he burst into tears. A bystander, who saw where the trouble lay, said to him, "Come, my boy, don't be so greedy. Be content with half the amount, and you'll be able to get your hand out without difficulty."

Do not attempt too much at once.

❧ 123 ❧

THE FROGS ASKING FOR A KING

Time was when the frogs were discontented because they had no one to rule over them: so they sent a deputation to Jupiter to ask him to give them a king. Jupiter, despising the folly of their request, cast a log into the pool where they lived, and said that that should be their king. The frogs were terrified at first by the splash, and scuttled away into the deepest parts

of the pool; but by and by, when they saw that the log remained motionless, one by one they ventured to the surface again, and before long, growing bolder, they began to feel such contempt for it that they even took to sitting upon it. Thinking that a king of that sort was an insult to their dignity, they sent to Jupiter a second time, and begged him to take away the sluggish king he had given them, and to give them another and a better one. Jupiter, annoyed at being pestered in this way, sent a stork to rule over them, who no sooner arrived among them than he began to catch and eat the frogs as fast as he could.

Let well enough alone.

124

The Olive Tree and the Fig Tree

An olive tree taunted a fig tree with the loss of her leaves at a certain season of the year. "You," she said, "lose your leaves every autumn, and are bare till the spring: whereas I, as you see, remain green and flourishing all the year round." Soon afterward there came a heavy fall of snow, which settled on the leaves of the olive so that she bent and broke under the weight; but the flakes fell harmlessly through the bare branches of the fig, which survived to bear many another crop.

125

The Lion and the Boar

One hot and thirsty day in the height of summer a lion and a boar came down to a little spring at the same moment to drink. In a trice they were quarreling as to who should drink first. The quarrel soon became a fight and they attacked one another with the utmost fury. Presently, stopping for a moment to take breath, they saw some vultures seated on a rock above evidently waiting for one of them to be killed, when they would fly down and feed upon the carcass. The sight sobered them at once, and they made up their quarrel, saying, "We had much better be friends than fight and be eaten by vultures."

❧ 126 ❧

THE FARMER AND HIS DOG

A Farmer who had gone into his field to mend a gap in one of his fences, found at his return the cradle in which he had left his only child asleep turned upside down, the clothes all torn and bloody, and his Dog lying near it, besmeared also with blood. Thinking that the animal had destroyed his child, he instantly dashed out his brains with the hatchet in his hand; when turning up the cradle, he found his child unhurt, and an enormous Serpent lying dead on the floor, killed by that faithful Dog whose courage and fidelity in preserving the life of his son deserved another kind of reward.

It is dangerous to give way to the blind
impulse of a sudden passion.

❧ 127 ❧

THE TWO THIEVES
AND THE BEAR

A couple of Thieves knowing of a Calf, that was kept in an Ox's stall, had determined to steal it away in the dark, and accordingly appointed the hour of midnight, for meeting at the place to accomplish their evil design: one of them was to keep watch on the outside, whilst the other was to go into the stall, and lift the Calf out of the window. On the night proposed, they accordingly went to the place; and one of them entered the window of the Ox's stall, whilst he that remained on watch, not without much fear of detection, desired his companion to make as much haste as possible: but he that was within answered, that the animal was so heavy and unmanageable, that he could not lift him from the ground, much less to the window: the other's impatience now increasing by the delay, he began to swear at him for his clumsy awkwardness, and at last told him to give the business up, if he could not accomplish it quickly, and make the best of his way out of the stall; for, if they remained in this manner till daylight, they should certainly be discovered. The other with many oaths replied, that he believed it was the devil himself he had to deal with; for, said he, "I cannot now even get out myself, he has got such fast hold of me."—The companion, no longer being able to stay with safety, ran off and left him to his fate. The fact was this: the Calf had been removed from the stall, soon after the Thieves had seen it there, to make room for a Bear that had been brought into the town as a show; and it was this great beast that the Thief had the misfortune to encounter, and who kept hugging him till the morning, when he was discovered by the master of the Bear and taken to prison.

A knave may gain more than an honest man for a day, but the honest man will gain more than the knave in a year.

128

THE WALNUT TREE

A walnut tree, which grew by the roadside, bore every year a plentiful crop of nuts. Everyone who passed by pelted its branches with sticks and stones, in order to bring down the fruit, and the tree suffered severely. "It is hard," it cried, "that the very persons who enjoy my fruit should thus reward me with insults and blows."

129

THE MAN AND THE LION

A man and a lion were companions on a journey, and in the course of conversation they began to boast about their prowess, and each claimed to be superior to the other in strength and courage. They were still arguing with some heat when they came to a crossroad where there was a statue of a man strangling a lion. "There!" said the man triumphantly, "look at that! Doesn't that prove to you that we are stronger than you?" "Not so fast, my friend," said the lion. "That is only your view of the case. If we lions could make statues, you may be sure that in most of them you would see the man underneath."

There are two sides to every question.

⚜ 130 ⚜

THE TORTOISE AND THE EAGLE

A tortoise, discontented with his lowly life, and envious of the birds he saw disporting themselves in the air, begged an eagle to teach him to fly. The eagle protested that it was idle for him to try, as nature had not provided him with wings; but the tortoise pressed him with entreaties and promises of treasure, insisting that it could only be a question of learning the craft of the air. So at length the eagle consented to do the best he could for him, and picked him up in his talons. Soaring with him to a great height in the sky he then let him go, and the wretched tortoise fell headlong and was dashed to pieces on a rock.

Vanity causes its own punishment.

⚘ 131 ⚘
THE SERPENT AND THE EAGLE

An eagle swooped down upon a serpent and seized it in his talons with the intention of carrying it off and devouring it. But the serpent was too quick for him and had its coils round him in a moment; and then there ensued a life-and-death struggle between the two. A countryman, who was a witness of the encounter, came to the assistance of the eagle, and succeeded in freeing him from the serpent and enabling him to escape. In revenge the serpent spat some of his poison into the man's drinking horn. Heated with his exertions, the man was about to slake his thirst with a draught from the horn, when the eagle knocked it out of his hand, and spilled its contents upon the ground.

One good turn deserves another.

⚘ 132 ⚘
THE ROGUE AND THE ORACLE

A rogue laid a wager that he would prove the Oracle at Delphi to be untrustworthy by procuring from it a false reply to an inquiry by himself. So he went to the temple on the appointed day with a small bird in his hand, which he concealed under the folds of his cloak, and asked whether what he held in his hand were alive

or dead. If the Oracle said "dead," he meant to produce the bird alive. If the reply was "alive," he intended to wring its neck and show it to be dead. But the Oracle was one too many for him, for the answer he got was this: "Stranger, whether the thing that you hold in your hand be alive or dead is a matter that depends entirely on your own will."

⚜ 133 ⚜

GRIEF AND HIS DUE

When Jupiter was assigning the various gods their privileges, it so happened that Grief was not present with the rest. But when all had received their share, he too entered and claimed his due. Jupiter was at a loss to know what to do, for there was nothing left for him. However, at last he decided that to him should belong the tears that are shed for the dead. Thus it is the same with Grief as it is with the other gods. The more devoutly men render to him his due, the more lavish is he of that which he has to bestow. It is not well, therefore, to mourn long for the departed; else Grief, whose sole pleasure is in such mourning, will be quick to send fresh cause for tears.

Do not grieve too long at the death of a loved one.

◁ 134 ▷

THE VAIN JACKDAW

J upiter announced that he intended to appoint a king over the birds, and named a day on which they were to appear before his throne, when he would select the most beautiful of them all to be their ruler. Wishing to look their best on the occasion they repaired to the banks of a stream, where they busied themselves in washing and preening their feathers. The jackdaw was there along with the rest, and realized that, with his ugly plumage, he would have no chance of being chosen as he was. So he waited till they were all gone, and then picked up the most gaudy of the feathers they had dropped, and fastened them about his own body, with the result that he looked

gayer than any of them. When the appointed day came, the birds assembled before Jupiter's throne; and, after passing them in review, he was about to make the jackdaw king, when all the rest set upon the king-elect, stripped him of his borrowed plumes, and exposed him for the jackdaw that he was.

It is not only fine feathers that make fine birds.

⚜ 135 ⚜
THE TRAVELER AND HIS DOG

A traveler was about to start on a journey, and said to his dog, who was stretching himself by the door, "Come, what are you yawning for? Hurry up and get ready. I mean you to go with me." But the dog merely wagged his tail and said quietly, "I'm ready, master. It's you I'm waiting for."

⚜ 136 ⚜
THE SHIPWRECKED MAN AND THE SEA

A shipwrecked man cast up on the beach fell asleep after his struggle with the waves. When he woke up, he bitterly reproached the sea for its treachery in enticing men with its smooth and smiling surface, and then, when they were well embarked, turning in fury upon them and sending both ship and sailors to destruction. The sea arose in the form of a woman, and replied, "Lay not the blame on me, O sailor, but on the winds. By nature I am as calm and safe as the land itself, but the winds fall upon me with their gusts and gales, and lash me into a fury that is not natural to me."

⚜ 137 ⚜
THE WILD BOAR AND THE FOX

A wild boar was engaged in whetting his tusks upon the trunk of a tree in the forest when a fox came by and, seeing what he was at, said to him, "Why are you doing that, pray? The huntsmen are not out today, and there are no other dangers at hand that I can see." "True, my friend," replied the boar, "but the instant my life is in danger I shall need to use my tusks. There'll be no time to sharpen them then."

It is too late to whet the sword when the trumpet sounds.

❧ 138 ❧

MERCURY AND
THE SCULPTOR

Mercury was very anxious to know in what estimation he was held by mankind; so he disguised himself as a man and walked into a sculptor's studio, where there were a number of statues finished and ready for sale. Seeing a statue of Jupiter among the rest, he inquired the price of it. "A crown," said the sculptor. "Is that all?" said he, laughing. "And (pointing to one of Juno) how much is that one?" "That," was the reply, "is half a crown." "And how much might you be wanting for that one over there, now?" he continued, pointing to a statue of himself. "That one?" said the sculptor. "Oh, I'll throw him in for nothing if you'll buy the other two."

❧ 139 ❧

THE FAWN AND
HIS MOTHER

A young fawn once said to his mother, "You are larger than a dog, and swifter, and more used to running, and you have your horns as a defense; why, then, O mother, do the hounds frighten you so?" She smiled, and said: "I know full well, my son, that all you say is true. I have the advantages you mention, but when I hear even the bark of a single dog I feel ready to faint, and fly away as fast as I can."

No arguments will give courage to the coward.

◁ 140 ▷
THE FOX AND THE LION

A fox who had never seen a lion one day met one, and was so terrified at the sight of him that he was ready to die with fear. After a time he met him again, and was still rather frightened, but not nearly so much as he had been when he met him first. But when he saw him for the third time he was so far from being afraid that he went up to him and began to talk to him as if he had known him all his life.

Familiarity breeds contempt.

141

THE EAGLE AND HIS CAPTOR

A man once caught an eagle, and after clipping his wings turned him loose among the fowls in his henhouse, where he moped in a corner, looking very dejected and forlorn. After a while his captor was glad enough to sell him to a neighbor, who took him home and let his wings grow again. As soon as he had recovered the use of them, the eagle flew out and caught a hare, which he brought home and presented to his benefactor. A fox observed this, and said to the eagle, "Don't waste your gifts on him! Go and give them to the man who first caught you; make *him* your friend, and then perhaps he won't catch you and clip your wings a second time."

142

THE BLACKSMITH AND HIS DOG

A blacksmith had a little dog, which used to sleep when his master was at work, but was very wide awake indeed when it was time for meals. One day his master pretended to be disgusted at this, and when he had thrown him a bone as usual, he said, "What on earth is the good of a lazy cur like you? When I am hammering away at my anvil, you just curl up and go

to sleep; but no sooner do I stop for a mouthful of food than you wake up and wag your tail to be fed."

Those who will not work deserve to starve.

⚜ 143 ⚜

THE STAG AT THE POOL

A thirsty stag went down to a pool to drink. As he bent over the surface he saw his own reflection in the water, and was struck with admiration for his fine spreading antlers, but at the same time he felt nothing but disgust for the weakness and slenderness of his legs. While he stood there looking at himself, he was seen and attacked by a lion; but in the chase which ensued, he soon drew away from his pursuer, and kept his lead as long as the ground over which he ran was open and free of trees. But coming presently to a wood, he was caught by his antlers in the branches, and fell a victim to the teeth and claws of his enemy. "Woe is me!" he cried with his last breath; "I despised my legs, which might have saved my life: but I gloried in my horns, and they have proved my ruin."

What is worth most is often valued least.

❧ 144 ❧
THE DOG AND THE SHADOW

A dog was crossing a plank bridge over a stream with a piece of meat in his mouth, when he happened to see his own reflection in the water. He thought it was another dog with a piece of meat twice as big; so he let go his own, and flew at the other dog to get the larger piece. But, of course, all that happened was that he got neither; for one was only a shadow, and the other was carried away by the current.

Beware lest you lose the substance
by grasping at the shadow.

⚜ 145 ⚜
MERCURY AND THE TRADESMEN

When Jupiter was creating man, he told Mercury to make an infusion of lies, and to add a little of it to the other ingredients which went to the making of the tradesmen. Mercury did so, and introduced an equal amount into each in turn—the tallow chandler, and the greengrocer, and the haberdasher, and all, till he came to the horse dealer, who was last on the list, when, finding that he had a quantity of the infusion still left, he put it all into him. This is why all tradesmen lie more or less, but they none of them lie like a horse dealer.

⚜ 146 ⚜
THE MICE AND THE WEASELS

There was war between the mice and the weasels, in which the mice always got the worst of it, numbers of them being killed and eaten by the weasels. So they called a council of war, in which an old mouse got up and said, "It's no wonder we are always beaten, for we have no generals to plan our battles and direct our movements in the field." Acting on his advice, they chose the biggest mice to be their leaders, and these, in order to be distinguished from the rank and file, provided themselves with helmets bearing large plumes of straw. They then led out the mice to battle, confident of victory; but they were defeated as usual, and were soon scampering as fast as they could to their holes. All made their way to safety without difficulty except the leaders, who were so hampered by the badges of their rank that they could not get into their holes, and fell easy victims to their pursuers.

Greatness carries its own penalties.

◁ 147 ▷
THE PEACOCK AND JUNO

The peacock was greatly discontented because he had not a beautiful voice like the nightingale, and he went and complained to Juno about it. "The nightingale's song," said he, "is the envy of all the birds; but whenever I utter a sound I become a laughingstock." The goddess tried to console him by saying, "You have not, it is true, the power of song, but then you far excel all the rest in beauty. Your neck flashes like the emerald, and your splendid tail is a marvel of gorgeous color." But the peacock was not appeased. "What is the use," said he, "of being beautiful, with a voice like mine?" Then Juno replied, with a shade of sternness in her tone, "Fate has allotted to all their destined gifts: to yourself beauty, to the eagle strength, to the nightingale song, and so on to all the rest in their degree. But you alone are dissatisfied with your portion. Make, then, no more complaints. For, if your present wish were granted, you would quickly find cause for fresh discontent."

Be content with your lot; one cannot
be first in everything.

⚜ 148 ⚜
THE BEAR AND THE FOX

A bear was once bragging about his generous feelings, and saying how refined he was compared with other animals. (There is, in fact, a tradition that a bear will never touch a dead body.) A fox, who heard him talking in this strain, smiled and said, "My friend, when you are hungry, I only wish you would confine your attention to the dead and leave the living alone."

A hypocrite deceives no one but himself.

The Bear and the Fox

THE ASS AND THE OLD PEASANT

An old peasant was sitting in a meadow watching his ass, which was grazing close by, when all of a sudden he caught sight of armed men stealthily approaching. He jumped up in a moment, and begged the ass to fly with him as fast as he could, "Or else," said he, "we shall both be captured by the enemy." But the ass just looked around lazily and said, "And if so, do you think they'll make me carry heavier loads than I have to now?" "No," said his master. "Oh, well, then," said the ass, "I don't mind if they do take me, for I shan't be any worse off."

150

THE ASS AND HIS MASTERS

A gardener had an ass which had a very hard time of it, what with scanty food, heavy loads, and constant beating. The ass therefore begged Jupiter to take him away from the gardener and hand him over to another master. So Jupiter sent Mercury to the gardener to bid him sell the ass to a potter, which he did. But the ass was as discontented as ever, for he had to work harder than before; so he begged Jupiter for relief a second time, and Jupiter very obligingly arranged that he should be sold to a tanner. But when the ass saw what his new master's trade was, he cried in despair, "Why wasn't I content to serve either of my former masters, hard as I had to work and badly as I was treated? For they would have buried me decently, but now I shall come in the end to the tanning vat."

Servants don't know a good master
till they have served a worse.

151

THE PACK ASS, THE WILD ASS, AND THE LION

A wild ass saw a pack ass jogging along under a heavy load, and taunted him with the condition of slavery in which he lived, in these words: "What a vile

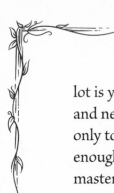

lot is yours compared with mine! I am free as the air, and never do a stroke of work; and, as for fodder, I have only to go to the hills and there I find far more than enough for my needs. But you! You depend on your master for food, and he makes you carry heavy loads every day and beats you unmercifully." At that moment a lion appeared on the scene, and made no attempt to molest the pack ass owing to the presence of the driver; but he fell upon the wild ass, who had no one to protect him, and without more ado made a meal of him.

It is no use being your own master unless you can stand up for yourself.

❧ 152 ❧
THE ANT

Ants were once men and made their living by tilling the soil. But, not content with the results of their own work, they were always casting longing eyes upon the crops and fruits of their neighbors, which they stole, whenever they got the chance, and added to their own store. At last their covetousness made Jupiter so angry that he changed them into ants. But, though their forms were changed, their nature remained the same: and so, to this day, they go about among the cornfields and gather the fruits of others' labor, and store them up for their own use.

You may punish a thief, but his bent remains.

⚜ 153 ⚜

THE OX AND THE FROG

Two little frogs were playing about at the edge of a pool when an ox came down to the water to drink, and by accident trod on one of them and crushed the life out of him. When the old frog missed him, she asked his brother where he was. "He is dead, mother," said the little frog; "an enormous big creature with four legs came to our pool this morning and trampled him down in the mud." "Enormous, was he? Was he as big as this?" said the frog, puffing herself out to look as big as possible. "Oh! Yes, much bigger," was the answer. The frog puffed herself out still more. "Was he as big as this?" said she. "Oh! Yes, yes, mother, *much* bigger," said the little frog. And yet again she puffed and puffed herself out till she was almost as round as a ball. "As big as . . .?" she began—but then she burst.

◁ 154 ▷
THE MAN AND THE IMAGE

A poor man had a wooden image of a god, to which he used to pray daily for riches. He did this for a long time, but remained as poor as ever, till one day he caught up the image in disgust and hurled it with all his strength against the wall. The force of the blow split open the head and a quantity of gold coins fell out upon the floor. The man gathered them up greedily, and said, "O you old fraud, you! When I honored you, you did me no good whatever; but no sooner do I treat you to insults and violence than you make a rich man of me!"

◁ 155 ▷
HERCULES AND THE WAGONER

A wagoner was driving his team along a muddy lane with a full load behind them, when the wheels of his wagon sank so deep in the mire that no efforts of his horses could move them. As he stood there, looking helplessly on, and calling loudly at intervals upon Hercules for assistance, the god himself appeared, and said to him, "Put your shoulder to the wheel, man, and goad on your horses, and then you may call on Hercules to assist you. If you won't lift a finger to help yourself, you can't expect Hercules or any one else to come to your aid."

Heaven helps those who help themselves.

❧ 156 ❧

THE POMEGRANATE, THE APPLE TREE, AND THE BRAMBLE

A Pomegranate and an apple tree were disputing about the quality of their fruits, and each claimed that its own was the better of the two. High words passed between them, and a violent quarrel was imminent, when a bramble impudently poked its head out of a neighboring hedge and said, "There, that's enough, my friends; don't let us quarrel."

❧ 157 ❧

THE LION, THE BEAR, AND THE FOX

A lion and a bear were fighting for possession of a kid, which they had both seized at the same moment. The battle was long and fierce, and at length both of them were exhausted, and lay upon the ground severely wounded and gasping for breath. A fox had all the time been prowling around and watching the fight, and when he saw the combatants lying there too weak to move, he slipped in and seized the kid, and ran off with it. They looked on helplessly, and one said to the other, "Here we've been mauling each other all this while, and no one the better for it except the fox!"

It sometimes happens that one man has all the toil, and another all the profit.

158

THE TROOPER AND HIS HORSE

As a Trooper was currying his Horse, he noticed that one of the shoe-nails had dropped out, yet he postponed for the present striking in another nail. Soon after he was summoned by sound of trumpet to join his corps, which was commanded to advance rapidly and charge the enemy. In the heat of the action the loose shoe fell off, his horse became lame, stumbled, and threw his rider to the ground. The Trooper was immediately slain by the enemy.

Small duties neglected become great perils.

159

THE TWO SOLDIERS AND THE ROBBER

Two soldiers traveling together were set upon by a robber. One of them ran away, but the other stood

his ground, and laid about him so lustily with his sword that the robber was fain to fly and leave him in peace. When the coast was clear the timid one ran back, and, flourishing his weapon, cried in a threatening voice, "Where is he? Let me get at him, and I'll soon let him know whom he's got to deal with." But the other replied, "You are a little late, my friend. I only wish you had backed me up just now, even if you had done no more than speak, for I should have been encouraged, believing your words to be true. As it is, calm yourself, and put up your sword. There is no further use for it. You may delude others into thinking you're as brave as a lion; but I know that, at the first sign of danger, you run away like a hare."

⚘ 160 ⚘

THE LION AND THE WILD ASS

A lion and a wild ass went out hunting together. The latter was to run down the prey by his superior speed, and the former would then come up and dispatch it. They met with great success; and when it came to sharing the spoil the lion divided it all into three equal portions. "I will take the first," said he, "because I am king of the beasts; I will also take the second, because, as your partner, I am entitled to half of what remains; and as for the third—well, unless you give it up to me and take yourself off pretty quick, the third, believe me, will make you feel very sorry for yourself!"

Might makes right.

⚜ 161 ⚜
THE MAN AND THE SATYR

A man and a satyr became friends, and determined to live together. All went well for a while, until one day in wintertime the satyr saw the man blowing on his hands. "Why do you do that?" he asked. "To warm my hands," said the man. That same day, when they sat down to supper together, they each had a steaming hot bowl of porridge, and the man raised his bowl to his mouth and blew on it. "Why do you do that?" asked the satyr. "To cool my porridge," said the man. The satyr got up from the table. "Good-bye," said he, "I'm going. I can't be friends with a man who blows hot and cold with the same breath."

_{§ 162 §}

THE IMAGE SELLER

A certain man made a wooden image of Mercury, and exposed it for sale in the market. As no one offered to buy it, however, he thought he would try to attract a purchaser by proclaiming the virtues of the image. So he cried up and down the market, "A god for sale! A god for sale! One who'll bring you luck and keep you lucky!" Presently one of the bystanders stopped him and said, "If your god is all you make him out to be, how is it you don't keep him and make the most of him yourself?" "I'll tell you why," replied he; "he brings gain, it is true, but he takes his time about it; whereas I want money at once."

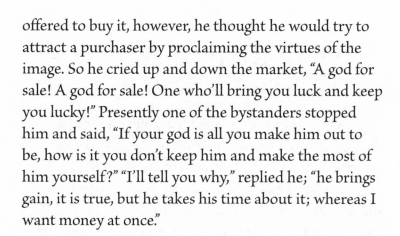

❦ 163 ❧

THE EAGLE AND THE ARROW

An eagle sat perched on a lofty rock, keeping a sharp lookout for prey. A huntsman, concealed in a cleft of the mountain and on the watch for game, spied him there and shot an arrow at him. The shaft struck him full in the breast and pierced him through and through. As he lay in the agonies of death, he turned his eyes upon the arrow. "Ah, cruel fate!" he cried, "that I should perish thus. But oh, fate more cruel still, that the arrow which kills me should be winged with an eagle's feathers!"

We often give our enemies the means
for our own destruction.

❦ 164 ❦

THE RICH MAN AND THE TANNER

A rich man took up his residence next door to a tanner, and found the smell of the tan yard so extremely unpleasant that he told him he must go. The tanner delayed his departure, and the rich man had to speak to him several times about it; and every time the tanner said he was making arrangements to move very shortly. This went on for some time, till at last the rich man got so used to the smell that he ceased to mind it, and troubled the tanner with his objections no more.

❦ 165 ❦

THE WOLF, THE MOTHER, AND HER CHILD

A hungry wolf was prowling about in search of food. By and by, attracted by the cries of a child, he came to a cottage. As he crouched beneath the window, he heard the mother say to the child, "Stop crying, do or I'll throw you to the wolf!" Thinking she really meant what she said, he waited there a long time in the expectation of satisfying his hunger. In the evening he heard the mother fondling her child and saying, "If the naughty wolf comes, he shan't get my little one. Daddy will kill him." The wolf got up in much disgust and walked away: "As for the people in that house," said he to himself, "you can't believe a word they say."

Do not trust the words of your enemies.

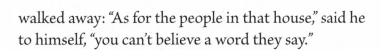

𝕔 166 𝕓

THE OLD WOMAN AND THE WINE JAR

An old woman picked up an empty wine jar which had once contained a rare and costly wine, and which still retained some traces of its exquisite bouquet. She raised it to her nose and sniffed at it again and again. "Ah," she cried, "how delicious must have been the liquid which has left behind so ravishing a smell."

◁ 167 ▷

THE SICK KITE

A Kite, who had been ill for a long time, begged of his mother to go to all the temples in the country, and see what prayers and promises could do for his recovery. The old Kite replied, "My son, unless you can think of an altar that neither of us has robbed, I fear that nothing can be done for you in that way."

Be in health what you wish to be when you are ill.

◁ 168 ▷

THE CAMEL

When men first saw the Camel, they were so frightened at his vast size that they fled away. After a time, perceiving the meekness and gentleness of his temper, they summoned courage enough to approach him. Soon afterwards, observing that he was an animal altogether deficient in spirit, they assumed such boldness as to put a bridle in his mouth, and to set a child to drive him.

Use serves to overcome dread.

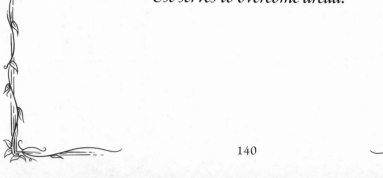

169

THE SOW AND THE WOLF

A Sow lay one day in the sty with her whole litter of pigs about her. A Wolf who longed for a small porker, but knew not how to get it, tried to worm himself into the good opinion of the mother. "How do you find yourself today, Mrs. Sow?" said he. "A little fresh air would certainly do you great good. Now, do go abroad and air yourself a little, and I will gladly mind your children till you return." "Many thanks for your offer," replied the Sow. "I know very well what kind of care you would take of my little ones, but if you really wish to be as obliging as you pretend to be, you will not show me your face again."

Services from strangers are to be suspected.

170

THE HEN AND THE SWALLOW

There was once a foolish Hen, that sat brooding upon a nest of Snakes' eggs. A Swallow perceiving it, flew to her, and told her what danger she was in. "Silly creature," said she, "you are hatching vipers. The moment they see the light, they will turn and wreak their venomous spite upon you."

Beware the consequences of your actions.

❦ 171 ❧

THE LIONESS AND THE VIXEN

A lioness and a vixen were talking together about their young, as mothers will, and saying how healthy and well-grown they were, and what beautiful coats they had, and how they were the image of their parents. "My litter of cubs is a joy to see," said the fox; and then she added, rather maliciously, "But I notice you never have more than one." "No," said the lioness grimly, "but that one's a lion."

Quality, not quantity.

❦ 172 ❧

THE VIPER AND THE FILE

A viper entered a carpenter's shop, and went from one to another of the tools, begging for something to eat. Among the rest, he addressed himself to the file, and asked for the favor of a meal. The file replied in a tone of pitying contempt, "What a simpleton you must be if you imagine you will get anything from me, who invariably take from everyone and never give anything in return."

The covetous are poor givers.

⚜ 173 ⚜
THE CAT AND THE COCK

A cat pounced on a cock, and cast about for some good excuse for making a meal off him, for cats don't as a rule eat cocks, and she knew she ought not to. At last she said, "You make a great nuisance of yourself at night by crowing and keeping people awake: so I am going to make an end of you." But the cock defended himself by saying that he crowed in order that men might wake up and set about the day's work in good time, and that they really couldn't very well do without him. "That may be," said the cat, "but whether they can or not, I'm not going without my dinner." And she killed and ate him.

The want of a good excuse never
kept a villain from crime.

❧ 174 ❧

THE GNAT AND THE BEE

A Gnat, half starved with cold and hunger, went one frosty morning to a beehive to beg charity; and offered to teach music in the Bee's family for her food and lodging. The Bee very civilly desired to be excused, "For," said she, "I bring up all my children to my own trade, that they may be able to get their living by their industry; and I am sure I am right, for see what that music, which you would teach my children, has brought you yourself to."

The worth of a calling is shown by its benefits.

❧ 175 ❧

THE TWO RATS

A cunning old Rat discovered in his rounds a most tempting piece of cheese, which was placed in a trap. But being well aware that if he touched it he would be caught, he slyly sought one of his young friends, and, under the mask of friendship, informed him of the prize. "I cannot use it myself," said he, "for I have just made a hearty meal." The inexperienced youngster thanked him with gratitude for the news, and heedlessly sprang upon the tempting bait; on which the trap closed and instantly destroyed him.

His companion, being now quite secure, quietly ate up the cheese.

Do not listen to every passerby.

 176

THE BLIND MAN AND THE LAME MAN

A Blind Man being stopped in a bad piece of road, met with a Lame Man, and entreated him to guide him through the difficulty he had got into. "How can I do that?" replied the Lame Man, "since I am scarce able to drag myself along?—but as you appear to be very strong, if you will carry me, we will seek our fortunes together. It will then be my interest to warn you of anything that may obstruct your way; your feet shall be my feet, and my eyes your eyes." "With all my heart," returned the Blind Man; "let us render each other our mutual services." So taking his lame companion on his back, they, by means of their union, traveled on with safety and pleasure.

From our wants and infirmities almost all the connections of society take their rise.

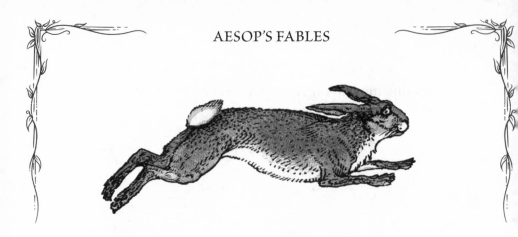

❧ 177 ❧

THE HARE AND THE TORTOISE

A hare was one day making fun of a tortoise for being so slow upon his feet. "Wait a bit," said the tortoise; "I'll run a race with you, and I'll wager that I win." "Oh, well," replied the hare, who was much amused at the idea, "let's try and see." And it was soon agreed that the fox should set a course for them, and be the judge. When the time came both started off together, but the hare was soon so far ahead that he thought he might as well have a rest. So down he lay and fell fast asleep. Meanwhile the tortoise kept plodding on, and in time reached the goal. At last the hare woke up with a start, and dashed on at his fastest, but only to find that the tortoise had already won the race.

Slow and steady wins the race.

❧ 178 ❧

THE SOLDIER AND HIS HORSE

A soldier gave his horse a plentiful supply of oats in time of war, and tended him with the utmost care, for he wished him to be strong to endure the hardships of the field, and swift to bear his master, when need arose, out of the reach of danger. But when the war was over he employed him on all sorts of drudgery, bestowing but little attention upon him, and giving him, moreover, nothing but chaff to eat. The time came when war broke out again, and the soldier saddled and bridled his horse, and, having put on his heavy coat of mail, mounted him to ride off and take the field. But the poor half-starved beast sank down under his weight, and said to his rider, "You will have to go into battle on foot this time. Thanks to hard work and bad food, you have turned me from a horse into an ass; and you cannot in a moment turn me back again into a horse."

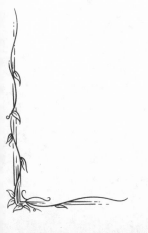
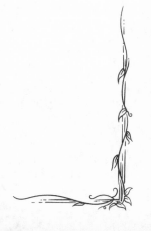

◁ 179 ▷
THE OXEN AND
THE BUTCHERS

O nce upon a time the oxen determined to be revenged upon the butchers for the havoc they wrought in their ranks, and plotted to put them to death on a given day. They were all gathered together discussing how best to carry out the plan, and the more violent of them were engaged in sharpening their horns for the fray, when an old ox got up upon his feet and said, "My brothers, you have good reason, I know, to hate these butchers, but, at any rate, they understand their trade and do what they have to do without causing unnecessary pain. But if we kill them, others, who have no experience, will be set to slaughter us, and will by their bungling inflict great sufferings upon us. For you may be sure that, even though all the butchers perish, mankind will never go without their beef."

Don't be in a hurry to change one evil for another.

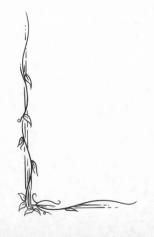

180

THE WOLF AND THE LION

A wolf stole a lamb from the flock, and was carrying it off to devour it at his leisure when he met a lion, who took his prey away from him and walked off with it. He dared not resist, but when the lion had gone some distance he said, "It is most unjust of you to take what's mine away from me like that." The lion laughed and called out in reply, "It was justly yours, no doubt! The gift of a friend, perhaps, eh?"

181

THE SHEEP, THE WOLF,
AND THE STAG

A stag once asked a sheep to lend him a measure of wheat, saying that his friend the wolf would be his surety. The sheep, however, was afraid that they meant to cheat her; so she excused herself, saying, "The wolf is in the habit of seizing what he wants and running off with it without paying, and you, too, can run much faster than I. So how shall I be able to come up with either of you when the debt falls due?"

Two blacks do not make a white.

❧ 182 ❧
THE LION AND THE THREE BULLS

T hree bulls were grazing in a meadow, and were watched by a lion, who longed to capture and devour them, but who felt that he was no match for the three so long as they kept together. So he began by false whispers and malicious hints to foment jealousies and distrust among them. This stratagem succeeded so well that ere long the bulls grew cold and unfriendly, and finally avoided each other and fed each one by himself apart. No sooner did the lion see this than he fell upon them one by one and killed them in turn.

The quarrels of friends are the opportunities of foes.

❧ 183 ❧
THE HORSE AND HIS RIDER

A young man, who fancied himself something of a horseman, mounted a horse which had not been properly broken in, and was exceedingly difficult to control. No sooner did the horse feel his weight in the saddle than he bolted, and nothing would stop him. A friend of the rider's met him in the road in his headlong career, and called out, "Where are you off to in such a hurry?" To which he, pointing to the horse, replied, "I've no idea: ask him."

✤ 184 ✤

THE GOAT AND THE VINE

A goat was straying in a vineyard, and began to browse on the tender shoots of a vine which bore several fine bunches of grapes. "What have I done to you," said the vine, "that you should harm me thus? Isn't there grass enough for you to feed on? All the same, even if you eat up every leaf I have, and leave me quite bare, I shall produce wine enough to pour over you when you are led to the altar to be sacrificed."

❦ 185 ❦
THE TWO POTS

Two pots, one of earthenware and the other of brass, were carried away down a river in flood. The brazen pot urged his companion to keep close by his side, and he would protect him. The other thanked him, but begged him not to come near him on any account: "For that," he said, "is just what I am most afraid of. One touch from you and I should be broken in pieces."

Equals make the best friends.

❦ 186 ❦
THE OLD HOUND

A hound who had served his master well for years, and had run down many a quarry in his time, began to lose his strength and speed owing to age. One day, when out hunting, his master started a powerful wild boar and set the hound at him. The latter seized the beast by the ear, but his teeth were gone and he could not retain his hold; so the boar escaped. His master began to scold him severely, but the hound interrupted him with these words: "My will is as strong as ever, master, but my body is old and feeble. You ought to honor me for what I have been instead of abusing me for what I am."

⚜ 187 ⚜

THE CLOWN AND THE COUNTRYMAN

A nobleman announced his intention of giving a public entertainment in the theatre, and offered splendid prizes to all who had any novelty to exhibit at the performance. The announcement attracted a crowd of conjurers, jugglers, and acrobats, and among the rest a clown, very popular with the crowd, who let it be known that he was going to give an entirely new turn. When the day of the performance came, the theatre was filled from top to bottom some time before the entertainment began. Several performers exhibited their tricks, and then the popular favorite came on empty-handed and alone. At once there was a hush of expectation: and he, letting his head fall upon his breast, imitated the squeak of a pig to such perfection that the audience insisted on his producing the animal, which, they said, he must have somewhere concealed about his person. He, however, convinced them that there was no pig there, and then the applause was deafening. Among the spectators was a countryman, who disparaged the clown's performance and announced that he would give a much superior exhibition of the same trick on the following day. Again the theatre was filled to overflowing, and again the clown gave his imitation amidst the cheers of the crowd. The countryman, meanwhile, before going on the stage, had secreted a young porker under his smock; and when the spectators derisively bade him do better if he could, he gave it a pinch in the ear and made it squeal loudly. But they all with one voice shouted out that the clown's imitation was much more true to life. Thereupon he produced the pig from under his smock and said sarcastically, "There, that shows what sort of judges you are!"

⚜ 188 ⚜

THE LARK AND THE FARMER

A lark nested in a field of corn, and was rearing her brood under cover of the ripening grain. One day, before the young were fully fledged, the farmer came to look at the crop, and, finding it yellowing fast, he said, "I must send around word to my neighbors to come and help me reap this field." One of the young larks overheard him, and was very much frightened, and asked her mother whether they hadn't better move house at once. "There's no hurry," replied she; "a man who looks to his friends for help will take his time about a thing." In a few days the farmer came by again, and saw that the grain was overripe and falling out of the ears upon the ground. "I must put it off no longer," he said; "This very day I'll hire the men and set them to work at once." The lark heard him and said to her young, "Come, my children, we must be off: he talks no more of his friends now, but is going to take things in hand himself."

Self-help is the best help.

❧ 189 ☙
THE LION AND THE ASS

A lion and an ass set up as partners and went a-hunting together. In course of time they came to a cave in which there were a number of wild goats. The lion took up his stand at the mouth of the cave, and waited for them to come out; while the ass went inside and brayed for all he was worth in order to frighten them out into the open. The lion struck them down one by one as they appeared; and when the cave was empty the ass came out and said, "Well, I scared them pretty well, didn't I?" "I should think you did," said the lion: "why, if I hadn't known you were an ass, I should have turned and run myself."

◁ 190 ▷
THE PROPHET

A prophet sat in the marketplace and told the fortunes of all who cared to engage his services. Suddenly there came running up one who told him that his house had been broken into by thieves, and that they had made off with everything they could lay hands on. He was up in a moment, and rushed off, tearing his hair and calling down curses on the miscreants. The bystanders were much amused, and one of them said, "Our friend professes to know what is going to happen to others, but it seems he's not clever enough to perceive what's in store for himself."

◁ 191 ▷
THE HOUND AND THE HARE

A young hound started a hare, and, when he caught her up, would at one moment snap at her with

his teeth as though he were about to kill her, while at another he would let go his hold and frisk about her, as if he were playing with another dog. At last the hare said, "I wish you would show yourself in your true colors! If you are my friend, why do you bite me? If you are my enemy, why do you play with me?"

He is no friend who plays double.

⊰ 192 ⊱

THE LION, THE MOUSE, AND THE FOX

A lion was lying asleep at the mouth of his den when a mouse ran over his back and tickled him so that he woke up with a start and began looking about everywhere to see what it was that had disturbed him. A fox, who was looking on, thought he would have a joke at the expense of the lion; so he said, "Well, this is the first time I've seen a lion afraid of a mouse." "Afraid of a mouse?" said the lion testily: "not I! It's his bad manners I can't stand."

Little liberties are great offenses.

⚜ 193 ⚜
THE TRUMPETER
TAKEN PRISONER

A trumpeter marched into battle in the van of the army and put courage into his comrades by his warlike tunes. Being captured by the enemy, he begged for his life, and said, "Do not put me to death; I have killed no one: indeed, I have no weapons, but carry with me only my trumpet here." But his captors replied, "That is only the more reason why we should take your life; for, though you do not fight yourself, you stir up others to do so."

He who incites strife is worse than
he who takes part in it.

⚜ 194 ⚜
THE WOLF AND THE CRANE

A wolf once got a bone stuck in his throat. So he went to a crane and begged her to put her long bill down his throat and pull it out. "I'll make it worth your while," he added. The crane did as she was asked, and got the bone out quite easily. The wolf thanked her warmly, and was just turning away, when she cried, "What about that fee of mine?" "Well, what about it?" snapped the wolf, baring his teeth as he spoke; "you can go about boasting that you once put your head into a wolf's mouth and didn't get it bitten off. What more do you want?"

In serving the wicked, expect no reward, and be thankful if you escape injury for your pains.

❦ 195 ❦

THE EAGLE, THE CAT, AND THE WILD SOW

An eagle built her nest at the top of a high tree; a cat with her family occupied a hollow in the trunk half-way down; and a wild sow and her young took up their quarters at the foot. They might have got on very well as neighbors had it not been for the evil cunning of the cat. Climbing up to the eagle's nest she said to the eagle, "You and I are in the greatest possible danger. That dreadful creature, the sow, who is always to be seen grubbing away at the foot of the tree, means to uproot it, that she may devour your family and mine at her ease." Having thus driven the eagle almost out of her senses with terror, the cat climbed down the tree, and said to the sow, "I must warn you against that dreadful bird, the eagle. She is only waiting her chance to fly down and carry off one of your little pigs when you take them out, to feed her brood with." She succeeded in frightening the sow as much as the eagle. Then she returned to her hole in the trunk, from which, feigning to be afraid, she never came forth by day. Only by night did she creep out unseen to procure food for her kittens. The eagle, meanwhile was afraid to stir from her nest, and the sow dared not leave her home among the roots: so that in time both they and their families perished of hunger, and their dead bodies supplied the cat with ample food for her growing family.

Gossips are to be seen and not heard.

❧ 196 ❧

THE WOLF AND THE SHEEP

A wolf was worried and badly bitten by dogs, and lay a long time for dead. By and by he began to revive, and, feeling very hungry, called out to a passing sheep and said, "Would you kindly bring me some water from the stream close by? I can manage about meat, if only I could get something to drink." But this sheep was no fool. "I can quite understand," said he, "that if I brought you the water, you would have no difficulty about the meat. Good morning."

Hypocritical speeches are easily seen through.

❧ 197 ❧

THE TUNA FISH AND THE DOLPHIN

A tuna fish was chased by a dolphin and splashed through the water at a great rate, but the dolphin gradually gained upon him, and was just about to seize him when the force of his flight carried the tuna onto a sandbank. In the heat of the chase the dolphin followed him, and there they both lay out of the water, gasping for dear life. When the tuna saw that his enemy was doomed like himself, he said, "I don't mind having to die now: for I see that he who is the cause of my death is about to share the same fate."

◁ 198 ▷

THE THREE TRADESMEN

The citizens of a certain city were debating about the best material to use in the fortifications which were about to be erected for the greater security of the town. A carpenter got up and advised the use of wood, which he said was readily procurable and easily worked. A stone-mason objected to wood on the ground that it was so inflammable, and recommended stones instead. Then a tanner got on his legs and said, "In my opinion there's nothing like leather."

Every man for himself.

◁ 199 ▷

THE MOUSE AND THE BULL

A bull gave chase to a mouse which had bitten him in the nose: but the mouse was too quick for him and slipped into a hole in a wall. The bull charged furiously into the wall again and again until he was tired out, and sank down on the ground exhausted with his efforts. When all was quiet, the mouse darted out and bit him again. Beside himself with rage he started to his feet, but by that time the mouse was back in his hole again, and he could do nothing but bellow and fume in helpless anger. Presently he heard a shrill little voice say from inside the wall, "You big fellows don't always have it your own way, you see: sometimes we little ones come off best."

The battle is not always to the strong.

⊰ 200 ⊱

THE HARE AND THE HOUND

A hound started a hare from her form, and pursued her for some distance; but as she gradually gained upon him, he gave up the chase. A rustic who had seen the race met the hound as he was returning, and taunted him with his defeat. "The little one was too much for you," said he. "Ah, well," said the hound, "don't forget it's one thing to be running for your dinner, but quite another to be running for your life."

Necessity is our strongest weapon.

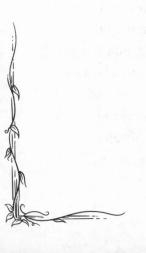

⚜ 201 ⚜

THE TOWN MOUSE AND THE COUNTRY MOUSE

A town mouse and a country mouse were acquaintances, and the country mouse one day invited his friend to come and see him at his home in the fields. The town mouse came, and they sat down to a dinner of barleycorns and roots, the latter of which had a distinctly earthy flavor. The fare was not much to the taste of the guest, and presently he broke out with "My poor dear friend, you live here no better than the ants. Now, you should just see how I fare! My larder is a regular horn of plenty. You must come and stay with me, and I promise you, you shall live on the fat of the land." So when he returned to town he took the country mouse with him, and showed him into a larder containing flour and oatmeal and figs and honey and dates. The country mouse had never seen anything like it, and sat down to enjoy the luxuries his friend provided: but before they had well begun, the door of the larder opened and some one came in. The two mice scampered off and hid themselves in a narrow and exceedingly uncomfortable hole. Presently, when all was quiet, they ventured out again; but some one else came in, and off they scuttled again. This was too much for the visitor. "Good-bye," said he, "I'm off. You live in the lap of luxury, I can see, but you are surrounded by dangers; whereas at home I can enjoy my simple dinner of roots and corn in peace."

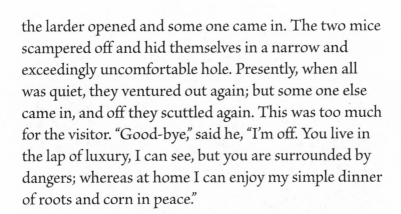

⊰ 202 ⊱

THE LION AND THE BULL

A lion saw a fine fat bull pasturing among a herd of cattle and cast about for some means of getting him into his clutches; so he sent him word that he was sacrificing a sheep, and asked if he would do him the honor of dining with him. The bull accepted the invitation, but, on arriving at the lion's den, he saw a great array of saucepans and spits, but no sign of a sheep; so he turned on his heel and walked quietly away. The lion called after him in an injured tone to ask the reason, and the bull turned around and said, "I have reason enough. When I saw all your preparations it struck me at once that the victim was to be a bull and not a sheep."

The net is spread in vain in sight of the bird.

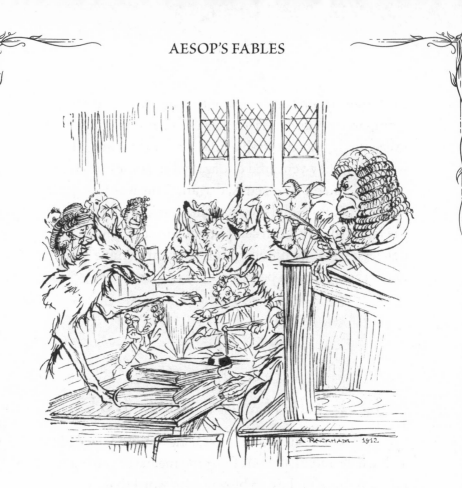

⚜ 203 ⚜

THE WOLF, THE FOX, AND THE APE

A wolf charged a fox with theft, which he denied, and the case was brought before an ape to be tried. When he had heard the evidence on both sides, the ape gave judgment as follows: "I do not think," he said, "that you, O wolf, ever lost what you claim; but all the same I believe that you, fox, are guilty of the theft, in spite of all your denials."

The dishonest get no credit, even if they act honestly.

❧ 204 ❧

THE EAGLE AND THE COCKS

There were two cocks in the same farmyard, and they fought to decide who should be master. When the fight was over, the beaten one went and hid himself in a dark corner; while the victor flew up on to the roof of the stables and crowed lustily. But an eagle espied him from high up in the sky, and swooped down and carried him off. Forthwith the other cock came out of his corner and ruled the roost without a rival.

Pride comes before a fall.

❧ 205 ❧

THE ESCAPED JACKDAW

A man caught a jackdaw and tied a piece of string to one of its legs, and then gave it to his children for a pet. But the jackdaw didn't at all like having to live with people; so, after a while, when he seemed to have become fairly tame and they didn't watch him so closely, he slipped away and flew back to his old haunts. Unfortunately, the string was still on his leg, and before long it got entangled in the branches of a tree and the jackdaw couldn't get free, try as he would. He saw it was all up with him, and cried in despair, "Alas, in gaining my freedom I have lost my life."

❧ 206 ❧

THE FARMER AND THE FOX

A farmer was greatly annoyed by a fox, which came prowling about his yard at night and carried off his fowls. So he set a trap for him and caught him; and in order to be revenged upon him, he tied a bunch of tow to his tail and set fire to it and let him go. As ill luck would have it, however, the fox made straight for the fields where the corn was standing ripe and ready for cutting. It quickly caught fire and was all burnt up, and the farmer lost all his harvest.

Revenge is a two-edged sword.

❧ 207 ❧

VENUS AND THE CAT

A cat fell in love with a handsome young man, and begged the goddess Venus to change her into a woman. Venus was very gracious about it, and changed her at once into a beautiful maiden, whom the young man fell in love with at first sight and shortly afterward married. One day Venus thought she would like to see whether the cat had changed her habits as well as her form; so she let a mouse run loose in the room where they were. Forgetting everything, the young woman had no sooner seen the mouse than up she jumped and was after it like a shot: at which the goddess was so disgusted that she changed her back again into a cat.

Venus and the Cat

⚜ 208 ⚜
THE OLD WOMAN AND HER MAIDS

A certain Old Woman had several Maids, whom she used to call to their work every morning at the crowing of the Cock. The Maids, finding it grievous to have their sweet sleep disturbed so early, killed the Cock, thinking when he was quiet they should enjoy their warm beds a little longer. But the Old Woman, no longer knowing what time it was, woke them up thereafter in the middle of the night.

Beware of falling from bad to worse.

⚜ 209 ⚜
INDUSTRY AND SLOTH

How many live in the world as useless as if they had never been born! They pass through life, like a bird through the air, and leave no track behind them; waste the prime of their days in deliberating what they shall do; and bring them to a period, without coming to any determination. An indolent young man, being asked why he lay in bed so long, jocosely and carelessly answered: "Every morning of my life I am hearing long causes. I have two fine girls, their names are Industry and Sloth, close at my bedside, as soon as ever I awake, pressing their different suits. One entreats me to get

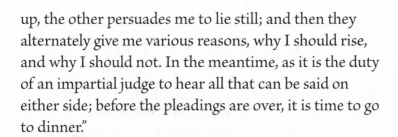

up, the other persuades me to lie still; and then they alternately give me various reasons, why I should rise, and why I should not. In the meantime, as it is the duty of an impartial judge to hear all that can be said on either side; before the pleadings are over, it is time to go to dinner."

Our term of life does not allow time
for long-protracted deliberation.

❦ 210 ❧

THE RIVER FISH AND THE SEA FISH

A large freshwater Pike was carried out to sea by a strong current. He gave himself great airs on account of what he considered his superior race and descent, and despised the Sea Fishes among whom he found himself. "You value yourself at a great price," said a little stranger, "but if ever it is our fate to come to the market, you will find that I am thought a good deal more of there than you."

Size does not control value.

❦ 211 ❦

THE STAG WITH ONE EYE

A stag, blind of one eye, was grazing close to the seashore and kept his sound eye turned towards the land, so as to be able to perceive the approach of the hounds, while the blind eye he turned towards the sea, never suspecting that any danger would threaten him from that quarter. As it fell out, however, some sailors, coasting along the shore, spied him and shot an arrow at him, by which he was mortally wounded. As he lay dying, he said to himself, "Wretch that I am! I bethought me of the dangers of the land, whence none assailed me: but I feared no peril from the sea, yet thence has come my ruin."

Misfortune often assails us from
an unexpected quarter.

❧ 212 ❧

THE CROW AND THE SWAN

A crow was filled with envy on seeing the beautiful white plumage of a swan, and thought it was due to the water in which the swan constantly bathed and swam. So he left the neighborhood of the altars, where he got his living by picking up bits of the meat offered in sacrifice, and went and lived among the pools and streams. But though he bathed and washed his feathers many times a day, he didn't make them any whiter, and at last died of hunger into the bargain.

You may change your habits, but not your nature.

❧ 213 ❧

THE FLY AND THE DRAFT MULE

A fly sat on one of the shafts of a cart and said to the mule who was pulling it, "How slow you are! Do mend your pace, or I shall have to use my sting as a goad." The mule was not in the least disturbed. "Behind me, in the cart," said he, "sits my master. He holds the reins, and flicks me with his whip, and him I obey, but I don't want any of your impertinence. I know when I may dawdle and when I may not."

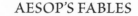

§ 214 ᛒ

THE COCK AND THE JEWEL

A cock, scratching the ground for something to eat, turned up a jewel that had by chance been dropped there. "Ho!" said he, "a fine thing you are, no doubt, and, had your owner found you, great would his joy have been. But for me, give me a single grain of corn before all the jewels in the world!"

The ignorant despise what is precious only because they cannot understand it.

⟨ 215 ⟩

THE WOLF AND
THE SHEPHERD

A wolf hung about near a flock of sheep for a long
time, but made no attempt to molest them.
The shepherd at first kept a sharp eye on him, for
he naturally thought he meant mischief. But as time
went by and the wolf showed no inclination to meddle
with the flock, he began to look upon him more as a
protector than as an enemy; and when one day some
errand took him to the city, he felt no uneasiness at
leaving the wolf with the sheep. But as soon as his
back was turned the wolf attacked them and killed the
greater number. When the shepherd returned and saw
the havoc he had wrought, he cried, "It serves me right
for trusting my flock to a wolf."

⟨ 216 ⟩

THE FARMER AND
THE STORK

A farmer set some traps in a field which he had lately
sown with corn, in order to catch the cranes which
came to pick up the seed. When he returned to look
at his traps he found several cranes caught, and among
them a stork, which begged to be let go, and said, "You
ought not to kill me: I am not a crane, but a stork, as

you can easily see by my feathers, and I am the most honest and harmless of birds." But the farmer replied, "It's nothing to me what you are: I find you among these cranes, who ruin my crops, and, like them, you shall suffer."

Birds of a feather flock together.

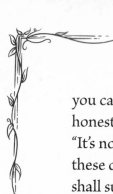

◁ 217 ▷

THE CHARGER AND THE MILLER

A horse, who had been used to carry his rider into battle, felt himself growing old and chose to work in a mill instead. He now no longer found himself stepping out proudly to the beating of the drums, but was compelled to slave away all day grinding the corn. Bewailing his hard lot, he said one day to the miller, "Ah me! I was once a splendid war-horse, gaily caparisoned, and attended by a groom whose sole duty was to see to my wants. How different is my present condition! I wish I had never given up the battlefield for the mill." The miller replied with asperity, "It's no use your regretting the past. Fortune has many ups and downs: you must just take them as they come."

❦ 218 ❧

THE GRASSHOPPER
AND THE OWL

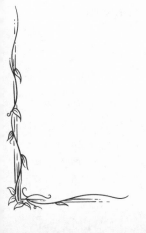

An owl, who lived in a hollow tree, was in the habit of feeding by night and sleeping by day; but her slumbers were greatly disturbed by the chirping of a grasshopper, who had taken up his abode in the branches. She begged him repeatedly to have some consideration for her comfort, but the grasshopper, if anything, only chirped the louder. At last the owl could stand it no longer, but determined to rid herself of the pest by means of a trick. Addressing herself to the grasshopper, she said in her most pleasant manner, "As I cannot sleep for your song, which, believe me, is as sweet as the notes of Apollo's lyre, I have a mind to taste some nectar, which Minerva gave me the other day. Won't you come in and join me?" The grasshopper was flattered by the praise of his song, and his mouth, too, watered at the mention of the delicious drink, so he said he would be delighted. No sooner had he got inside the hollow where the owl was sitting than she pounced upon him and ate him up.

⚜ 219 ⚜

THE GRASSHOPPER
AND THE ANTS

One fine day in winter some ants were busy drying their store of corn, which had got rather damp during a long spell of rain. Presently up came a grasshopper and begged them to spare her a few grains, "For," she said, "I'm simply starving." The ants stopped work for a moment, though this was against their principles. "May we ask," said they, "what you were doing with yourself all last summer? Why didn't you collect a store of food for the winter?" "The fact is," replied the grasshopper, "I was so busy singing that I hadn't the time." "If you spent the summer singing," replied the ants, "you can't do better than spend the winter dancing." And they chuckled and went on with their work.

It is best to prepare for days of necessity.

❧ 220 ☙

THE FARMER AND THE VIPER

One winter a farmer found a viper frozen and numb with cold, and out of pity picked it up and placed it in his bosom. The viper was no sooner revived by the warmth than it turned upon its benefactor and inflicted a fatal bite upon him; and as the poor man lay dying, he cried, "I have only got what I deserved, for taking compassion on so villainous a creature."

Kindness is thrown away upon the evil.

❧ 221 ☙

THE TWO FROGS

Two frogs were neighbors. One lived in a marsh, where there was plenty of water, which frogs love: the other in a lane some distance away, where all the water to be had was that which lay in the ruts after rain. The marsh frog warned his friend and pressed him to come and live with him in the marsh, for he would find his quarters there far more comfortable and—what was still more important—more safe. But the other refused, saying that he could not bring himself to move from a place to which he had become accustomed. A few days afterward a heavy wagon

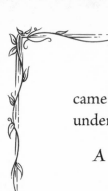

came down the lane, and he was crushed to death under the wheels.

A willful man will have his way to his own hurt.

⚜ 222 ⚜

THE COBBLER
TURNED DOCTOR

A very unskillful cobbler, finding himself unable to make a living at his trade, gave up mending boots and took to doctoring instead. He gave out that he had the secret of a universal antidote against all poisons, and acquired no small reputation, thanks to his talent for puffing himself. One day, however, he fell very ill; and the king of the country bethought him that he would test the value of his remedy. Calling, therefore, for a cup, he poured out a dose of the antidote, and, under pretense of mixing poison with it, added a little water, and commanded him to drink it. Terrified by the fear of being poisoned, the cobbler confessed that he knew nothing about medicine, and that his antidote was worthless. Then the king summoned his subjects and addressed them as follows: "What folly could be greater than yours? Here is this cobbler to whom no one will send his boots to be mended, and yet you have not hesitated to entrust him with your lives!"

◁ 223 ▷
THE ASS, THE COCK, AND THE LION

An ass and a cock were in a cattle pen together. Presently a lion, who had been starving for days, came along and was just about to fall upon the ass and make a meal of him when the cock, rising to his full height and flapping his wings vigorously, uttered a tremendous crow. Now, if there is one thing that frightens a lion, it is the crowing of a cock: and this one had no sooner heard the noise than he fled. The ass was mightily elated at this, and thought that, if the lion couldn't face a cock, he would be still less likely to stand up to an ass: so he ran out and pursued him. But when the two had got well out of sight and hearing of the cock, the lion suddenly turned upon the ass and ate him up.

❦ 224 ❦
THE BELLY AND THE MEMBERS

The members of the body once rebelled against the belly. "You," they said to the belly, "live in luxury and sloth, and never do a stroke of work; while we not only have to do all the hard work there is to be done, but are actually your slaves and have to minister to all your wants. Now, we will do so no longer, and you can shift for yourself for the future." They were as good as their word, and left the belly to starve. The result was just what might have been expected: the whole body soon began to fail, and the members and all shared in the general collapse. And then they saw too late how foolish they had been.

As in the body, so in the state, each member in his proper sphere must work for the common good.

❦ 225 ❦
THE BALD MAN AND THE FLY

A fly settled on the head of a bald man and bit him. In his eagerness to kill it, he hit himself a smart slap. But the fly escaped, and said to him in derision,

"You tried to kill me for just one little bite; what will you do to yourself now, for the heavy smack you have just given yourself?" "Oh, for that blow I bear no grudge," he replied, "for I never intended myself any harm; but as for you, you contemptible insect, who live by sucking human blood, I'd have borne a good deal more than that for the satisfaction of dashing the life out of you!"

Revenge will hurt the avenger.

◁ 226 ▷
THE HORSE AND THE HOG

Hog that was lazily lying in the sun saw a War-
Horse advancing, on his way to the battlefield.
The Horse was gaily caparisoned, and proudly spurned
the ground, as if impatient to charge the enemy. The
Hog half lifted his head, and, grunting, said to him,
"What a fool you are to be so ready to rush to your
death!" "Your speech," replied the Horse, "fits well a vile
animal, that only lives to get fat and be killed by the
knife. If I die on the field, I die where duty calls me, and
I shall leave the memory of a good name behind."

*'Tis not death but the manner of
it which is important.*

◁ 227 ▷
THE ANGLER AND
THE LITTLE FISH

A Fisherman who had caught a very small Fish was
about to throw him into his basket. The little
fellow, gasping, pleaded thus for his life: "What! you
are never going to keep such a minnow as I am, not one
quarter grown! Fifty like me wouldn't make a decent
dish. Do throw me back, and come and catch me
again when I am bigger." "It's all very well to say 'Catch
me again,' my little fellow," replied the Man, "but you

know you'll make yourself very scarce for the future. You're big enough now to make one in a frying-pan, so in you go."

No time like the present.

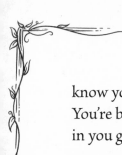

⚜ 228 ⚜

AESOP AT PLAY

An Athenian once found Aesop joining merrily in the sports of some children. He ridiculed him for his want of gravity, and Aesop good-temperedly took up a bow, unstrung it, and laid it at his feet. "There, friend," said he; "that bow, if kept always strained, would lose its spring, and probably snap. Let it go free sometimes, and it will be the fitter for use when it is wanted."

Wise play makes wise work.

⚜ 229 ⚜

THE FOX AND THE TIGER

A skillful Archer coming into the woods, directed his arrows so well that the beasts fled in dismay. The Tiger, however, told them not to be afraid, for he would singly engage their enemy, and drive him from their domain. He had scarcely spoken, when an arrow

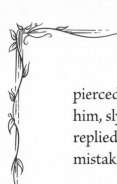

pierced his ribs and lodged in his side. The Fox asked him, slyly, what he thought of his opponent now. "Ah!" replied the Tiger, writing with pain, "I find that I was mistaken in my reckoning."

Knowledge is power.

⚘ 230 ⚘

THE FOX IN THE WELL

An unlucky Fox having fallen into a Well, was able, by dint of great efforts, to keep his head barely above water. While he was there struggling, and sticking his claws into the side of the Well, a Wolf came by and looked in. "What! my dear brother," said he, with affected concern, "can it really be you that I see down there? How cold you must feel! How long have you been in? How came you to fall in? I am so pained to see you. Do tell me all about it!" "The end of a rope would be of more use to me than all your pity," answered the Fox. "Just help me to set my foot once more on solid ground, and you shall have the whole story."

Say well is good, but do well is better.

❦ 231 ❧

HONOR, PRUDENCE, AND PLEASURE

Honor, Prudence, and Pleasure undertook to keep house together. Honor was to govern the family, Prudence to provide for it, and Pleasure to conduct its arrangements. For some time they went on exceedingly well, and with great propriety; but, after a while, Pleasure getting the upper hand, began to carry mirth to extravagance, and filled the house with gay, idle, riotous company, and the consequent expenses threatened the ruin of the establishment. Upon this Honor and Prudence, finding it absolutely necessary to break up the partnership, determined to quit the house, and leave Pleasure to go on her own way. This could not continue long, as she soon brought herself to poverty, and came a-begging to her former companions, Honor and Prudence, who had now settled in another habitation. However, they would never afterward admit Pleasure to be a partner in their household, but sent for her occasionally, on holidays, to make them merry, and in return, they maintained her out of their alms.

Intemperance has a smiling and alluring aspect, but a dreadful retinue.

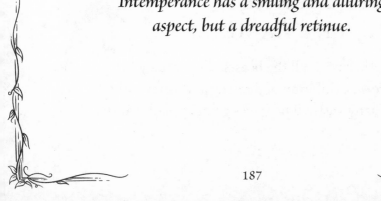

❧ 232 ❧
THE ASS AND THE WOLF

An ass was feeding in a meadow, and, catching sight of his enemy the wolf in the distance, pretended to be very lame and hobbled painfully along. When the wolf came up, he asked the ass how he came to be so lame, and the ass replied that in going through a hedge he had trodden on a thorn, and he begged the wolf to pull it out with his teeth, "In case," he said, "when you eat me, it should stick in your throat and hurt you very much." The wolf said he would, and told the ass to lift up his foot, and gave his whole mind to getting out the thorn. But the ass suddenly let out with his heels and fetched the wolf a fearful kick in the mouth, breaking his teeth; and then he galloped off at full speed. As soon as he could speak the wolf growled to himself, "It serves me right: my father taught me to kill, and I ought to have stuck to that trade instead of attempting to cure."

❧ 233 ❧
THE MONKEY AND THE CAMEL

At a gathering of all the beasts, the monkey gave an exhibition of dancing and entertained the company vastly. There was great applause at the finish, which excited the envy of the camel and made him desire to win the favor of the assembly by the same means. So he got up from his place and began dancing, but he cut such a ridiculous figure as he plunged about, and made such a grotesque exhibition of his ungainly person, that the beasts all fell upon him with ridicule and drove him away.

It is absurd to ape our betters.

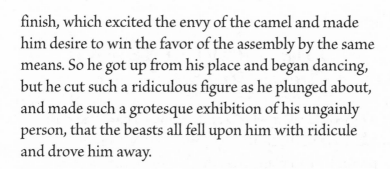

✦ 234 ✦
THE SICK MAN AND THE DOCTOR

A sick man received a visit from his doctor, who asked him how he was. "Fairly well, doctor," said he, "but I find I sweat a great deal." "Ah," said the doctor, "that's a good sign." On his next visit he asked the same question, and his patient replied, "I'm much as usual, but I've taken to having shivering fits, which leave me cold all over." "Ah," said the doctor, "that's a good sign too." When he came the third time and inquired as before about his patient's health, the sick man said that he felt very feverish. "A very good sign," said the doctor; "you are doing very nicely indeed." Afterward a friend came to see the invalid, and on asking him how he did, received this reply: "My dear friend, I'm dying of good signs."

⚘ 235 ⚘

THE TRAVELERS AND THE PLANE TREE

Two travelers were walking along a bare and dusty road in the heat of a summer's day. Coming presently to a plane tree, they joyfully turned aside to shelter from the burning rays of the sun in the deep shade of its spreading branches. As they rested, looking up into the tree, one of them remarked to his companion, "What a useless tree the plane is! It bears no fruit and is of no service to man at all." The plane tree interrupted him with indignation. "You ungrateful creature!" it cried. "You come and take shelter under me from the scorching sun, and then, in the very act of enjoying the cool shade of my foliage, you abuse me and call me good for nothing!"

Many a service is met with ingratitude.

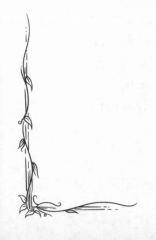

The Travelers and the Plane Tree

⚜ 236 ⚜
THE FLEA AND THE OX

A flea once said to an ox, "How comes it that a big strong fellow like you is content to serve mankind, and do all their hard work for them, while I, who am no bigger than you see, live on their bodies and drink my fill of their blood, and never do a stroke for it all?" To which the ox replied, "Men are very kind to me, and so I am grateful to them: they feed and house me well, and every now and then they show their fondness for me by patting me on the head and neck."

"They'd pat me, too," said the flea, "if I let them: but I take good care they don't, or there would be nothing left of me."

⚜ 237 ⚜
THE BIRDS, THE BEASTS, AND THE BAT

The birds were at war with the beasts, and many battles were fought with varying success on either side. The bat did not throw in his lot definitely with either party, but when things went well for the birds he was found fighting in their ranks; when, on the other hand, the beasts got the upper hand, he was to be found among the beasts. No one paid any attention to him while the war lasted: but when it was over, and peace was restored, neither the birds nor the beasts would have anything to do with so double-faced a traitor, and so he remains to this day a solitary outcast from both.

He winds up friendless who plays both sides against the middle.

⚜ 238 ⚜

THE MAN AND HIS TWO SWEETHEARTS

A man of middle age, whose hair was turning grey, had two sweethearts, an old woman and a young one. The elder of the two didn't like having a lover who looked so much younger than herself; so, whenever he came to see her, she used to pull the dark hairs out of his head to make him look old. The younger, on the other hand, didn't like him to look so much older than herself, and took every opportunity of pulling out the grey hairs, to make him look young. Between them, they left not a hair in his head, and he became perfectly bald.

Those who seek to please everybody please nobody.

239

THE EAGLE, THE JACKDAW, AND THE SHEPHERD

One day a jackdaw saw an eagle swoop down on a lamb and carry it off in its talons. "My word," said the jackdaw, "I'll do that myself." So it flew high up into the air, and then came shooting down with a great whirring of wings on to the back of a big ram. It had no sooner alighted than its claws got caught fast in the wool, and nothing it could do was of any use: there it stuck, flapping away, and only making things worse instead of better. By and by up came the shepherd. "Oho," he said, "so that's what you'd be doing, is it?" And he took the jackdaw, and clipped its wings and carried it home to his children. It looked so odd that they didn't know what to make of it. "What sort of bird is it, father?" they asked. "It's a jackdaw," he replied, "and nothing but a jackdaw: but it wants to be taken for an eagle."

If you attempt what is beyond your power, your trouble will be wasted and you court not only misfortune but ridicule.

ꕥ 240 ꕤ
THE WOLF AND THE BOY

A wolf, who had just enjoyed a good meal and was in a playful mood, caught sight of a boy lying flat upon the ground, and, realizing that he was trying to hide, and that it was fear of himself that made him do this, he went up to him and said, "Aha, I've found you, you see; but if you can say three things to me, the truth of which cannot be disputed, I will spare your life." The boy plucked up courage and thought for a moment, and then he said, "First, it is a pity you saw me; secondly, I was a fool to let myself be seen; and thirdly, we all hate wolves because they are always making unprovoked attacks upon our flocks." The wolf replied, "Well, what you say is true enough from your point of view; so you may go."

241

THE MILLER, HIS SON, AND THEIR ASS

A miller, accompanied by his young son, was driving his ass to market in hopes of finding a purchaser for him. On the road they met a troop of girls, laughing and talking, who exclaimed, "Did you ever see such a pair of fools? To be trudging along the dusty road when they might be riding!" The miller thought there was sense in what they said; so he made his son mount the ass, and himself walked at the side. Presently they met some of his old cronies, who greeted them and said, "You'll spoil that son of yours, letting him ride while you toil along on foot! Make him walk, young lazybones! It'll do him all the good in the world." The miller followed their advice, and took his son's place on the back of the ass while the boy trudged along behind. They had not gone far when they overtook a party of women and children, and the miller heard them say, "What a selfish old man! He himself rides in comfort, but lets his poor little boy follow as best he can on his own legs!" So he made his son get up behind him. Further along the road they met some travelers, who asked the miller whether the ass he was riding was his own property, or a beast hired for the occasion. He replied that it was his own, and that he was taking it to market to sell. "Good heavens!" said they, "with a load like that the poor beast will be so exhausted by the time he gets there that no one will look at him. Why, you'd do better to carry him!" "Anything to please you," said the old man, "we can but try." So they got off, tied the ass's legs together with a rope and slung him on a pole, and at last reached the town, carrying him between them. This was so absurd a sight that the people ran out in crowds to laugh at it, and chaffed the father and son unmercifully, some even calling them lunatics. They had then got to a bridge over the river, where the ass, frightened by the noise and his unusual situation, kicked and struggled till he broke the ropes that bound him, and fell into the water and was drowned. Whereupon the unfortunate miller, vexed and ashamed, made the best of his way home again, convinced that in trying to please all he had pleased none, and had lost his ass into the bargain.

Try to please all and you end up pleasing none.

⁂ 242 ⁂
THE LAMB CHASED
BY A WOLF

A wolf was chasing a lamb, which took refuge in a temple. The wolf urged it to come out of the precincts, and said, "If you don't, the priest is sure to catch you and offer you up in sacrifice on the altar." To which the lamb replied, "Thanks, I think I'll stay where I am. I'd rather be sacrificed any day than be eaten up by a wolf."

❧ 243 ❧
THE STAG AND THE VINE

A stag, pursued by the huntsmen, concealed himself under cover of a thick vine. They lost track of him and passed by his hiding-place without being aware that he was anywhere near. Supposing all danger to be over, he presently began to browse on the leaves of the vine. The movement drew the attention of the returning huntsmen, and one of them, supposing some animal to be hidden there, shot an arrow at a venture into the foliage. The unlucky stag was pierced to the heart, and, as he expired, he said, "I deserve my fate for my treachery in feeding upon the leaves of my protector."

Ingratitude sometimes brings its own punishment.

⚜ 244 ⚜

THE ARCHER AND THE LION

An archer went up into the hills to get some sport
with his bow, and all the animals fled at the sight
of him with the exception of the lion, who stayed
behind and challenged him to fight. But he shot an
arrow at the lion and hit him, and said, "There, you see
what my messenger can do: just you wait a moment
and I'll tackle you myself." The lion, however, when he
felt the sting of the arrow, ran away as fast as his legs
could carry him. A fox, who had seen it all happen,
said to the lion, "Come, don't be a coward: why don't
you stay and show fight?" But the lion replied, "You
won't get me to stay, not you: why, when he sends a
messenger like that before him, he must himself be
a terrible fellow to deal with."

*Give a wide berth to those who can
do damage at a distance.*

⚜ 245 ⚜

THE WOLF AND THE GOAT

A wolf caught sight of a goat browsing above him on
the scanty herbage that grew on the top of a steep
rock; and being unable to get at her, tried to induce her
to come lower down. "You are risking your life up there,
madam, indeed you are," he called out: "pray take my

advice and come down here, where you will find plenty of better food." The goat turned a knowing eye upon him. "It's little you care whether I get good grass or bad," said she: "what you want is to eat me."

Beware of a friend with an ulterior motive.

The Wolf and the Goat

❦ 246 ❧
THE SICK STAG

A stag fell sick and lay in a clearing in the forest, too weak to move from the spot. When the news of his illness spread, a number of the other beasts came to inquire after his health, and they one and all nibbled a little of the grass that grew around the invalid till at last there was not a blade within his reach. In a few days he began to mend, but was still too feeble to get up and go in search of fodder; and thus he perished miserably of hunger owing to the thoughtlessness of his friends.

Evil companions bring more hurt than profit.

❦ 247 ❧
THE ASS AND THE MULE

A certain man who had an ass and a mule loaded them both up one day and set out upon a journey. So long as the road was fairly level, the ass got on very well: but by and by they came to a place among the hills where the road was very rough and steep, and the ass was at his last gasp. So he begged the mule to relieve him of a part of his load: but the mule refused. At last, from sheer weariness, the ass stumbled and fell down a steep place and was killed. The driver was in despair, but he did the best he could: he added the ass's load to the mule's, and he also flayed the ass and put his skin on

the top of the double load. The mule could only just manage the extra weight, and, as he staggered painfully along, he said to himself, "I have only got what I deserved: if I had been willing to help the ass at first, I should not now be carrying his load and his skin into the bargain."

An ounce of prevention is worth a pound of cure.

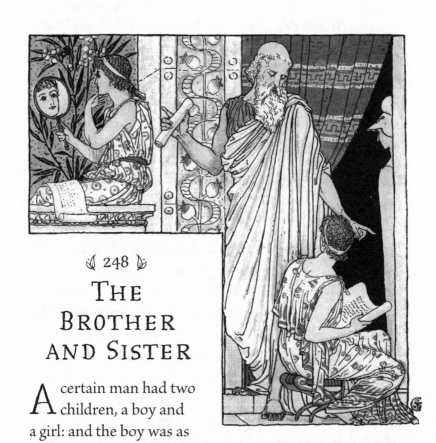

৬ 248 ৬

THE
BROTHER
AND SISTER

A certain man had two children, a boy and a girl: and the boy was as good-looking as the girl was plain. One day, as they were playing together in their mother's chamber, they chanced upon a mirror and saw their own features for the first time. The boy saw what a handsome fellow he was, and began to boast to his sister about his good looks: she, on her part, was ready to cry with vexation when she was aware of her plainness, and took his remarks as an insult to herself. Running to her father, she told him of her brother's conceit, and accused him of meddling with his mother's things. He laughed and kissed them both, and said, "My children, learn from now onwards to make a good use of the glass. You, my boy, strive to be as good as it shows you to be handsome; and you, my girl, resolve to make up for the plainness of your features by the sweetness of your disposition."

⁂ 249 ⁂
THE HEIFER AND THE OX

A heifer went up to an ox, who was straining hard at the plow, and sympathized with him in a rather patronizing sort of way on the necessity of his having to work so hard. Not long afterward there was a festival in the village and everyone kept holiday. But, whereas the ox was turned loose into the pasture, the heifer was seized and led off to sacrifice. "Ah," said the ox, with a grim smile, "I see now why you were allowed to have such an idle time. It was because you were always intended for the altar."

He laughs best that laughs last.

THE KINGDOM OF THE LION

W hen the lion reigned over the beasts of the earth
he was never cruel or tyrannical, but as gentle
and just as a king ought to be. During his reign he called
a general assembly of the beasts, and drew up a code
of laws under which all were to live in perfect equality
and harmony. The wolf and the lamb, the tiger and the
stag, the leopard and the kid,
the dog and the hare, all
should dwell side by side
in unbroken peace and
friendship. The hare
said, "Oh! How I have
longed for this day
when the weak take
their place without
fear by the side of
the strong!"

THE ASS AND HIS DRIVER

A n ass was being driven down a mountain road, and
after jogging along for a while sensibly enough he
suddenly quitted the track and rushed to the edge of a
precipice. He was just about to leap over the edge when
his driver caught hold of his tail and did his best to pull

him back. But pull as he might he couldn't get the ass to budge from the brink. At last he gave up, crying, "All right, then, get to the bottom your own way; but it's the way to sudden death, as you'll find out quick enough."

A willful beast must go his own way.

⊲ 252 ⊳
THE LION AND THE HARE

A lion found a hare sleeping in her form, and was just going to devour her when he caught sight of a passing stag. Dropping the hare, he at once made for the bigger game; but finding, after a long chase, that he could not overtake the stag, he abandoned the attempt and came back for the hare. When he reached the spot, however, he found she was nowhere to be seen, and he had to go without his dinner. "It serves me right," he said; "I should have been content with what I had got, instead of hankering after a better prize."

A bird in the hand is worth two in the bush.

⚜ 253 ⚜
THE WOLVES AND THE DOGS

Once upon a time the wolves said to the dogs, "Why should we continue to be enemies any longer? You are very like us in most ways. The main difference between us is one of training only. We live a life of freedom; but you are enslaved to mankind, who beat you, and put heavy collars around your necks, and compel you to keep watch over their flocks and herds for them, and, to crown all, they give you nothing but bones to eat. Don't put up with it any longer, but hand over the flocks to us, and we will all live on the fat of the land and feast together." The dogs allowed themselves to be persuaded by these words, and accompanied the wolves into their den. But no sooner were they well inside than the wolves set upon them and tore them to pieces.

Traitors richly deserve their fate.

⚜ 254 ⚜
THE BULL AND THE CALF

A full-grown bull was struggling to force his huge bulk through the narrow entrance to a cow house where his stall was, when a young calf came up and said to him, "If you'll step aside a moment, I'll show you

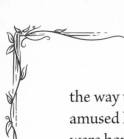

the way to get through." The bull turned upon him an amused look. "I knew that way," said he, "before you were born."

✥ 255 ✥

THE TREES AND THE AX

A woodman went into the forest and begged of the trees the favor of a handle for his ax. The principal trees at once agreed to so modest a request, and unhesitatingly gave him a young ash sapling, out of which he fashioned the handle he desired. No sooner had he done so than he set to work to fell the noblest trees in the wood. When they saw the use to which he was putting their gift, they cried, "Alas! Alas! We are undone, but we are ourselves to blame. The little we gave has cost us all. Had we not sacrificed the rights of the ash, we might ourselves have stood for ages."

They are foolish who give their enemies the means of destroying them.

⚘ 256 ⚘
THE ASTRONOMER

There was once an astronomer whose habit it was to go out at night and observe the stars. One night, as he was walking about outside the town gates, gazing up absorbed into the sky and not looking where he was going, he fell into a dry well. As he lay there groaning, some one passing by heard him, and, coming to the edge of the well, looked down and, on learning what had happened, said, "If you really mean to say that you were looking so hard at the sky that you didn't even see where your feet were carrying you along the ground, it appears to me that you deserve all you've got."

⚘ 257 ⚘
THE LABORER AND THE SNAKE

A laborer's little son was bitten by a snake and died of the wound. The father was beside himself with grief, and in his anger against the snake he caught up an ax and went and stood close to the snake's hole, and watched for a chance of killing it. Presently the snake came out, and the man aimed a blow at it, but only succeeded in cutting off the tip of its tail before it wriggled in again. He then tried to get it to come out a second time, pretending that he wished to make up the

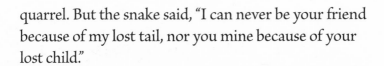
quarrel. But the snake said, "I can never be your friend because of my lost tail, nor you mine because of your lost child."

> *Injuries are never forgotten in the*
> *presence of those who caused them.*

❦ 258 ❧
THE CAGED BIRD AND THE BAT

A singing bird was confined in a cage which hung outside a window, and had a way of singing at night when all other birds were asleep. One night a bat came and clung to the bars of the cage, and asked the bird why she was silent by day and sang only at night. "I have a very good reason for doing so," said the bird: "it was once when I was singing in the daytime that a fowler was attracted by my voice, and set his nets for me and caught me. Since then I have never sung except by night." But the bat replied, "It is no use your doing that now when you are a prisoner: if only you had done so before you were caught, you might still have been free."

> *Precautions are useless after the event.*

⚘ 259 ⚘
THE ASS AND HIS PURCHASER

A man who wanted to buy an ass went to market, and, coming across a likely-looking beast, arranged with the owner that he should be allowed to take him home on trial to see what he was like. When he reached home, he put him into his stable along with the other asses. The newcomer took a look round, and immediately went and chose a place next to the laziest and greediest beast in the stable. When the master saw this he put a halter on him at once, and led him off and handed him over to his owner again. The latter was a good deal surprised to see him back so soon, and said, "Why, do you mean to say you have tested him already?" "I don't want to put him through any more tests," replied the other: "I could see what sort of beast he is from the companion he chose for himself."

A man is known by the company he keeps.

⚘ 260 ⚘
THE KID AND THE WOLF

A kid strayed from the flock and was chased by a wolf. When he saw he must be caught he turned around and said to the wolf, "I know, sir, that I can't escape being eaten by you; and so, as my life is bound to be short, I pray you let it be as merry as may be. Will you not play me a tune to dance to before I die?" The wolf saw no objection to having some music before his dinner: so he took out his pipe and began to play, while the kid danced before him. Before many minutes were passed the gods who guarded the flock heard the sound and came up to see what was going on. They no sooner clapped eyes on the wolf than they gave chase and drove him away. As he ran off, he turned and said to the kid, "It's what I thoroughly deserve: my trade is the butcher's, and I had no business to turn piper to please you."

In time of dire need, clever thinking is key.

⁜ 261 ⁜

THE DEBTOR AND HIS SOW

A man of Athens fell into debt and was pressed for
the money by his creditor; but he had no means
of paying at the time, so he begged for delay. But the
creditor refused and said he must pay at once. Then the
debtor fetched a sow—the only one he had—and took
her to market to offer her for sale. It happened that his
creditor was there too. Presently a buyer came along
and asked if the sow produced good litters. "Yes," said
the debtor, "very fine ones; and the remarkable thing is
that she produces females at the Mysteries and males
at the Panathenea." (Festivals these were; and the
Athenians always sacrifice a sow at one, and a boar at
the other; while at the Dionysia they sacrifice a kid.) At
that the creditor, who was standing by, put in, "Don't be
surprised, sir; why, still better, at the Dionysia this sow
has kids!"

⁜ 262 ⁜

THE BALD HUNTSMAN

A man who had lost all his hair took to wearing
a wig, and one day he went out hunting. It was
blowing rather hard at the time, and he hadn't gone far
before a gust of wind caught his hat and carried it off,
and his wig too, much to the amusement of the hunt.

But he quite entered into the joke, and said, "Ah, well! The hair that wig is made of didn't stick to the head on which it grew, so it's no wonder it won't stick to mine."

◁ 263 ▷

THE HERDSMAN AND THE LOST BULL

A herdsman was tending his cattle when he missed a young bull, one of the finest of the herd. He went at once to look for him, but, meeting with no success in his search, he made a vow that, if he should discover the thief, he would sacrifice a calf to Jupiter. Continuing his search, he entered a thicket, where he presently espied a lion devouring the lost bull. Terrified with fear, he raised his hands to heaven and cried, "Great Jupiter, I vowed I would sacrifice a calf to thee if I should discover the thief; but now a full-grown bull I promise thee if only I myself escape unhurt from his clutches."

◁ 264 ▷

THE HOUND AND THE FOX

A hound, roaming in the forest, spied a lion, and being well used to lesser game, gave chase, thinking he would make a fine quarry. Presently the lion perceived that he was being pursued; so, stopping short, he rounded on his pursuer and gave a loud roar. The hound immediately turned tail and fled. A fox, seeing him running away, jeered at him and said, "Ho! Ho! There goes the coward who chased a lion and ran away the moment he roared!"

◁ 265 ▷

THE MULE

One morning a mule, who had too much to eat and too little to do, began to think himself a very fine fellow indeed, and frisked about saying, "My father was undoubtedly a high-spirited horse and I take after him entirely." But very soon afterward he was put into the harness and compelled to go a very long way with a heavy load behind him. At the end of the day, exhausted by his unusual exertions, he said dejectedly to himself, "I must have been mistaken about my father; he can only have been an ass after all."

Every truth has two sides.

❦ 266 ❧

THE FATHER AND HIS DAUGHTERS

A man had two daughters, one of whom he gave in marriage to a gardener, and the other to a potter. After a time he thought he would go and see how they were getting on; and first he went to the gardener's wife. He asked her how she was, and how things were going with herself and her husband. She replied that on the whole they were doing very well. "But," she continued, "I do wish we could have some good rain. The garden wants it badly." Then he went on to the potter's wife and made the same inquiries of her. She replied that she and her husband had nothing to complain of. "But," she went on, "I do wish we could have some nice dry weather, to dry the pottery." Her father looked at her with a humorous expression on his face. "You want dry weather," he said, "and your sister wants rain. I was going to ask in my prayers that your wishes should be granted; but now it strikes me I had better not refer to the subject."

You can't please everybody.

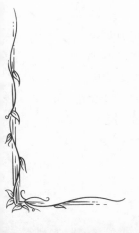

⚜ 267 ⚜
THE THIEF AND
THE INNKEEPER

A thief hired a room at an inn, and stayed there some days on the lookout for something to steal. No opportunity, however, presented itself, till one day, when there was a festival to be celebrated, the innkeeper appeared in a fine new coat and sat down before the door of the inn for an airing. The thief no sooner set eyes upon the coat than he longed to get possession of it. There was no business doing, so he went and took a seat by the side of the innkeeper, and began talking to him. They conversed together for some time, and then the thief suddenly yawned and howled like a wolf. The innkeeper asked him in some concern what ailed him. The thief replied, "I will tell you about myself, sir, but first I must beg you to take charge of my clothes for me, for I intend to leave them with you. Why I have these fits of yawning I cannot tell. Maybe they are sent as a punishment for my misdeeds; but, whatever the reason, the facts are that when I have yawned three times I become a ravening wolf and fly at men's throats." As he finished speaking he yawned a second time and howled again as before. The innkeeper, believing every word he said, and terrified at the prospect of being confronted with a wolf, got up hastily and started to run indoors; but the thief caught him by the coat and tried to stop him, crying, "Stay, sir, stay, and take charge of my clothes, or else I shall never see them again." As he spoke he opened his mouth and began to yawn for the third time. The innkeeper, mad with the fear of being eaten by a wolf, slipped out of his coat, which remained in the other's hands, and bolted into the inn and locked the door behind him; and the thief then quietly stole off with his spoil.

Every tale is not to be believed.

⚜ 268 ⚜

THE PACK ASS AND THE WILD ASS

A wild ass, who was wandering idly about, one day came upon a pack ass lying at full length in a sunny spot and thoroughly enjoying himself. Going up to him, he said, "What a lucky beast you are! Your sleek coat shows how well you live: how I envy you!" Not long after the wild ass saw his acquaintance again, but this time he was carrying a heavy load, and his driver was following behind and beating him with a thick stick. "Ah, my friend," said the wild ass, "I don't envy you any more: for I see you pay dear for your comforts."

Advantages that are dearly bought
are doubtful blessings.

The Frogs and the Well

269

THE FROGS AND THE WELL

Two frogs lived together in a marsh. But one hot summer the marsh dried up, and they left it to look for another place to live in, for frogs like damp places if they can get them. By and by they came to a deep well, and one of them looked down into it, and said to the other, "This looks a nice cool place. Let us jump in and settle here." But the other, who had a wiser head on his shoulders, replied, "Not so fast, my friend. Supposing this well dried up like the marsh, how should we get out again?"

Look before you leap.

270

THE CRAB AND THE FOX

A crab once left the seashore and went and settled in a meadow some way inland, which looked very nice and green and seemed likely to be a good place to feed in. But a hungry fox came along and spied the crab and caught him. Just as he was going to be eaten up, the crab said, "This is just what I deserve; for I had no business to leave my natural home by the sea and settle here as though I belonged to the land."

Be content with your lot.

⚜ 271 ⚜

THE FOX AND THE GRASSHOPPER

A grasshopper sat chirping in the branches of a tree. A fox heard her, and, thinking what a dainty morsel she would make, he tried to get her down by a trick. Standing below in full view of her, he praised her song in the most flattering terms, and begged her to descend, saying he would like to make the acquaintance of the owner of so beautiful a voice. But she was not to be taken in, and replied, "You are very much mistaken, my dear sir, if you imagine I am going to come down. I keep well out of the way of you and your kind ever since the day when I saw numbers of grasshoppers' wings strewn about the entrance to a fox's earth."

⚜ 272 ⚜

THE FARMER, HIS BOY, AND THE ROOKS

A farmer had just sown a field of wheat, and was keeping a careful watch over it, for numbers of rooks and starlings kept continually settling on it and eating up the grain. Along with him went his boy, carrying a sling; and whenever the farmer asked for the sling the starlings understood what he said and warned the rooks and they were off in a moment. So the farmer hit on a trick. "My lad," said he, "we must get the better of these birds somehow. After this, when I want the sling, I won't say 'sling,' but just 'humph,' and you must then hand me the sling quickly." Presently back came the whole flock. "Humph!" said the farmer; but the starlings took no notice, and he had time to sling several stones among them, hitting one on the head, another in the legs, and another in the wing, before they got out of range. As they made all haste away they met some cranes, who asked them what the matter was. "Matter?" said one of the rooks; "it's those rascals, men, that are the matter. Don't you go near them. They have a way of saying one thing and meaning another which has just been the death of several of our poor friends."

◁ 273 ▷

THE ASS AND THE DOG

An ass and a dog were on their travels together, and, as they went along, they found a sealed packet lying on the ground. The ass picked it up, broke the seal, and found it contained some writing, which he proceeded to read out aloud to the dog. As he read on it turned out to be all about grass and barley and hay— in short, all the kinds of fodder that asses are fond of. The dog was a good deal bored with listening to all this, till at last his impatience got the better of him, and he cried, "Just skip a few pages, friend, and see if there isn't something about meat and bones." The ass glanced

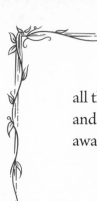

all through the packet, but found nothing of the sort, and said so. Then the dog said in disgust, "Oh, throw it away, do. What's the good of a thing like that?"

⚜ 274 ⚜
THE ASS CARRYING THE IMAGE

A certain man put an image on the back of his ass to take it to one of the temples of the town. As they went along the road all the people they met uncovered and bowed their heads out of reverence for the image; but the ass thought they were doing it out of respect for himself, and began to give himself airs accordingly. At last he became so conceited that he imagined he could do as he liked, and, by way of protest against the load he was carrying, he came to a full stop and flatly declined to proceed any further. His driver, finding him so obstinate, hit him hard and long with his stick, saying the while, "Oh, you dunderheaded idiot, do you suppose it's come to this, that men pay worship to an ass?"

Rude shocks await those who take to themselves the credit that is due to others.

❦ 275 ❧

THE ATHENIAN AND THE THEBAN

An Athenian and a Theban were on the road together, and passed the time in conversation, as is the way of travelers. After discussing a variety of subjects they began to talk about heroes, a topic that tends to be more fertile than edifying. Each of them was lavish in his praises of the heroes of his own city, until eventually the Theban asserted that Hercules was the greatest hero who had ever lived on earth, and now occupied a foremost place among the gods; while the Athenian insisted that Theseus was far superior, for his fortune had been in every way supremely blessed, whereas Hercules had at one time been forced to act as a servant. And he gained his point, for he was a very glib fellow, like all Athenians; so that the Theban, who was no match for him in talking, cried at last in some disgust, "All right, have your way; I only hope that, when our heroes are angry with us, Athens may suffer from the anger of Hercules, and Thebes only from that of Theseus."

◁ 276 ▷

THE GOATHERD
AND THE GOAT

A goatherd was one day gathering his flock to return to the fold, when one of his goats strayed and refused to join the rest. He tried for a long time to get her to return by calling and whistling to her, but the goat took no notice of him at all; so at last he threw a stone at her and broke one of her horns. In dismay, he begged her not to tell his master. But she replied, "You silly fellow, my horn would cry aloud even if I held my tongue."

It's no use trying to hide what can't be hidden.

❦ 277 ❧

THE SHEEP AND THE DOG

Once upon a time the sheep complained to the shepherd about the difference in his treatment of themselves and his dog. "Your conduct," said they, "is very strange and, we think, very unfair. We provide you with wool and lambs and milk and you give us nothing but grass, and even that we have to find for ourselves. But you get nothing at all from the dog, and yet you feed him with tidbits from your own table." Their remarks were overheard by the dog, who spoke up at once and said, "Yes, and quite right, too. Where would you be if it wasn't for me? Thieves would steal you! Wolves would eat you! Indeed, if I didn't keep constant watch over you, you would be too terrified even to graze!" The sheep were obliged to acknowledge that he spoke the truth, and never again made a grievance of the regard in which he was held by his master.

⚜ 278 ⚜

THE FALCON AND THE GOOSE

A Goose who had strong reasons for thinking that the time of his sacrifice was near at hand, carefully avoided coming into close quarters with any of the farm servants or domestics of the estate on which he lived. A glimpse that he had once caught of the kitchen, with its blazing fire, and the cook, chopping off the heads of some of his companions, had been sufficient to keep him ever after in dread. Hence, one day when he was wanted for roasting, all the calling, clucking, and coaxing of the cook's assistants were in vain. "How deaf and dull you must be," said a Falcon who noticed this, "not to hear when you are called, or to see when you are wanted! You should take pattern by me. I never let my master call me twice." "Ah," answered the Goose, "if Falcons were called, like Geese, to be run upon a spit and set before the kitchen fire, they would be just as slow to come, and just as hard of hearing, as I am now."

The errand makes the difference.

❧ 279 ❧
THE ASS AND THE LITTLE DOG

The Ass observing how great a favorite a Little Dog was with his Master, how much caressed and fondled, and fed with choice bits at every meal—and for no other reason, that he could see, but skipping and frisking about and wagging his tail—resolved to imitate him, and see whether the same behavior would not bring him similar favors. Accordingly, the Master was no sooner come home from walking, and seated in his easy-chair, than the Ass came into the room, and danced around him with many an awkward gambol. The Man could not help laughing aloud at the odd sight. The joke, however, became serious, when the Ass, rising on his hind-legs, laid his forefeet upon his Master's shoulders, and braying in his face in the most fascinating manner, would fain have jumped into his lap. The Man cried out for help, and one of his servants running in with a good stick, laid it unmercifully on the bones of the poor Ass, who was glad to get back to his stable.

A place for everyone, and everyone in his place.

The Lion, Jupiter, and the Elephant

❧ 280 ❧
THE LION, JUPITER, AND THE ELEPHANT

The lion, for all his size and strength, and his sharp teeth and claws, is a coward in one thing: he can't bear the sound of a cock crowing, and runs away whenever he hears it. He complained bitterly to Jupiter for making him like that; but Jupiter said it wasn't his fault: he had done the best he could for him, and, considering this was his only failing, he ought to be well content. The lion, however, wouldn't be comforted, and was so ashamed of his timidity that he wished he might die. In this state of mind, he met the elephant and had a talk with him. He noticed that the great beast cocked up his ears all the time, as if he were listening for something, and he asked him why he did so. Just then a gnat came humming by, and the elephant said, "Do you see that wretched little buzzing insect? I'm terribly afraid of its getting into my ear: if it once gets in, I'm dead and done for." The lion's spirits rose at once when he heard this: "For," he said to himself, "if the elephant, huge as he is, is afraid of a gnat, I needn't be so much ashamed of being afraid of a cock, who is ten thousand times bigger than a gnat."

❧ 281 ☙

THE SHEPHERD
AND THE WOLF

A shepherd found a wolf's cub straying in the pastures, and took him home and reared him along with his dogs. When the cub grew to his full size, if ever a wolf stole a sheep from the flock, he used to join the dogs in hunting him down. It sometimes happened that the dogs failed to come up with the thief, and, abandoning the pursuit, returned home. The wolf would on such occasions continue the chase by himself, and when he overtook the culprit, would stop and share the feast with him, and then return to the shepherd. But if some time passed without a sheep being carried off by the wolves, he would steal one himself and share his plunder with the dogs. The shepherd's suspicions were aroused, and one day he caught him in the act; and, fastening a rope around his neck, hung him on the nearest tree.

*What's bred in the bone is sure to
come out in the flesh.*

282

THE PIG AND THE SHEEP

A pig found his way into a meadow where a flock of sheep were grazing. The shepherd caught him, and was proceeding to carry him off to the butcher's when he set up a loud squealing and struggled to get free. The sheep rebuked him for making such a to-do, and said to him, "The shepherd catches us regularly and drags us off just like that, and we don't make any fuss." "No, I dare say not," replied the pig, "but my case and yours are altogether different. He only wants you for wool, but he wants me for bacon."

283

THE GARDENER AND HIS DOG

A gardener's dog fell into a deep well, from which his master used to draw water for the plants in his garden with a rope and a bucket. Failing to get the dog out by means of these, the gardener went down into the well himself in order to fetch him up. But the dog thought he had come to make sure of drowning him; so he bit his master as soon as he came within reach, and hurt him a good deal, with the result that he left the dog to his fate and climbed out of the well, remarking, "It serves me quite right for trying to save so determined a suicide."

⚜ 284 ⚜
THE LION IN LOVE

A lion fell deeply in love with the daughter of a
cottager and wanted to marry her. But her father
was unwilling to give her to so fearsome a husband,
and yet didn't want to offend the lion; so he hit upon
the following expedient. He went to the lion and said,
"I think you will make a very good husband for my
daughter; but I cannot consent to your union unless
you let me draw your teeth and pare your nails, for my
daughter is terribly afraid of them." The lion was so
much in love that he readily agreed that this should be
done. When once, however, he was thus
disarmed, the cottager was afraid of
him no longer, but drove him away
with his club.

❦ 285 ❧
THE RIVERS AND THE SEA

O nce upon a time all the rivers combined to protest against the action of the sea in making their waters salt. "When we come to you," said they to the sea, "we are sweet and drinkable; but when once we have mingled with you, our waters become as briny and unpalatable as your own." The sea replied shortly, "Keep away from me and you'll remain sweet."

❦ 286 ❧
THE BEEKEEPER

A thief found his way into an apiary when the beekeeper was away, and stole all the honey. When the keeper returned and found the hives empty, he was very much upset and stood staring at them for some time. Before long the bees came back from gathering honey, and, finding their hives overturned and the keeper standing by, they made for him with their stings. At this he fell into a passion and cried, "You ungrateful scoundrels, you let the thief who stole my honey get off scot-free, and then you go and sting me who have always taken such care of you!"

*When you hit back make sure you
have got the right man.*

⚜ 287 ⚜

THE PHILOSOPHER AMONG THE TOMBS

A sage Philosopher, who was well versed in all knowledge, natural as well as moral, was one day found in a cemetery deeply absorbed in contemplating two human skeletons which lay before him; the one that of a duke, the other of a common beggar. When, after some time, he made this exclamation: "If skillful anatomists have made it appear that the bones, nerves, muscles, and entrails of all men are made after the same manner and form, surely this is a most convincing proof that true nobility is situated in the mind, and not in the blood."

The rich and the poor meet together in death.

⚜ 288 ⚜

THE CATS AND THE MONKEY

Two Cats having stolen some cheese, could not agree about dividing the prize. In order, therefore, to settle the dispute, they consented to refer the matter to a Monkey. The proposed judge very readily accepted the office, and, producing a balance, put a part into each scale. "Let me see," said he, "ah—this lump outweighs the other." And he bit off a considerable piece in order to make it balance. The opposite scale was now the heavier, which afforded our conscientious judge reason for a second mouthful. "Hold, hold!" said the two Cats, who began to be alarmed for the event, "give us our respective shares and we are satisfied." "If you are satisfied," returned the Monkey, "Justice is not; a cause of this nature is by no means so soon determined." He continued to nibble first one piece then the other, till the poor Cats, seeing their cheese gradually diminishing, entreated him to give himself no further trouble, but to award them what remained. "Not so fast, I beseech you, friends," replied the Monkey; "we owe Justice to ourselves as well as to you. What remains is due to me as a fee." Upon which he crammed the whole into his mouth, and with great gravity dismissed the Court.

Those who dance must pay the piper.

◁ 289 ▷

THE DIAMOND AND
THE GLOWWORM

A Diamond happened to fall from the solitaire of a young lady as she was walking one evening on a terrace in her garden. A Glowworm, who had beheld it sparkle in its descent, soon as the gloom of night had eclipsed its luster began to mock and to insult it. Art thou that wondrous thing that vaunteth of such prodigious brightness? Where now is all thy boasted brilliancy? Alas, in an evil hour has fortune thrown thee within the reach of my superior blaze. Conceited insect, replied the gem, that oweth thy feeble glimmer to the darkness that surrounds thee; know, that my luster bears the test of day, and even derives its chief advantage from that distinguishing light, which discovers thee to be no more than a dark and paltry worm.

To be set in a strong point of light is as favorable to merit as it is to imposture.

⚜ 290 ⚜
THE PLAGUE AMONG THE BEASTS

A mortal distemper once raged among the Beasts, and swept away prodigious numbers. After it had continued some time without abatement, the Beasts decided that it was a judgment inflicted upon them for their sins, and a day was appointed for a general confession; when it was agreed that he who appeared to be the greatest sinner should suffer death as an atonement for the rest. The Fox was appointed father confessor upon the occasion; and the Lion, with great generosity, condescended to be the first in making public confession. "For my part," said he, "I must acknowledge I have been an enormous offender. I have killed many innocent Sheep in my time; nay, once, but it was a case of necessity, I made a meal of the Shepherd." The Fox, with much gravity, owned that these in any other but the king, would have been inexpiable crimes; but that His Majesty had certainly a right to a few silly Sheep; nay, and to the Shepherd, too, in case of necessity. The judgment of the Fox was applauded by all the larger animals; and the Tiger, the Leopard, the Bear, and the Wolf made confession of many sins of the like nature; which were all excused with the same lenity and mercy, and their crimes accounted so venial as scarce to deserve the name of offenses. At last, a poor penitent Ass, with great contrition, acknowledged that once going through the churchyard, being very hungry and tempted by the sweetness of the grass, he had cropped a little of it, not more, however, in quantity than the tip of his tongue; he was very sorry for the misdemeanor, and hoped— "Hope!" exclaimed the Fox, with singular zeal; "what canst thou hope for after the commission of so heinous a crime? What! eat the churchyard grass! Oh, sacrilege! This, this is the flagrant wickedness, my brethren, which has drawn the wrath of Heaven upon our heads, and this the notorious offender whose death must make atonement for all our transgressions." So saying, he ordered his entrails for sacrifice, and the Beasts went to dinner upon the rest of his carcass.

It is easy to find fault with the helpless.

❦ 291 ❧

THE WOLF AND THE HORSE

A wolf on his rambles came to a field of oats, but, not being able to eat them, he was passing on his way when a horse came along. "Look," said the wolf, "here's a fine field of oats. For your sake I have left it untouched, and I shall greatly enjoy the sound of your teeth munching the ripe grain." But the horse replied, "If wolves could eat oats, my fine friend, you would hardly have indulged your ears at the cost of your belly."

There is no virtue in giving to others
what is useless to oneself.

The Wolf and the Horse

292

THE BAT, THE BRAMBLE, AND THE SEAGULL

A bat, a bramble, and a seagull went into partnership and determined to go on a trading voyage together. The bat borrowed a sum of money for his venture; the bramble laid in a stock of clothes of various kinds; and the seagull took a quantity of lead. And so they set out. By and by a great storm came on, and their boat with all the cargo went to the bottom, but the three travelers managed to reach land. Ever since then the seagull flies to and fro over the sea, and every now and then dives below the surface, looking for the lead he's lost; while the bat is so afraid of meeting his creditors that he hides away by day and only comes out at night to feed; and the bramble catches hold of the clothes of every one who passes by, hoping some day to recognize and recover the lost garments.

All men are more concerned to recover what they lose than to acquire what they lack.

293

THE DOG AND THE WOLF

A dog was lying in the sun before a farmyard gate when a wolf pounced upon him and was just going to eat him up. But he begged for his life and said,

239

"You see how thin I am and what a wretched meal I should make you now. But if you will only wait a few days my master is going to give a feast. All the rich scraps and pickings will fall to me and I shall get nice and fat. Then will be the time for you to eat me." The wolf thought this was a very good plan and went away. Some time afterward he came to the farmyard again, and found the dog lying out of reach on the stable roof. "Come down," he called, "and be eaten. You remember our agreement?" But the dog said coolly, "My friend, if ever you catch me lying down by the gate there again, don't you wait for any feast."

Once bitten, twice shy.

❦ 294 ❦

THE WASP AND THE SNAKE

A wasp settled on the head of a snake, and not only stung him several times, but clung obstinately to the head of his victim. Maddened with pain the snake tried every means he could think of to get rid of the creature, but without success. At last he became desperate, and crying, "Kill you I will, even at the cost of my own life," he laid his head with the wasp on it under the wheel of a passing wagon, and they both perished together.

❧ 295 ❧
THE EAGLE AND
THE BEETLE

An eagle was chasing a hare, which was running for dear life and was at her wits' end to know where to turn for help. Presently she espied a beetle, and begged it to aid her. So when the eagle came up the beetle warned her not to touch the hare, which was under its protection. But the eagle never noticed the beetle because it was so small, seized the hare and ate her up. The beetle never forgot this, and used to keep an eye on the eagle's nest, and whenever the eagle laid an egg it climbed up and rolled it out of the nest and broke it. At last the eagle got so worried over the loss of her eggs that she went up to Jupiter, who is the special protector of eagles, and begged him to give her a safe place to nest in; so he let her lay her eggs in his lap. But the beetle noticed this and made a ball of dirt the size of an eagle's egg, and flew up and deposited it in Jupiter's lap. When Jupiter saw the dirt, he stood up to shake it out of his robe, and, forgetting about the eggs, he shook them out too, and they were broken just as before. Ever since then, they say, eagles never lay their eggs at the season when beetles are about.

The weak will sometimes find ways to
avenge an insult, even upon the strong.

❧ 296 ❧

THE FOWLER AND
THE LARK

A fowler was setting his nets for little birds when a lark came up to him and asked him what he was doing. "I am engaged in founding a city," said he, and with that he withdrew to a short distance and concealed himself. The lark examined the nets with great curiosity, and presently, catching sight of the bait, hopped on to them in order to secure it, and became entangled in the meshes. The fowler then ran up quickly and captured her. "What a fool I was!" said she. "But at any rate, if that's the kind of city you are founding, it'll be a long time before you find fools enough to fill it."

❧ 297 ❧

THE FISHERMAN PIPING

A fisherman who could play the flute went down one day to the seashore with his nets and his flute; and, taking his stand on a projecting rock, began to play a tune, thinking that the music would bring the fish jumping out of the sea. He went on playing for some time, but not a fish appeared. So at last he threw down his flute and cast his net into the sea, and made a great haul of fish. When they were landed and he saw them leaping about on the shore, he cried, "You rascals! You wouldn't dance when I piped; but now I've stopped, you can do nothing else!"

To do the right thing at the right season is a great art.

The Fisherman Piping

◊ 298 ◊

THE WEASEL AND THE MAN

A man once caught a weasel, which was always sneaking about the house, and was just going to drown it in a tub of water, when it begged hard for its life, and said to him, "Surely you haven't the heart to put me to death? Think how useful I have been in clearing your house of the mice and lizards which used to infest it, and show your gratitude by sparing my life." "You have not been altogether useless, I grant you," said the man. "But who killed the fowls? Who stole the meat? No, no! You do much more harm than good, and die you shall."

◊ 299 ◊

THE PLOWMAN, THE ASS, AND THE OX

A plowman yoked his ox and his ass together, and set to work to plow his field. It was a poor makeshift of a team, but it was the best he could do, as he had but a single ox. At the end of the day, when the beasts were loosed from the yoke, the ass said to the ox, "Well, we've had a hard day. Which of us is to carry the master home?" The ox looked surprised at the question. "Why," said he, "you, to be sure, as usual."

DEMADES AND HIS FABLE

Demades the orator was once speaking in the assembly at Athens; but the people were very inattentive to what he was saying, so he stopped and said, "Gentlemen, I should like to tell you one of Aesop's fables." This made everyone listen intently. Then Demades began, "Demeter, a swallow, and an eel were once traveling together, and came to a river without a bridge: the swallow flew over it, and the eel swam across." And then he stopped. "What happened to Demeter?" cried several people in the audience. "Demeter," he replied, "is very angry with you for listening to fables when you ought to be minding public business."

301

THE MONKEY AND THE DOLPHIN

When people go on a voyage they often take with them lapdogs or monkeys as pets to wile away the time. Thus it fell out that a man returning to Athens from the East had a pet monkey on board with him. As they neared the coast of Attica a great storm burst upon them, and the ship capsized. All on board were thrown into the water, and tried to save themselves by swimming, the monkey among the rest. A dolphin saw him, and, supposing him to be a man, took him on his back and began swimming towards the shore. When they got near Piræus, which is the port of Athens, the dolphin asked the monkey if he was an Athenian. The monkey replied that he was, and added that he came of a very distinguished family. "Then, of course, you know Piræus," continued the dolphin. The monkey thought he was referring to some high official or other, and replied, "Oh, yes, he's a very old friend of mine." At that, detecting his hypocrisy, the dolphin was so disgusted that he dived below the surface, and the unfortunate monkey was quickly drowned.

Those who pretend to be what they are not,
sooner or later find themselves in deep water.

◁ 302 ▷

THE CROW AND THE SNAKE

A hungry crow spied a snake lying asleep in a sunny spot, and, picking it up in his claws, he was carrying it off to a place where he could make a meal of it without being disturbed, when the snake reared its head and bit him. It was a poisonous snake, and the bite was fatal, and the dying crow said, "What a cruel fate is mine! I thought I had made a lucky find, and it has cost me my life!"

◁ 303 ▷

THE DOGS AND THE FOX

S ome dogs once found a lion's skin, and were worrying it with their teeth. Just then a fox came by, and said, "You think yourselves very brave, no doubt; but if that were a live lion you'd find his claws a good deal sharper than your teeth."

It is easy to kick a man that is down.

◁ 304 ▷

THE NIGHTINGALE AND THE HAWK

A nightingale was sitting on a bough of an oak and singing, as her custom was. A hungry hawk presently spied her, and darting to the spot seized her in his talons. He was just about to tear her in pieces when she begged him to spare her life. "I'm not big enough," she pleaded, "to make you a good meal. You ought to seek your prey among the bigger birds." The hawk eyed her with some contempt. "You must think me very simple," said he, "if you suppose I am going to give up a certain prize on the chance of a better of which I see at present no signs."

৶ 305 ৸

THE ROSE AND THE AMARANTH

A rose and an amaranth* blossomed side by side in a garden, and the amaranth said to her neighbor, "How I envy you your beauty and your sweet scent! No wonder you are such a universal favorite." But the rose replied with a shade of sadness in her voice, "Ah, my dear friend, I bloom but for a time. My petals soon wither and fall, and then I die. But your flowers never fade, even if they are cut; for they are everlasting."

Greatness carries its own penalties.

* Amaranth means undying flower.

◁ 306 ▷

THE MAN, THE HORSE, THE OX, AND THE DOG

One winter's day, during a severe storm, a horse, an ox, and a dog came and begged for shelter in the house of a man. He readily admitted them, and, as they were cold and wet, he lit a fire for their comfort; and he put oats before the horse, and hay before the ox, while he fed the dog with the remains of his own dinner. When the storm abated, and they were about to depart, they determined to show their gratitude in the following way. They divided the life of man among them, and each endowed one part of it with the qualities which were peculiarly his own. The horse took youth, and hence young men are high-mettled and impatient of restraint; the ox took middle age, and accordingly men in middle life are steady and hard-working; while the dog took old age, which is the reason why old men are so often peevish and ill-tempered, and, like dogs, attached chiefly to those who look to their comfort, while they are disposed to snap at those who are unfamiliar or distasteful to them.

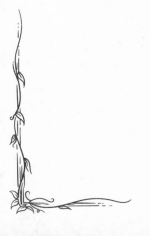

❧ 307 ❧
THE WOLVES, THE SHEEP, AND THE RAM

The wolves sent a deputation to the sheep with proposals for a lasting peace between them, on condition of their giving up the sheep-dogs to instant death. The foolish sheep agreed to the terms; but an old ram, whose years had brought him wisdom, interfered and said, "How can we expect to live at peace with you? Why, even with the dogs at hand to protect us, we are never secure from your murderous attacks!"

❧ 308 ❧
THE SWAN

The swan is said to sing but once in its life—when it knows that it is about to die. A certain man, who had heard of the song of the swan, one day saw one of these birds for sale in the market, and bought it and took it home with him. A few days later he had some friends to dinner, and produced the swan, and bade it sing for their entertainment; but the swan remained silent. In course of time, when it was growing old, it became aware of its approaching end and broke into a sweet, sad song. When its owner heard it, he said angrily, "If the creature only sings when it is about to die, what a fool I was that day I wanted to hear its song! I ought to have wrung its neck instead of merely inviting it to sing."

◁ 309 ▷
THE SNAKE AND JUPITER

A snake suffered a good deal from being constantly trodden upon by man and beast, owing partly to the length of his body and partly to his being unable to raise himself above the surface of the ground; so he went and complained to Jupiter about the risks to which he was exposed. But Jupiter had little sympathy for him. "I dare say," said he, "that if you had bitten the first that trod on you, the others would have taken more trouble to look where they put their feet."

◁ 310 ▷
THE WOLF AND HIS SHADOW

A wolf, who was roaming about on the plain when the sun was getting low in the sky, was much impressed by the size of his shadow, and said to himself, "I had no idea I was so big. Fancy my being afraid of a lion! Why, I, not he, ought to be king of the beasts." And, heedless of danger, he strutted about as if there could be no doubt at all about it. Just then a lion sprang upon him and began to devour him. "Alas," he cried, "had I not lost sight of the facts, I shouldn't have been ruined by my fancies."

❧ 311 ☙

THE PLOWMAN AND THE WOLF

A plowman loosed his oxen from the plow, and led them away to the water to drink. While he was absent a half-starved wolf appeared on the scene, and went up to the plow and began chewing the leather straps attached to the yoke. As he gnawed away desperately in the hope of satisfying his craving for food, he somehow got entangled in the harness, and, taking fright, struggled to get free, tugging at the traces as if he would drag the plow along with him. Just then the plowman came back, and seeing what was happening, he cried, "Ah, you old rascal, I wish you would give up thieving for good and take to honest work instead."

312

MERCURY AND THE MAN BITTEN BY AN ANT

A man once saw a ship go down with all its crew, and commented severely on the injustice of the gods. "They care nothing for a man's character," said he, "but let the good and the bad go to their deaths together." There was an ant heap close by where he was standing, and, just as he spoke, he was bitten in the foot by an ant. Turning in a temper to the ant heap he stamped upon it and crushed hundreds of unoffending ants. Suddenly Mercury appeared, and belabored him with his staff, saying as he did so, "You villain, where's your nice sense of justice now?"

313

THE WILY LION

A lion watched a fat bull feeding in a meadow, and his mouth watered when he thought of the royal feast he would make, but he did not dare to attack him, for he was afraid of his sharp horns. Hunger, however, presently compelled him to do something; and as the use of force did not promise success, he determined to resort to artifice. Going up to the bull in friendly fashion, he said to him, "I cannot help saying how much I admire your magnificent figure. What a fine head! What powerful shoulders and thighs! But, my dear friend, what in the world makes you wear those ugly horns? You must find them as awkward as they are unsightly. Believe me, you would do much better without them." The bull was foolish enough to be persuaded by this flattery to have his horns cut off; and, having now lost his only means of defense, fell an easy prey to the lion.

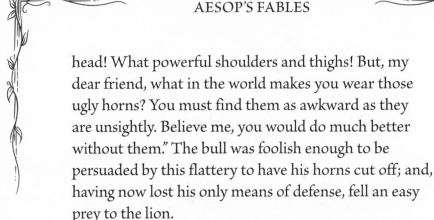

❦ 314 ❧

THE PARROT AND THE CAT

A man once bought a parrot and gave it the run of his house. It reveled in its liberty, and presently flew up on to the mantelpiece and screamed away to its heart's content. The noise disturbed the cat, who was asleep on the hearth rug. Looking up at the intruder, she said, "Who may you be, and where have you come from?" The parrot replied, "Your master has just bought me and brought me home with him." "You impudent bird," said the cat, "how dare you, a newcomer, make a noise like that? Why, I was born here, and have lived here all my life, and yet, if I venture to mew, they throw things at me and chase me all over the place." "Look here, mistress," said the parrot, "you just hold your tongue. My voice they delight in; but yours—yours is a perfect nuisance."

❧ 315 ❧

THE STAG AND THE LION

A stag was chased by the hounds, and took refuge in a cave, where he hoped to be safe from his pursuers. Unfortunately the cave contained a lion, to whom he fell an easy prey. "Unhappy that I am," he cried, "I am saved from the power of the dogs only to fall into the clutches of a lion."

Out of the frying pan and into the fire.

❧ 316 ❧

THE IMPOSTOR

A certain man fell ill, and, being in a very bad way, he made a vow that he would sacrifice a hundred oxen to the gods if they would grant him a return to health. Wishing to see how he would keep his vow, they caused him to recover in a short time. Now, he hadn't an ox in the world, so he made a hundred little oxen out of tallow and offered them up on an altar, at the same time saying, "Ye gods, I call you to witness that I have discharged my vow." The gods determined to be even with him, so they sent him a dream, in which he was bidden to go to the seashore and fetch a hundred crowns which he was to find there. Hastening in

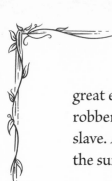

great excitement to the shore, he fell in with a band of robbers, who seized him and carried him off to sell as a slave. And when they sold him, a hundred crowns was the sum he fetched.

Do not promise more than you can perform.

❧ 317 ❧

The Dogs and the Hides

O nce upon a time a number of dogs, who were famished with hunger, saw some hides steeping in a river, but couldn't get at them because the water was too deep. So they put their heads together, and decided to drink away at the river till it was shallow enough for them to reach the hides. But long before that happened they burst themselves with drinking.

Attempt not impossibilities.

❦ 318 ❦

THE LION, THE FOX, AND THE ASS

A lion, a fox, and an ass went out hunting together. They had soon taken a large booty, which the lion requested the ass to divide between them. The ass divided it all into three equal parts, and modestly begged the others to take their choice; at which the lion, bursting with fury, sprang upon the ass and tore him to pieces. Then, glaring at the fox, he bade him make a fresh division. The fox gathered almost the whole in one great heap for the lion's share, leaving only the smallest possible morsel for himself. "My dear friend," said the lion, "how did you get the knack of it so well?" The fox replied, "Me? Oh, I took a lesson from the ass."

Happy is he who learns from the misfortunes of others.

❧ 319 ❧

THE OWL AND THE NIGHTINGALE

A formal solemn Owl had many years made his habitation in a grove among the ruins of an old monastery, and had pored so often over some moldy manuscripts, the stupid relics of a monkish library, that he grew infected with the pride and pedantry of the place; and, mistaking gravity for wisdom, he would sit whole days with his eyes half shut, fancying himself profoundly learned. It happened as he sat one evening, half buried in meditation, and half asleep, that a Nightingale, unluckily perching near him, began her melodious lays. He started from his reverie, and with a horrid screech interrupting her song—"Be gone," cried he, "thou impertinent minstrel, nor distract with noisy dissonance my sublime contemplations; and know, vain songster, that harmony consists in truth alone, which is gained by laborious study; and not in languishing notes, fit only to soothe the ear of a lovesick maid." "Conceited pedant," returned the Nightingale, "whose wisdom lies only in the feathers that muffle up thy unmeaning face; music is a natural and rational entertainment, and though not adapted to the ears of an Owl, has ever been relished and admired by all who are possessed of true taste and elegance."

It is natural for a pedant to despise those arts which polish our manners, and would extirpate pedantry.

320

THE DOG AND THE OYSTER

A Dog, used to eating eggs, saw an Oyster; and, opening his mouth to its widest extent, swallowed it down with the utmost relish, supposing it to be an egg. Soon afterwards suffering great pain in his stomach, he said, "I deserve all this torment, for my folly in thinking that everything round must be an egg."

They who act without sufficient thought,
will often fall into unsuspected danger.

321

THE THRUSH AND THE SWALLOW

A young Thrush, who lived in an orchard, once became acquainted with a Swallow. A friendship sprang up between them, and the Swallow, after skimming the orchard and the neighboring meadow, would every now and then come to visit the Thrush. The Thrush, hopping from branch to branch, would welcome him with his most cheerful note. "Oh, mother!" said he to his parent, one day, "never did any creature have such a friend as I have in this same Swallow." "Nor did any mother," replied the parent Bird, "ever have such a silly son as I have in this same Thrush. Long before the approach of winter, your friend will

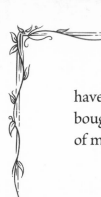

have left you, and while you sit shivering on a leafless bough, he will be sporting under sunny skies hundreds of miles away."

Unequal friendships do not last.

⚔ 322 ⚔

THE FROG AND THE MOUSE

A Frog and a Mouse, who had long been rivals for the sovereignty of a certain marsh, and had many a skirmish and running fight together, agreed one day to settle the matter, once for all, by a fair and open combat. They met, and each, armed with the point of a bulrush for a spear, was ready to fight to the death. The combat began in earnest, and there is no knowing how it might have ended, had not a Kite, seeing them from afar, pounced down and carried off both heroes in her talons.

Peace brings security.

⚔ 323 ⚔

THE FIGHTING COCKS

Two Cocks fought for the sovereignty of the farm-yard. One was severely beaten, and ran and hid

himself in a hole. The conqueror flew to the top of an outhouse, there clapped his wings, and crowed out "Victory!" Just then an Eagle made a swoop, seized him, and carried him off. The other, seeing this from his hiding-place, came out, and, shaking off the recollection of his late disgrace, strutted about among his Hens with all the dignity imaginable.

Pride goes before a fall.

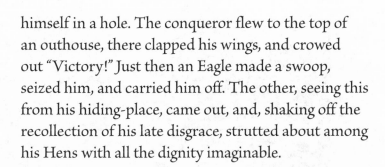

⚜ 324 ⚜

THE LION'S SHARE

The Lion and several other Beasts once agreed to live peaceably together in the forest, sharing equally all the spoils of hunting. One day, a fine fat Stag fell into a snare set by the Goat, who thereupon called the rest together. The Lion divided the Stag into four parts. Taking the best piece for himself, he said, "This is mine, of course, as I am the Lion;" taking another portion, he added, "This too is mine by right—the right, if you must know, of the strongest." Further, putting aside the third piece, "That's for the most valiant," said he; "and as for the remaining part, touch it if you dare."

Might makes right.

❦ 325 ❧

THE GNAT AND THE LION

A gnat once went up to a lion and said, "I am not in the least afraid of you. I don't even allow that you are a match for me in strength. What does your strength amount to after all? That you can scratch with your claws and bite with your teeth—just like a woman in a temper—and nothing more. But I'm stronger than you. If you don't believe it, let us fight and see." So saying, the gnat sounded his horn, and darted in and bit the lion on the nose. When the lion felt the sting, in his haste to crush him he scratched his nose badly, and made it bleed, but failed altogether to hurt the gnat, which buzzed off in triumph, elated by its victory. Presently, however, it got entangled in a spider's web, and was caught and eaten by the spider, thus falling prey to an insignificant insect after having triumphed over the king of the beasts.

The Gnat and the Lion

❧ 326 ❧

THE FOWLER, THE PARTRIDGE, AND THE COCK

O ne day, as a fowler was sitting down to a scanty supper of herbs and bread, a friend dropped in unexpectedly. The larder was empty, so he went out and caught a tame partridge, which he kept as a decoy, and was about to wring her neck when she cried, "Surely you won't kill me? Why, what will you do without me next time you go fowling? How will you get the birds to come to your nets?" He let her go at this, and went to his henhouse, where he had a plump young cock. When the cock saw what he was after, he too pleaded for his life, and said, "If you kill me, how will you know the time of night? And who will wake you up in the morning when it is time to get to work?" The fowler, however, replied, "You are useful for telling the time, I know; but, for all that, I can't send my friend supperless to bed." And therewith he caught him and wrung his neck.

327

The Farmer and His Dogs

A farmer was snowed up in his farmstead by a severe storm, and was unable to go out and procure provisions for himself and his family. So he first killed his sheep and used them for food. Then, as the storm still continued, he killed his goats. And, last of all, as the weather showed no signs of improving, he was compelled to kill his oxen and eat them. When his dogs saw the various animals being killed and eaten in turn, they said to one another, "We had better get out of this or we shall be the next to go!"

328

The Eagle and the Fox

An eagle and a fox became great friends and determined to live near one another. They thought that the more they saw of each other the better friends they would be. So the eagle built a nest at the top of a high tree, while the fox settled in a thicket at the foot of it and produced a litter of cubs. One day the fox went out foraging for food, and the eagle, who also wanted food for her young, flew down into the thicket, caught up the fox's cubs, and carried them up into the tree for a meal for herself and her family. When the fox came back, and found out what had happened, she was not so much sorry for the loss of her cubs as furious

because she couldn't get at the eagle and pay her out for her treachery. So she sat down not far off and cursed her. But it wasn't long before she had her revenge. Some villagers happened to be sacrificing a goat on a neighboring altar, and the eagle flew down and carried off a piece of burning flesh to her nest. There was a strong wind blowing, and the nest caught fire, with the result that her fledglings fell half-roasted to the ground. Then the fox ran to the spot and devoured them in full sight of the eagle.

Do unto others as you would have them do unto you.

⚜ 329 ⚜

THE BUTCHER AND HIS CUSTOMERS

Two Men were buying meat at a butcher's stall in the marketplace, and, while the butcher's back was turned for a moment, one of them snatched up a joint and hastily thrust it under the other's cloak, where it could not be seen. When the butcher turned round, he missed the meat at once, and charged them with having stolen it; but the one who had taken it said he hadn't got it, and the one who had got it said he hadn't taken it. The butcher felt sure they were deceiving him, but he

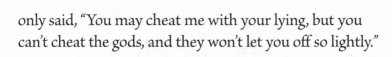

only said, "You may cheat me with your lying, but you can't cheat the gods, and they won't let you off so lightly."

Prevarication often amounts to perjury.

❧ 330 ☙
HERCULES AND MINERVA

Hercules was once traveling along a narrow road when he saw lying on the ground in front of him what appeared to be an apple, and as he passed he stamped upon it with his heel. To his astonishment, instead of being crushed it doubled in size; and, on his attacking it again and smiting it with his club, it swelled up to an enormous size and blocked up the whole road. Upon this he dropped his club, and stood looking at it in amazement. Just then Minerva appeared, and said to him, "Leave it alone, my friend; that which you see before you is the Apple of Discord. If you do not meddle with it, it remains small as it was at first, but if you resort to violence it swells into the thing you see."

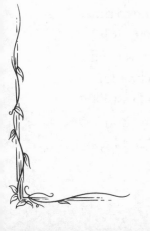

⚜ 331 ⚜
THE FOX WHO SERVED A LION

A lion had a fox to attend on him, and whenever they went hunting the fox found the prey and the lion fell upon it and killed it, and then they divided it between them in certain proportions. But the lion always got a very large share, and the fox a very small one, which didn't please the latter at all; so he determined to set up on his own account. He began by trying to steal a lamb from a flock of sheep. But the shepherd saw him and set his dogs on him. The hunter was now the hunted, and was very soon caught and dispatched by the dogs.

Better servitude with safety than freedom with danger.

⚜ 332 ⚜
THE QUACK DOCTOR

A certain man fell sick and took to his bed. He consulted a number of doctors from time to time, and they all, with one exception, told him that his life was in no immediate danger, but that his illness would probably last a considerable time. The one who took a different view of his case, who was also the last to be consulted, bade him prepare for the worst: "You have not twenty-four hours to live," said he, "and I fear

I can do nothing." As it turned out, however, he was quite wrong; for at the end of a few days the sick man quitted his bed and took a walk abroad, looking, it is true, as pale as a ghost. In the course of his walk he met the doctor who had prophesied his death. "Dear me," said the latter, "how do you do? You are fresh from the other world, no doubt. Pray, how are our departed friends getting on there?" "Most comfortably," replied the other, "for they have drunk the water of oblivion, and have forgotten all the troubles of life. By the way, just before I left, the authorities were making arrangements to prosecute all the doctors, because they won't let sick men die in the course of nature, but use their arts to keep them alive. They were going to charge you along with the rest, till I assured them that you were no doctor, but a mere impostor."

❧ 333 ❧

THE LION, THE WOLF, AND THE FOX

A lion, infirm with age, lay sick in his den, and all the beasts of the forest came to inquire after his health with the exception of the fox. The wolf thought this was a good opportunity for paying off old scores against the fox, so he called the attention of the lion to his absence, and said, "You see, sire, that we have all come to see how you are except the fox, who hasn't come near you, and doesn't care whether you are well or ill."

Just then the fox came in and heard the last words of the wolf. The lion roared at him in deep displeasure, but he begged to be allowed to explain his absence, and said, "Not one of them cares for you so much as I, sire, for all the time I have been going around to the doctors and trying to find a cure for your illness." "And may I ask if you have found one?" said the lion. "I have, sire," said the fox, "and it is this: you must flay a wolf and wrap yourself in his skin while it is still warm." The lion accordingly turned to the wolf and struck him dead with one blow of his paw, in order to try the fox's prescription; but the fox laughed and said to himself, "That's what comes of stirring up ill-will."

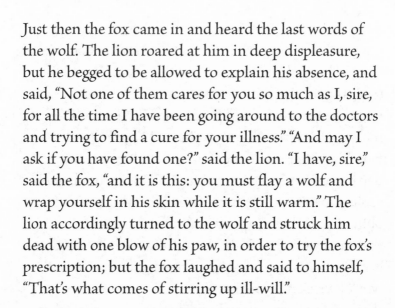

⚜ 334 ⚜

HERCULES AND PLUTUS

When Hercules was received among the gods and was entertained at a banquet by Jupiter, he responded courteously to the greetings of all with the exception of Plutus, the god of wealth. When Plutus approached him, he cast his eyes upon the ground, and turned away and pretended not to see him. Jupiter was surprised at this conduct on his part, and asked why, after having been so cordial with all the other gods, he had behaved like that to Plutus. "Sire," said Hercules, "I do not like Plutus, and I will tell you why. When we were on earth together I always noticed that he was to be found in the company of scoundrels."

⅏ 335 ⅏

THE FOX AND THE LEOPARD

A fox and a leopard were disputing about their looks, and each claimed to be the more handsome of the two. The leopard said, "Look at my smart coat; you have nothing to match that." But the fox replied, "Your coat may be smart, but my wits are smarter still."

⅏ 336 ⅏

THE FOX, THE FLIES, AND THE HEDGEHOG

A fox, in swimming across a rapid river, was swept away by the current and carried a long way downstream in spite of his struggles, until at last, bruised and exhausted, he managed to scramble onto dry ground from a backwater. As he lay there unable to move, a swarm of horseflies settled on him and sucked his blood undisturbed, for he was too weak even to

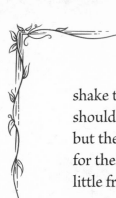

shake them off. A hedgehog saw him, and asked if he should brush away the flies that were tormenting him; but the fox replied, "Oh, please, no, not on any account, for these flies have sucked their fill and are taking very little from me now; but, if you drive them off, another swarm of hungry ones will come and suck all the blood I have left, and leave me without a drop in my veins."

⛦ 337 ⛦

THE CROW AND THE RAVEN

A crow became very jealous of a raven, because the latter was regarded by men as a bird of omen which foretold the future, and was accordingly held in great respect by them. She was very anxious to get the same sort of reputation herself; and, one day, seeing some travelers approaching, she flew on to a branch of a tree at the roadside and cawed as loud as she could. The travelers were in some dismay at the sound, for they feared it might be a bad omen; till one of them, spying the crow, said to his companions, "It's all right, my friends, we can go on without fear, for it's only a crow and that means nothing."

Those who pretend to be something they are not only make themselves ridiculous.

⚜ 338 ⚜
THE WITCH

A witch professed to be able to avert the anger of the gods by means of charms, of which she alone possessed the secret; and she drove a brisk trade, and made a fat livelihood out of it. But certain persons accused her of black magic and carried her before the judges, and demanded that she should be put to death for dealings with the devil. She was found guilty and condemned to death; and one of the judges said to her as she was leaving the dock, "You say you can avert the anger of the gods. How comes it, then, that you have failed to disarm the enmity of men?"

⚜ 339 ⚜
THE OLD MAN AND DEATH

An old man cut himself a bundle of faggots in a wood and started to carry them home. He had a long way to go, and was tired out before he had got much more than halfway. Casting his burden on the ground, he called upon death to come and release him from his life of toil. The words were scarcely out of his mouth when, much to his dismay, death stood before him and professed his readiness to serve him. He was almost frightened out of his wits, but he had enough presence of mind to stammer out, "Good sir, if you'd be so kind, pray help me up with my burden again."

How sorry we would be if many of our wishes were granted.

⚜ 340 ⚜
THE MISER

A miser sold everything he had, and melted down his hoard of gold into a single lump, which he buried secretly in a field. Every day he went to look at it, and would sometimes spend long hours gloating over his treasure. One of his men noticed his frequent visits to the spot, and one day watched him and discovered

his secret. Awaiting his opportunity, he went one night and dug up the gold and stole it. Next day the miser visited the place as usual, and, finding his treasure gone, fell to tearing his hair and groaning over his loss. In this condition he was seen by one of his neighbors, who asked him what his trouble was. The miser told him of his misfortune; but the other replied, "Don't take it so much to heart, my friend; put a brick into the hole, and take a look at it every day. You won't be any worse off than before, for even when you had your gold it was of no earthly use to you."

The true value of money is not in
its possession but in its use.

⊲ 341 ⊳
THE FOXES AND THE RIVER

A number of foxes assembled on the bank of a river and wanted to drink; but the current was so strong and the water looked so deep and dangerous that they didn't dare to do so, but stood near the edge encouraging one another not to be afraid. At last one of them, to shame the rest, and show how brave he was, said, "I am not a bit frightened! See, I'll step right into the water!" He had no sooner done so than the current swept him off his feet. When the others saw him being carried downstream they cried, "Don't go and leave us! Come back and show us where we too can drink with

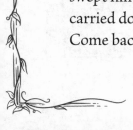

safety." But he replied, "I'm afraid I can't yet. I want to go to the seaside, and this current will take me there nicely. When I come back I'll show you with pleasure."

⊲ 342 ⊳
THE HORSE AND THE STAG

There was once a horse who used to graze in a meadow which he had all to himself. But one day a stag came into the meadow, and said he had as good a right to feed there as the horse, and moreover chose all the best places for himself. The horse, wishing to be revenged upon his unwelcome visitor, went to a man and asked if he would help him to turn out the stag. "Yes," said the man, "I will by all means; but I can only do so if you let me put a bridle in your mouth and mount on your back." The horse agreed to this, and the two together very soon turned the stag out of the pasture. But when that was done, the horse found to his dismay that in the man he had got a master for good.

Liberty is too huge a price to pay for revenge.

❧ 343 ❧

THE FOX AND THE BRAMBLE

In making his way through a hedge, a fox missed his footing and caught at a bramble to save himself from falling. Naturally, he got badly scratched, and in disgust he cried to the bramble, "It was your help I wanted, and see how you have treated me! I'd sooner have fallen outright." The bramble, interrupting him, replied, "You must have lost your wits, my friend, to catch at me, who am myself always catching at others."

To the selfish, all are selfish.

❧ 344 ❧

THE FOX AND THE SNAKE

A snake, in crossing a river, was carried away by the current, but managed to wriggle onto a bundle of thorns which was floating by, and was thus carried at a great rate downstream. A fox caught sight of it from the bank as it went whirling along, and called out, "Gad! The passenger fits the ship!"

⚜ 345 ⚜
THE LION, THE FOX,
AND THE STAG

A lion lay sick in his den, unable to provide himself with food. So he said to his friend the fox, who came to ask how he did, "My good friend, I wish you would go to yonder wood and beguile the big stag, who lives there, to come to my den. I have a fancy to make my dinner off a stag's heart and brains." The fox went to the wood and found the stag and said to him, "My dear sir, you're in luck. You know the lion, our king. Well, he's at the point of death, and has appointed you his successor to rule over the beasts. I hope you won't forget that I was the first to bring you the good news. And now I must be going back to him; and, if you take my advice, you'll come too and be with him at the last." The stag was highly flattered, and followed the fox to the lion's den, suspecting nothing. No sooner had he got inside than the lion sprang upon him, but he misjudged his spring, and the stag got away with only his ears torn, and returned as fast as he could to the shelter of the wood. The fox was much mortified, and the lion, too, was dreadfully disappointed, for he was getting very hungry in spite of his illness. So he begged the fox to have another try at coaxing the stag to his den. "It'll be almost impossible this time," said the fox, "but I'll try." And off he went to the wood a second time, and found the stag resting and trying to recover from his fright.

As soon as he saw the fox he cried, "You scoundrel, what do you mean by trying to lure me to my death like that? Take yourself off, or I'll do you to death with my horns." But the fox was entirely shameless. "What a coward you were," said he. "Surely you didn't think the lion meant any harm? Why, he was only going to whisper some royal secrets into your ear when you went off like a scared rabbit. You have rather disgusted him, and I'm not sure he won't make the wolf king instead, unless you come back at once and show you've got some spirit. I promise you he won't hurt you, and I will be your faithful servant."

The stag was foolish enough to be persuaded to return, and this time the lion made no mistake, but overpowered him, and feasted right royally upon his carcass. The fox, meanwhile, watched his chance and, when the lion wasn't looking, filched away the brains to reward him for his trouble. Presently the lion began searching for them, of course without success; and the fox, who was watching him, said, "I don't think it's much use your looking for the brains. A creature who twice walked into a lion's den can't have got any."

⚘ 346 ⚘

THE MAN WHO LOST HIS SPADE

A man was engaged in digging over his vineyard, and one day on coming to work he missed his spade.

Thinking it may have been stolen by one of his laborers, he questioned them closely, but they one and all denied any knowledge of it. He was not convinced by their denials, and insisted that they should all go to the town and take an oath in a temple that they were not guilty of the theft. This was because he had no great opinion of the simple country deities, but thought that the thief would not pass undetected by the shrewder gods of the town. When they got inside the gates the first thing they heard was the town crier proclaiming a reward for information about a thief who had stolen something from the city temple. "Well," said the man to himself, "it strikes me I had better go back home again. If these town gods can't detect the thieves who steal from their own temples, it's scarcely likely they can tell me who stole my spade."

◁ 347 ▷

THE PARTRIDGE AND
THE FOWLER

A fowler caught a partridge in his nets, and was just about to wring its neck when it made a piteous appeal to him to spare its life and said, "Do not kill me, but let me live and I will repay you for your kindness by decoying other partridges into your nets." "No," said the fowler, "I will not spare you. I was going to kill you anyhow, and after that treacherous speech you thoroughly deserve your fate."

❦ 348 ❦
THE RUNAWAY SLAVE

A slave, being discontented with his lot, ran away from his master. He was soon missed by the latter, who lost no time in mounting his horse and setting out in pursuit of the fugitive. He presently came up with him, and the slave, in the hope of avoiding capture, slipped into a treadmill and hid himself there. "Aha," said his master, "that's the very place for you, my man!"

❦ 349 ❦
THE HUNTER AND
THE WOODMAN

A hunter was searching in the forest for the tracks of a lion, and, catching sight presently of a woodman engaged in felling a tree, he went up to him and asked him if he had noticed a lion's footprints anywhere about, or if he knew where his den was. The woodman answered, "If you will come with me, I will show you the lion himself." The hunter turned pale with fear, and his teeth chattered as he replied, "Oh, I'm not looking for the lion, thanks, but only for his tracks."

The hero is brave in deeds as well as words.

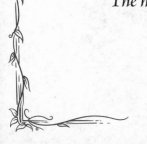

৶ 350 ৡ
THE HORSE AND THE ASS

A horse, proud of his fine harness, met an ass on the high road. As the ass with his heavy burden moved slowly out of the way to let him pass, the horse cried out impatiently that he could hardly resist kicking him to make him move faster. The ass held his peace, but did not forget the other's insolence. Not long afterward the horse became broken-winded, and was sold by his owner to a farmer. One day, as he was drawing a dung cart, he met the ass again, who in turn derided him and said, "Aha! You never thought to come to this, did you, you who were so proud! Where are all your gay trappings now?"

Better humble security than gilded danger.

351

THE DOG CHASING A WOLF

A dog was chasing a wolf, and as he ran he thought what a fine fellow he was, and what strong legs he had, and how quickly they covered the ground. "Now, there's this wolf," he said to himself, "what a poor creature he is; he's no match for me, and he knows it and so he runs away." But the wolf looked round just then and said, "Don't you imagine I'm running away from you, my friend. It's your master I'm afraid of."

352

THE HAWK, THE KITE, AND THE PIGEONS

The pigeons in a certain dovecote were persecuted by a kite, who every now and then swooped down and carried off one of their number. So they invited a hawk into the dovecote to defend them against their enemy. But they soon repented of their folly; for the hawk killed more of them in a day than the kite had done in a year.

Avoid a remedy that is worse than the disease.

❧ 353 ❧

THE WOMAN AND THE FARMER

A woman, who had lately lost her husband, used to go every day to his grave and lament her loss. A farmer, who was engaged in plowing not far from the spot, set eyes upon the woman and desired to have her for his wife. So he left his plow and came and sat by her side, and began to shed tears himself. She asked him why he wept; and he replied, "I have lately lost my wife, who was very dear to me, and tears ease my grief." "And I," said she, "have lost my husband." And so for a while they mourned in silence. Then he said, "Since you and I are in like case, shall we not do well to marry and live together? I shall take the place of your dead husband, and you, that of my dead wife." The woman consented to the plan, which indeed seemed reasonable enough, and they dried their tears. Meanwhile, a thief had come and stolen the oxen which the farmer had left with his plow. On discovering the theft, he beat his breast and loudly bewailed his loss. When the woman heard his cries, she came and said, "Why, are you weeping still?" To which he replied, "Yes, and I mean it this time."

❧ 354 ☙

PROMETHEUS AND THE MAKING OF MAN

At the bidding of Jupiter, Prometheus set about the creation of man and the other animals. Jupiter, seeing that mankind, the only rational creatures, were far outnumbered by the irrational beasts, bade him redress the balance by turning some of the latter into men. Prometheus did as he was bidden, and this is the reason why some people have the forms of men but the souls of beasts.

❧ 355 ☙

THE SWALLOW AND THE CROW

A swallow was once boasting to a crow about her birth. "I was once a princess," said she, "the daughter of a king of Athens, but my husband used me cruelly, and cut out my tongue for a slight fault. Then, to protect me from further injury, I was turned by Juno into a bird." "You chatter quite enough as it is," said the crow. "What you would have been like if you hadn't lost your tongue, I can't think."

Fair weather friends are not worth much.

⚜ 356 ⚜
THE TRAVELER
AND FORTUNE

A traveler, exhausted with fatigue after a long journey, sank down at the very brink of a deep well and presently fell asleep. He was within an ace of falling in, when Dame Fortune appeared to him and touched him on the shoulder, cautioning him to move further away. "Wake up, good sir, I pray you," she said. "Had you fallen into the well, the blame would have been thrown not on your own folly but on me, Fortune."

Everyone is more or less master of his own fate.

❦ 357 ❧

THE GOATHERD AND THE WILD GOATS

A goatherd was tending his goats out at pasture when he saw a number of wild goats approach and mingle with his flock. At the end of the day he drove them home and put them all into the pen together. Next day the weather was so bad that he could not take them out as usual, so he kept them at home in the pen, and fed them there. He only gave his own goats enough food to keep them from starving, but he gave the wild goats as much as they could eat and more; for he was very anxious for them to stay, and he thought that if he fed them well they wouldn't want to leave him. When the weather improved, he took them all out to pasture again; but no sooner had they got near the hills than the wild goats broke away from the flock and scampered off. The goatherd was very much disgusted at this, and roundly abused them for their ingratitude. "Rascals!" he cried, "to run away like that after the way I've treated you!" Hearing this, one of them turned round and said, "Oh, yes, you treated us all right—too well, in fact; it was just that which put us on our guard. If you treat newcomers like ourselves so much better than your own flock, it's more than likely that, if another lot of strange goats joined yours, we should then be neglected in favor of the last comers."

*Old friends cannot with impunity
be sacrificed for new ones.*

◁ 358 ▷

THE NIGHTINGALE AND THE SWALLOW

A swallow, conversing with a nightingale, advised her to quit the leafy coverts where she made her home, and to come and live with men, like herself, and nest under the shelter of their roofs. But the nightingale replied, "Time was when I too, like yourself, lived among men. But the memory of the cruel wrongs I then suffered makes them hateful to me, and never again will I approach their dwellings."

The scene of past sufferings revives painful memories.

◁ 359 ▷

THE HUNTER AND THE HORSEMAN

A hunter went out after game, and succeeded in catching a hare, which he was carrying home with him when he met a man on horseback, who said to him, "You have had some sport I see, sir," and offered to buy it. The hunter readily agreed; but the horseman had no sooner got the hare in his hands than he set spurs to his horse and went off at full gallop. The hunter ran after him for some little distance; but it soon dawned upon him that he had been tricked, and he gave up trying to overtake the horseman, and, to save his face, called after him as loud as he could, "All right, sir, all right, take your hare. It was meant all along as a present."

◁ 360 ▷
JUPITER AND THE CAMEL

The Camel once upon a time complained to Jupiter that he was not as well served as he ought to be in the means of defense and offense. "The Bull," said he, "has horns; the Boar, tusks; and the Lion and Tiger, formidable claws and fangs that make them feared and respected on all sides. I, on the other hand, have to put up with the abuse of all who choose to insult me." Jupiter angrily told him that if he would take the trouble to think, he would see that he was given qualities shared by no other Beast; and that, as a punishment for his foolish complaint, his ears should be shortened.

Man does not always know what is best for him.

◁ 361 ▷
THE WOODCOCK AND THE MALLARD

A Woodcock and a Mallard were feeding together in some marshy ground at the back of a mill-pond.

"Dear me," said the squeamish Woodcock, "in what a voracious and beastly manner you devour all that comes before you! Neither snail, frog, toad, nor any kind of filth can escape the fury of your enormous appetite. All alike goes down without measure and without distinction. What an odious vice is gluttony!" "Good lack!" replied the Mallard; "pray, how came you to be my accuser? And whence has your excessive delicacy a right to censure my plain eating? Is it a crime to satisfy one's hunger? Or is it not, indeed, a virtue rather to be pleased with the food which nature offers us? Surely, I would sooner be charged with gluttony than with that finical and sickly appetite on which you are pleased to ground your superiority of taste. What a silly vice is daintiness!" Thus endeavoring to palliate their respective passions, our epicures parted with a mutual contempt. The Mallard, hastening to devour some garbage, which was in reality a bait, immediately gorged a hook, through mere greediness and oversight; while the Woodcock, flying through a glade in order to seek his favorite fare, was entangled in a net spread across for that purpose; falling each of them a sacrifice to their different, but equal foibles.

A voracious appetite, and a fondness for dainties, equally take off our attention from more material concerns.

◁ 362 ▷

THE WOMAN AND HER HEN

A Woman had a Hen that laid an egg every day. The Fowl was of a superior breed, and the eggs were very fine, and sold for a good price. The Woman thought that by giving the hen twice as much food as she had been in the habit of giving, the bird might be brought to lay two eggs a day instead of one. So the quantity of food was doubled. The Hen thereupon grew very fat, and stopped laying altogether.

Figures are not always facts.

◁ 363 ▷

THE WOLF, THE SHE-GOAT, AND THE KID

A She-Goat, leaving her house one morning to look for food, told her Kid to bolt the door, and to open to no one who did not give as a password, "A plague on the Wolf, and all his tribe." A Wolf who was lurking about, unseen by the Goat, heard her words, and when she was gone, came and tapped at the door, and imitating her voice, said, "A plague on the Wolf, and all his tribe." He made sure that the door would be opened at once; but the Kid, whose suspicions were aroused, replied: "Show me your beard and I will let you in at once."

Double proof is surest.

❧ 364 ❧
THE TWO TRAVELERS

As two Men were traveling through a wood, one of them took up an axe which he saw lying upon the ground. "Look here," said he to his companion, "I have found an axe." "Don't say 'I have found it,'" replied the other, "but 'We have found it.' As we are companions, we ought to share it between us." The first would not, however, consent. They had not gone far, when they heard the owner of the axe calling after them in a great passion. "We are in for it!" said he who had the axe. "Nay," answered the other, "say, 'I am in for it!'—not we. You would not let me share the prize, and I am not going to share the danger."

He who shares the danger ought to share the prize.

❧ 365 ❧
THE CAT AND THE SPARROWS

A great friendship once existed between a Sparrow and a Cat, to whom, when quite a kitten, the Bird had been given. When they were playing together, the bold Sparrow would often fly into little mimic rages, and peck the Cat with his bill, while Pussy would beat him off with only half-opened claws; and though this sport would often wax warm, there was never real anger between them. It happened, however, that the Bird made the acquaintance of another Sparrow, and being both of them saucy fellows, they soon fell out and quarreled in earnest. The little friend of the Cat, in these fights, generally fared the worst; and one day he came trembling all over with passion, and besought the Cat to avenge his wrongs for him. Pussy thereupon pounced on the offending stranger, and speedily crunched him up and swallowed him. "I had no idea before that Sparrows were so nice," said the Cat to herself, for her blood was now stirred; and as quick as thought her little playmate was seized and sent to join his enemy.

Trouble is more easily started than stopped.

◁ 366 ▷

THE LION, THE TIGER, AND THE FOX

A Lion and a Tiger happened to come together over the dead body of a Fawn that had been recently shot. A fierce battle ensued, and as each animal was in the prime of his age and strength, the combat was long and furious. At last they lay stretched on the ground panting, bleeding, and exhausted, each unable to lift a paw against the other. An impudent Fox coming by at the time, stepped in and carried off before their eyes the prey on account of which they had both fought so

savagely. "Woe betide us," said the Lion, "that we should suffer so much to serve a Fox!"

It often happens that one has the toil and another the profit.

THE ARCHER AND THE DOVE

An Archer, seeing a Dove among the branches of an oak, raised his bow and aimed at the Bird. Just then an Adder, on which unknowingly he had trodden, bit him in the leg. Feeling the poison spreading in his veins, he threw down his bow, and exclaimed, "Fate has justly brought destruction on me while I was contriving the death of another!"

He that mischief hatcheth, mischief always catcheth.

THE WOLVES AND THE SHEEP

Once upon a time, the Wolves sent an embassy to the Sheep, desiring that there might be a lasting peace between them. "Why," said the Messengers, "should we be forever at war? These wicked Dogs are the cause of it all; they are always barking at us and making us mad.

Now if you will give up your Dogs, we will send you our children as hostages of peace." The silly Sheep agreed to the proposal and dismissed the Dogs. The Wolves gave up their Whelps. But the young Wolves cried for their mothers, and the Wolves then claimed that the peace had been broken, and set upon the Sheep, who, deprived of their defenders, the Dogs, could make no resistance, but fell an easy prey to their enemies.

Make no truce with a sworn enemy.

⚜ 369 ⚜

THE FROGS AND THE FIGHTING BULLS

A Frog one day, peeping out of a marsh, saw two Bulls fighting at some distance off in the meadow. "Alas! my friends," cried he to his fellow Frogs, "whatever will become of us?" "Why, what are you frightened at?" asked one of the Frogs; "what can their quarrels have to do with us? They are only proving which shall be master of the herd." "True," answered the first, "and it is just that which causes my fear, for the one

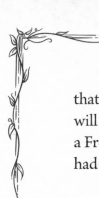

that is beaten will take refuge here in the marshes, and will tread us to death." And so it happened; and many a Frog, in dying, had sore proof that the fears which he had thought to be groundless were not so in fact.

Coming events cast their shadows before.

❧ 370 ❧

THE ASS, THE APE, AND THE MOLE

An Ass and an Ape were one day grumbling together over their grievances. "My ears are so long that people laugh at me," said the Ass; "I wish I had horns like the Ox." "And I," said the Ape, "am really ashamed to turn my back upon any one. Why should not I have a fine bushy tail as well as that saucy fellow the Fox?" "Hold your tongues, both of you," said a Mole that overheard them, "and be thankful for what you have. The poor Moles have no horns at all, and no tail to speak of, and are nearly blind as well."

We should never complain so long as there
are others worse off than ourselves.

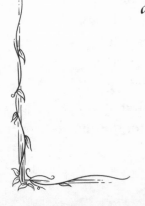

◁ 371 ▷
THE BEGGAR AND HIS DOG

A Beggar and his Dog sat at the gate of a noble Courtier, and were preparing to make a meal on a bowl of fragments from the Kitchenmaid. A poor dependent of his Lordship's, who had been sharing the singular favor of a dinner at the steward's table, was struck with their appearance, and stopped a little to observe them. The Beggar, hungry and voracious as any Courtier in Christendom, seized with greediness the choicest morsels, and swallowed them himself; the residue was divided into portions for his children. A scrag was thrust into one pocket for honest Jack, a crust into another for bashful Tom, and a luncheon of cheese was wrapped up with care for the little favorite of his hopeful family. In short, if anything was thrown to the Dog, it was a bone so closely picked, that it scarce afforded a pittance to keep life and soul together. How exactly alike, said the dependent, is this poor Dog's case and mine! He is watching for a dinner from a master who cannot spare it; I for a place from a needy Lord, whose wants perhaps are greater than my own; and whose relations, more clamorous than any of this Beggar's brats. Shrewdly was it said by an ingenious writer, a Courtier's Dependent is a Beggar's Dog.

The misery of depending upon patrons whose charity has too much to do at home.

◁ 372 ▷

THE PARTRIDGE
AND THE COCKS

A certain man having taken a Partridge, cut his wings and put him into a little yard where he kept Game-Cocks. The Cocks were not at all civil to the newcomer, who at first put his treatment down to the fact of his being a stranger. When, however, he found that they frequently fought and nearly killed each other, he ceased to wonder that they did not respect him.

*Those who do not treat their own
kindred well make poor friends.*

◁ 373 ▷

THE
COUNTRYMAN
AND THE
SNAKE

A Villager, one frosty day in the depth of winter, found a Snake under a hedge almost dead with the cold. Having pity on the poor creature, he brought it home, and

laid it on the hearth near the fire. Revived by the heat, it reared itself up, and with dreadful hissings flew at the wife and children of its benefactor. The Man, hearing their cries, rushed in, and, seizing a mattock, soon cut the Snake in pieces. "Vile wretch!" said he; "is this the reward you make to him who saved your life? Die, as you deserve; but a single death is too good for you."

Ingratitude is a crime.

⚜ 374 ⚜
THE SPIDER AND THE SILKWORM

A Spider busied in spreading his web from one side of the room to the other, was asked by an industrious Silkworm, to what end he spent so much time and labor, in making such a number of lines and circles. The Spider angrily replied, Do not disturb me, thou ignorant thing; I transmit my ingenuity to posterity, and fame is the object of my wishes. Just as he had spoken, Susan the chambermaid, coming into the room to feed her silkworms, saw the Spider at his work; and with one stroke of her broom, sweeps him away, and destroys at once his labors and his hopes of fame.

He that is employed in works of use, generally advantages himself or others; while he who toils for fame alone must expect to often lose his labor.

❧ 375 ☙

THE DOG AND THE CROCODILE

A Dog, running along the banks of the Nile, grew thirsty, but fearing to be seized by the monsters of that river, he would not stop to quench his thirst, but lapped as he ran. A Crocodile, raising his head above the surface of the water, asked him why he was in such a hurry? "I have often wished to meet you," added he, "and feel sure I should like you immensely. So why not stay and chat awhile?" "You do me great honor," replied the Dog, "but I am afraid the pleasure would be all on your side; and, to tell the truth, it is to avoid such companions as you that I am in such haste."

We can never be too carefully guarded against a connection with persons of bad character.

❧ 376 ☙

THE WOLF AND THE FOX

The Wolves and Foxes once selected one of their number to be their ruler. The Wolf that was chosen was a plausible, smooth-spoken rascal, and on a very early day he addressed an assembly of his subjects as follows: "One thing," he said, "is of such vital importance, and will tend so much to our general welfare, that I cannot impress it too strongly upon your attention. Nothing cherishes true brotherly feeling and promotes the general good so much as the suppression of all selfishness. Let each one of you, then, share with any hungry brother who may be near whatever in hunting may fall to your lot." "Hear, hear!" cried a Fox, who had listened to the speech; "and of course you yourself will begin with the fat Sheep that you hid yesterday in a corner of your lair."

Practice what you preach.

⚜ 377 ⚜
CAESAR AND THE SLAVE

During a visit that Tiberius Caesar paid to one of his country residences, he observed that whenever he walked in the grounds, a certain Slave was always a little way ahead of him, busily watering the paths. Turn which way he would, go where he might, there was the fellow still fussing about with his watering-pot. He felt sure that he was making himself thus needlessly officious in the hope of thereby gaining his liberty. In making a Slave free, a part of the ceremony consisted in giving him a gentle stroke on one side of the face. Hence, when the man came running up in eager expectation, at the call of the Emperor, the latter said to him, "I have for a long time observed you meddling where you had nothing to do, and while you might have been better employed elsewhere. You are mistaken if

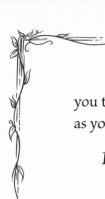

you think I can afford a box on the ear at so low a price as you bid for it."

Being busy does not always mean being useful.

🙙 378 🙚

THE SWALLOW AND OTHER BIRDS

A Farmer, sowing his fields with flax, was observed by a Swallow, who, like the rest of her tribe, had traveled a good deal and was very clever. Among other things, she knew that of this same flax, when it grew up, nets and snares would be made, to entrap her little friends, the Birds of the country. Hence, she earnestly besought them to help her in picking up and eating the hateful seed, before it had time to spring from the ground. But food of a much nicer kind was then so plentiful, and it was so pleasant to fly about and sing, thinking of nothing, that they paid no attention to her entreaties. By and by the blades of the flax appeared above the ground, and the anxiety of the Swallow was renewed. "It is not yet too late," said she; "pull it all up, blade by blade, and you may then escape the fate which is otherwise in store for you. You cannot, like me, fly to other countries when danger threatens you here." The little Birds, however, took no notice of the Swallow, except to consider her a very troublesome person, whom silly fears had set beside herself. In

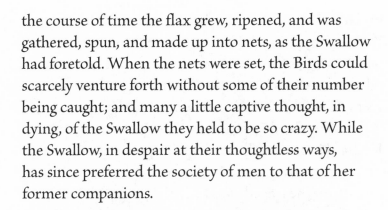

the course of time the flax grew, ripened, and was gathered, spun, and made up into nets, as the Swallow had foretold. When the nets were set, the Birds could scarcely venture forth without some of their number being caught; and many a little captive thought, in dying, of the Swallow they held to be so crazy. While the Swallow, in despair at their thoughtless ways, has since preferred the society of men to that of her former companions.

Prevention is better than cure.

❧ 379 ❧
THE FOX AND THE CAT

A Fox and a Cat, traveling together, beguiled the tediousness of their journey by moralizing. "Of all the moral virtues," exclaimed Reynard, "mercy is surely the noblest! What say you, my sage friend, is it not so?" "Undoubtedly," replied the Cat, with a most demure countenance; "nothing is more becoming in a creature of any sensibility than compassion." While they were thus complimenting each other on the wisdom of their views, a Wolf darted out from a wood upon a flock of Sheep which were feeding in an adjacent meadow, and without being in the least affected by the piteous cries of a poor Lamb, devoured it before their eyes. "Horrible cruelty!" exclaimed the Cat. "Why does he not feed on vermin, instead of making

his barbarous meals on such innocent creatures?"
Reynard agreed with his friend in the observation, to
which he added some very pathetic remarks on the
odiousness of such conduct. Their indignation was
rising in its warmth and zeal when they arrived at a
little cottage by the wayside, where the tenderhearted
Reynard immediately cast his eye upon a fine Cock
that was strutting about in the yard. And now, adieu
moralizing, he leaped over the pales, and without any
sort of scruple, demolished his prize in an instant. In
the meanwhile, a plump Mouse, which ran out of the
stable, totally put to flight our Cat's philosophy, who
fell to the repast without the least commiseration.

It is a common habit to talk of what is right
and good, and to do what is quite the reverse.

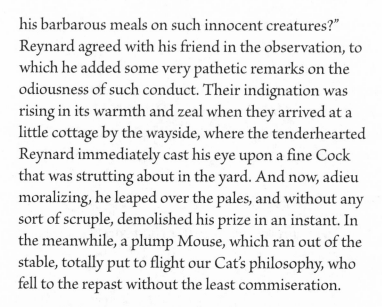

❧ 380 ❧
THE GARDENER AND
HIS LANDLORD

A simple sort of Country Fellow, who rented a
cottage and small garden on the outskirts of a park
belonging to a great Squire, was much annoyed at the
havoc which a certain Hare made with his choice and
delicate young vegetables. So off went the Man, one
morning, to complain to the Squire. "This Hare," said
he, "laughs at all snares. He has a charm which keeps
off all the sticks and stones that I throw at him. In plain

truth, I believe he is no Hare at all, but a wizard in disguise." "Nay, were he the father of all wizards," replied the Squire, who was a great hunter, "my Dogs will make short work with him. We'll come tomorrow, and see about it." The next morning came the Squire with his pack of Hounds, and a score of friends, huntsmen and others. The Gardener was at breakfast, and felt bound to ask them to partake. They did so, and made great inroads upon his store of provisions. "Now, then, let us beat for the Hare," cried the Squire; and the hunstmen blew their horns with deafening noise, and the Dogs flew here and there in search of the Hare, who was soon started from under a big cabbage where he had gone for shelter. Across the garden ran the Hare, and after him went the Dogs. Alas for the beds, the frames, the flowers! Through the hedge went the Hare, and over the beds and through the hedge after him went the Squire, the friends, the huntsmen, horses and all. A wreck indeed did the place look, when they were gone. "Ah!" cried the Countryman, "fool that I was to go to the great for help! Here is more damage done in half an hour than all the Hares in the province would have made in a year!"

Do not ask others to do what you can do yourself.

❦ 381 ❧
THE WOLF IN DISGUISE

A Wolf who by his frequent visits to a flock of sheep in his neighborhood, began to be extremely well known to them, thought it expedient, for the more successfully carrying on of his depredations, to appear in a new character. To this end, he disguised himself in a shepherd's habit; and, resting his forefeet upon a stick, which served him by way of crook, he softly made his approach toward the fold. It happened that the shepherd and his dog were both of them extended on the grass, fast asleep, so that he would certainly have succeeded in his project, if he had not imprudently attempted to imitate the shepherd's voice. The horrid noise awakened them both; when the Wolf, encumbered with his disguise, and finding it impossible either to resist, or to flee, yielded up his life an easy prey to the shepherd's dog.

There would be little chance of detecting hypocrisy were it not always addicted to over-act its part.

❦ 382 ❧
THE ANT AND THE FLY

An Ant and a Fly one day disputed as to their respective merits. "Vile creeping insect!" said the Fly to the Ant, "can you for a moment compare yourself with me? I soar on the wing like a bird. I enter the

palaces of kings, and alight on the heads of princes, nay, of emperors, and only quit them to adorn the yet more attractive brow of beauty. Besides, I visit the altars of the gods. Not a sacrifice is offered but is first tasted by me. Every feast, too, is open to me. I eat and drink of the best, instead of living for days on two or three grains of corn as you do." "All that's very fine," replied the Ant; "but listen to me. You boast of your feasting, but you know that your diet is not always so choice, and you are sometimes forced to eat what nothing should induce me to touch. As for alighting on the heads of kings and emperors, you know very well that whether you pitch on the head of an emperor, or of an ass (and it is as often on the one as the other), you are shaken off from both with impatience. And, then, the 'altars of the gods,' indeed! There and everywhere else you are looked upon as nothing but a nuisance. In the winter, too, while I feed at my ease on the fruit of my toil, I often see your friends dying with cold, hunger, and fatigue. I lose my time now in talking to you. Chattering will fill neither my bin nor my cupboard."

Bread earned by toil is sweet.

◁ 383 ▷
THE SHEPHERD TURNED MERCHANT

A Shepherd, that kept his Sheep at no great distance from the sea, one day drove them close to the

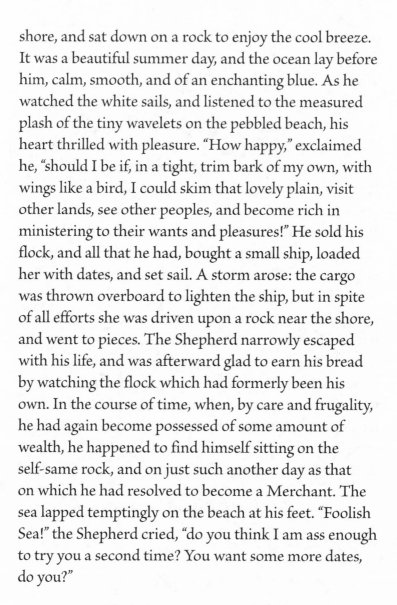

shore, and sat down on a rock to enjoy the cool breeze. It was a beautiful summer day, and the ocean lay before him, calm, smooth, and of an enchanting blue. As he watched the white sails, and listened to the measured plash of the tiny wavelets on the pebbled beach, his heart thrilled with pleasure. "How happy," exclaimed he, "should I be if, in a tight, trim bark of my own, with wings like a bird, I could skim that lovely plain, visit other lands, see other peoples, and become rich in ministering to their wants and pleasures!" He sold his flock, and all that he had, bought a small ship, loaded her with dates, and set sail. A storm arose: the cargo was thrown overboard to lighten the ship, but in spite of all efforts she was driven upon a rock near the shore, and went to pieces. The Shepherd narrowly escaped with his life, and was afterward glad to earn his bread by watching the flock which had formerly been his own. In the course of time, when, by care and frugality, he had again become possessed of some amount of wealth, he happened to find himself sitting on the self-same rock, and on just such another day as that on which he had resolved to become a Merchant. The sea lapped temptingly on the beach at his feet. "Foolish Sea!" the Shepherd cried, "do you think I am ass enough to try you a second time? You want some more dates, do you?"

Experience is a sure teacher.

❧ 384 ❧
THE CATS AND THE MICE

I n former times a fierce and lasting war raged
between the Cats and Mice, in which, time after
time, the latter had to fly. One day when the Mice in
council were discussing the cause of their ill-luck, the
general opinion seemed to be that it was the difficulty
of knowing, in the heat of the conflict, who were their
leaders, that led to their defeat and utter rout. So it
was decided that in future each captain should have
his head decorated with some thin straws, so that all
the Mice would then know to whom they were to look
for orders. After the Mice had drilled and disciplined
their numbers, they once more gave battle to the Cats;
but again they met with no better success, being utterly
routed. The greater part reached their holes in safety,
but the captains were prevented by their strange head-
gear from entering their retreats, and fell prey to their
cruel pursuers.

*Those who have the greatest honor,
have the gravest danger.*

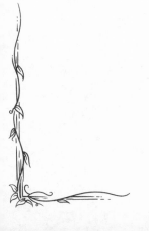

❧ 385 ❧
THE BEE AND THE FLY

A Bee observing a Fly frisking about her hive, asked him in a very angry tone what he did there. "Is it for such fellows as you," said she, "to intrude into the company of the queens of the air?" "You have great reason, truly," replied the Fly, "to be out of humor. I am sure they must be mad who would have any concern with so quarrelsome a nation." "And why so, may I ask?" returned the enraged Bee. "We have the best laws and are governed by the best policy in the world. We feed upon the most fragrant flowers, and all our business is to make honey; honey, which equals nectar, low, tasteless wretch, who lives upon nothing but vile things." "We live as we can," rejoined the Fly. "Poverty, I hope, is no crime; but passion is one, I am sure. The honey you make is sweet, I grant you, but your heart is all bitterness; for to be revenged on an enemy you will destroy your own life, and are so foolish in your rage as to do more mischief to yourselves than to your enemy. Take my word for it, one had better have fewer talents, and use them more wisely."

Well-governed communities should
make well-governed individuals.

◁ 386 ▷

THE LION, AND THE ASSES AND HARES

Upon the breaking out of a war between the Birds and the Beasts, the Lion summoned all his subjects to appear in arms at a certain time and place, upon pain of his high displeasure. A number of Hares and Asses made their appearance on the field. Several of the commanders were for turning them off as creatures utterly unfit for service. "Do not be too hasty," said the Lion; "the Asses will do very well for trumpeters, and the Hares will make excellent messengers."

Everything has its use.

◁ 387 ▷

A MAN BITTEN BY A DOG

A Man, who had been sadly bitten by a Dog, was advised by an old woman to cure the wound by rubbing a piece of bread in it, and giving it to the Dog that had bitten him. He did so, and Aesop, passing by at the time, asked him what he was about. The Man told him, and Aesop replied, "I am glad you do it privately, for if the rest of the Dogs of the town were to see you, we should be eaten up alive."

Season counsel with sense.

❧ 388 ❧

THE FOX AND THE MASK

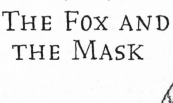

A Fox was one day rummaging in the house of an actor, and came across a very beautiful Mask. Putting his paw on the forehead he said, "What a handsome face we have here! It is a pity that it should want brains."

Beauty without brains nothing gains.

❧ 389 ❧

THE CREAKING WHEEL

A Coachman hearing one of the Wheels of his coach make a great noise, and perceiving that it was the worst one of the four, asked how it came to take such a liberty. The Wheel answered that from the beginning of time grumbling had always been the privilege of the weak.

Much smoke, little fire.

⚜ 390 ⚜
THE MOUNTAIN IN LABOR

In olden times, a mighty rumbling was heard in a Mountain. This lasted a long time, until all the country round about was shaken. The people flocked together, from far and near, to see what would come of the upheaval. After many days of waiting and wise prophesyings from the crowd—out came a Mouse.

Do not make much ado about nothing.

⚜ 391 ⚜
THE ENVIOUS MAN AND THE COVETOUS

Two Men, one a Covetous fellow, and the other thoroughly possessed by the passion of envy, came together to present their petitions to Jupiter. The god sent Apollo to deal with their requests. Apollo told them that whatsoever should be granted to the first who asked, the other should receive double. The Covetous Man forbore to speak, waiting in order that he might receive twice as much as his companion. The Envious Man, in the spitefulness of his heart, thereupon prayed that one of his own eyes might be put out, knowing that the other would have to lose both of his.

Envy shoots at another and wounds itself.

❧ 392 ❧
THE PEACOCK AND THE MAGPIE

The Birds once met together to choose a king, and among others the Peacock was a candidate. Spreading his showy tail, and stalking up and down with affected grandeur, he caught the eyes of the silly multitude by his brilliant appearance, and was elected by acclamation. Just as they were going to proclaim him, the Magpie stepped forth into the midst of the assembly, and thus addressed the new king: "May it please your majesty-elect to permit a humble admirer to propose a question. As our king, we put our lives and fortunes in your hands. If, therefore, the Eagle, the Vulture, and the Kite should in the future, as they have in times past, make a descent upon us, what means would you take for our defense?" This pithy question opened the eyes of the Birds to the weakness of their choice. They cancelled the election, and have ever since regarded the Peacock as a vain pretender, and considered the Magpie to be as good a speaker as any of their number.

The crowd is caught by display.

❦ 393 ❧

THE FLYING-FISH AND THE DOLPHIN

A Flying-Fish, being pursued by a Dolphin, swam for safety into shallow water. Seeing the Dolphin still after him, he came too far into shore, and was thrown by the waves high and dry on the sand. The Dolphin, eager in pursuit, and unable to stop himself, was also stranded. The Flying-Fish, beholding the Dolphin in the same condition as himself, said, "Now I die with pleasure, for I see my enemy has met the same fate."

Revenge is sweet.

❦ 394 ❧

THE THIEF AND HIS MOTHER

A little Boy, who went to school, stole one of his schoolfellow's books and took it home. His Mother, so far from correcting him, took the book and sold it, and gave him an apple for his pains. In the course of time the Boy became a Thief, and at last was tried for his life and condemned. He was led to the gallows, a great crowd of people following, and among them his Mother, weeping bitterly. Seeing her, he prayed the officers to grant him the favor of a few parting words with her, and his request was freely granted. He went to his Mother, put his arm round her neck, and making as though he would whisper something in her ear, bit it off. Her cry of pain drew everybody's eyes upon them, and great was the indignation, that at such a time he should add another violence to his list of crimes. "Nay, good people," said he, "do not be deceived. My first theft was of a book, which I gave to my Mother. Had she whipped me for it, instead of praising me, I should not have come to the gallows now that I am a man."

Spare the rod, spoil the child.

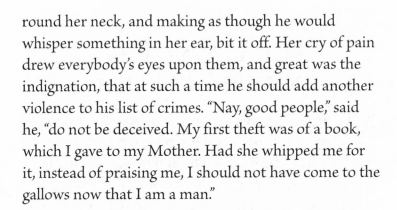

⚜ 395 ⚜

THE FOX AND THE HEDGEHOG

A Fox, swimming across a river, was drifted along by the stream, and carried by an eddy into a nook on the opposite bank. He lay there exhausted, and unable for a time to scramble up. To add to his misfortunes

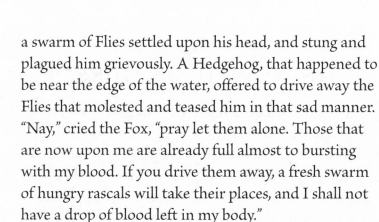

a swarm of Flies settled upon his head, and stung and plagued him grievously. A Hedgehog, that happened to be near the edge of the water, offered to drive away the Flies that molested and teased him in that sad manner. "Nay," cried the Fox, "pray let them alone. Those that are now upon me are already full almost to bursting with my blood. If you drive them away, a fresh swarm of hungry rascals will take their places, and I shall not have a drop of blood left in my body."

Old trials are better borne than new ones.

⚜ 396 ⚜
THE DOVE AND THE ANT

An Ant going to a river to drink, fell in, and was carried along in the stream. A Dove pitied her condition, and threw into the river a small twig, by means of which the Ant gained the shore. The Ant afterwards, seeing a man with a bow aiming at the Dove, stung him in the foot sharply, and made him miss his aim, and so saved the Dove's life.

The grateful heart will always find
a way to be of service.

397

THE COUNCIL OF HORSES

Upon a time, a neighing steed, who grazed among a numerous breed, with mutiny had fired the train, and spread dissension through the plain. On matters that concerned the State, the Council met in grand debate. A Colt, whose eyeballs flamed with ire, elate with strength and youthful fire, in haste stepped forth before the rest, and thus the listening throng addressed: "Good gods! how abject is our race, condemned to slavery and disgrace! Shall we our servitude retain, because our sires have borne the chain? Consider, friends, your strength and might; 'tis conquest to assert your right. How cumb'rous is the gilded coach! The pride of man is our reproach. Were we designed for daily toil; to drag the ploughshare through the soil; to sweat in harness through the road; to groan beneath the carrier's load? How feeble are the two-legged kind! What force is in our nerves combined! Shall, then, our nobler jaws submit to foam, and champ the galling bit?

Shall haughty man my back bestride? Shall the sharp spur provoke my side? Forbid it, heavens! Reject the rein; your shame, your infamy, disdain. Let him the lion first control, and still the tiger's famished growl; let us, like them, our freedom claim, and make him tremble at our name."

A general nod approved the cause, and all the circle neighed applause. When, lo! with grave and solemn face, a Steed advanced before the race, with age and long experience wise; around he cast his thoughtful eyes, and to the murmurs of the train thus spoke the Nestor of the plain: "When I had health and strength like you, the toils of servitude I knew; now grateful man rewards my pains, and gives me all these wide domains. At will I crop the year's increase; my latter life is rest and peace. I grant, to man we lend our pains, and aid him to correct the plains; but doth he not divide the care through all the labors of the year? How many thousand structures rise, to fence us from inclement skies! For us he bears the sultry day, and stores up all our winter's hay: he sows, he reaps the harvest's grain; we share the toil and share the gain. Since every creature was decreed to aid each other's mutual need, appease your discontented mind, and act the part by Heaven assigned." The tumult ceased. The colt submitted, and, like his ancestors, was bitted.

Those who know their station in life
know the greatest contentment.

◁ 398 ▷

THE FOX AND THE WOOD-CUTTER

A Fox having been hunted hard, and run a long chase, saw a Wood-Cutter at work, and begged him to help him to some hiding-place. The Man said he might go into his cottage, which was close by. He was no sooner in, than the Huntsmen came up. "Have you

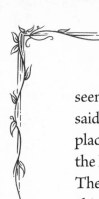

seen a Fox pass this way?" said they. The Wood-Cutter said, "No," but pointed at the same time towards the place where the Fox lay. The Huntsmen did not take the hint, however, and made off again at full speed. The Fox, who had seen all that took place through a chink in the wall, thereupon came out, and was walking away without a word. "Why, how now?" said the Man; "haven't you the manners to thank your host before you go?" "Yes, yes," said the Fox; "if your deeds had been as honest as your words, I would have given you thanks."

Sincerity is shown by the heart.

⚜ 399 ⚜

THE LYNX AND THE MOLE

Under the covert of a thick wood, at the foot of a tree, as a Lynx lay whetting his teeth and waiting for his prey, he espied a Mole half buried under a hillock of her own raising. "Alas, poor creature," said the Lynx, "how much I pity you! Surely, Jupiter has been very unkind, to debar you from the light of day which rejoices the whole creation. You are certainly not above half alive, and it would be doing you a service to make an end of you." "I thank you for your kindness," replied the Mole, "but I think I have fully as much vivacity as my state and circumstances require. For the rest, I am perfectly well contented with the faculties which Jupiter has given me, who, I am sure, wants not our direction in distributing his gifts. I have not, 'tis true, your piercing eyes, but I have ears which answer all my purposes. Hark! for example, I am warned by a noise which I hear behind you, to flee from danger." So saying, she crept into the earth, while a javelin from the arm of a hunter pierced the quick-sighted Lynx to the heart.

Let none criticize nature.

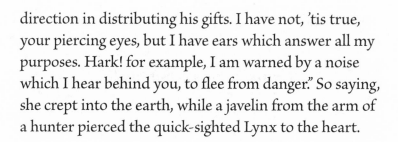

❧ 400 ❧

THE HORSE AND THE LION

A Lion, who had got old and infirm, saw a fine plump Nag, and longed for a bit of him. Knowing that the animal would prove too fleet for him in the chase, he had recourse to artifice. He gave out to all the Beasts that, having spent many years in studying physic, he was now prepared to heal any malady or distemper with which they might be afflicted. He hoped by that means to get admittance among them, and so find a chance of satisfying his appetite. The Horse, who had doubts of the Lion's honesty, came up limping, pretending that he had run a thorn into one of his hind feet, which gave him great pain. The Lion asked that the foot might be shown to him, and pored over it with a mock earnest air. The Horse, slyly looking round, saw that he was preparing to spring, and vigorously sending out both his heels at once, gave the Lion such a kick in the face, that it laid him stunned and sprawling upon the ground.

Then laughing at the success of his trick, he trotted merrily away.

Over-craftiness defeats itself.

◊ 401 ◊
JUPITER'S LOTTERY

Jupiter, in order to please mankind, directed Mercury to give notice that he had established a lottery, in which there were no blanks; and that amongst a variety of other valuable chances, wisdom was the highest prize. It was Jupiter's command that in this lottery some of the gods should also become adventurers. The tickets being disposed of, and the wheels placed, Mercury was employed to preside at the drawing. It happened that the best prize fell to Minerva, upon which a general murmur ran through the assembly, and hints were thrown out that Jupiter had used some unfair practices to secure this desirable lot to his daughter. Jupiter, that he might at once punish and silence these impious clamors of the human race, presented them with folly in the place of wisdom; with which they went away perfectly well contented, and from that time, the greatest fools have always looked upon themselves as the wisest men.

Folly, passing with men for wisdom, makes each contented with his own share of understanding.

402

THE OWLS, THE BATS, AND THE SUN

The Owls, Bats, and several other Birds of night used to meet together in a thick shade, where they abused their neighbors in a very sociable manner. Their satire at last fell upon the Sun, whom they all agreed to be very troublesome, impertinent, and inquisitive. The Sun chanced to overhear his critics, but contented himself with replying: "Ladies, I care little for your opinion, but I wonder how you dare abuse one who could in an instant destroy you; however, the only answer I shall give you or the revenge I shall take of you, is to shine on."

Gossips are best answered by silence.

403

THE BEES, THE DRONES, AND THE WASP

A party of Drones got into a hive, and laying claim to the honey and comb which they found there, tried to force the Bees to quit. The Bees, however, made a sturdy resistance. Finally the Drones agreed to their proposal that the dispute should be referred for judgment to the Wasp. The Wasp, pretending that it was a hard matter to decide, directed both parties to make and fill some comb before him in court, so that he might see whose production most resembled the property in dispute. The Bees at once set to work, but the Drones refused the trial; so the verdict was given by Judge Wasp in favor of the Bees.

A tree is known by its fruit.

⊰ 404 ⊱

THE CUCKOO, THE HEDGE-SPARROW, AND THE OWL

A lazy Cuckoo, too idle to make a comfortable home for herself and her offspring, laid her eggs in the nest built by the Hedge-Sparrow who, taking the charge wholly on herself, hatched them, and bred up the young with maternal attention, till such time as they were enabled to provide for themselves, when they took wing and fled. Upon this the worthless Cuckoo came gossiping to the Owl, complaining of the misconduct of the Hedge-Sparrow in treating her with so little attention, in return for the confidence she had shown in entrusting her with the care of her precious young brood. "Would you believe it?" continued the Cuckoo. "The ungrateful birds have flown off without paying me any of those duties which are the natural right of a mother from her offspring!" "Peace, peace," replied the sage Owl, "nor expect that from others which you cannot give in return. The obligation lies wholly on your side to the charitable Hedge-Sparrow, for her kindness to your helpless young, whom you had abandoned; and remember this, that before you teach gratitude to others, you should learn yourself to be grateful."

Ne'er-do-wells always find flaws in their neighbors.

⊰ 405 ⊱
THE ASS AND THE GRASSHOPPERS

An Ass having heard some Grasshoppers chirping was highly enchanted; and, desiring to possess the same charms of melody, demanded what sort of food they lived on, to give them such beautiful voices. They replied, "The dew." The Ass resolved that he would live only upon dew, and in a short time died of hunger.

No two people can be treated alike.

◁ 406 ▷

THE SHEEP AND THE BRAMBLE

A Sheep, during a severe storm, wandered into a thicket for shelter, and there lay so snug and warm that he soon fell fast asleep. The clouds clearing away, and the winds returning to rest, inclined the Sheep to return to his pasture. But, ah! what was his situation: a Bramble had laid such a firm hold of his fleece, that it was left as a forfeit for the protection the thicket had given him.

He who makes his bed must lie in it.

◁ 407 ▷

THE EMIGRANT MICE

A Mouse, weary of living in the continual alarm attendant on the carnage committed among her nation by cats and traps, thus addressed herself to the tenant of a hole near her own: "An excellent thought has just come into my head; I read in some book, which I gnawed a few days ago, that there is a fine country called the Indies, in which mice are in much greater security than here. In that region the sages believe that the soul of a mouse has been that of a king, a great captain, or some wonderful saint, and that after death it will probably enter the body of a beautiful woman

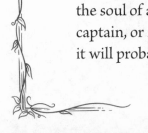

or mighty potentate. If I recollect rightly, this is called metempsychosis. Under this idea they treat all animals with paternal charity, and build and endow hospitals for mice, where they are fed like people of consequence. Come then, my good sister, let us hasten to a country the customs of which are so excellent, and where justice is done to our merits." "But, sister," replied her neighbor, "do not cats enter these hospitals? If they do, metempsychosis must take place very soon, and in great numbers; and a talon or a tooth might make a fakir or a king, a miracle we can do very well without." "Do not fear," said the first mouse. "In these countries order is completely established; the cats have their houses as well as we ours, and they have their hospitals for the sick separate from ours." After this conversation our two mice set out together, contriving the evening before she set sail to creep along the cordage of a vessel that was to make a long voyage. They got under weigh, and were enraptured with the sight of the sea which took them from the abominable shores on which cats exercise their tyranny. The voyage was pleasant, and they reached Surat, not like merchants to acquire riches, but to receive good treatment from the Hindoos. They had scarcely entered one of the houses fitted up for mice when they aspired to the best accommodation. One of them pretended to recollect having formerly been a Brahmin on the coast of Malabar, and the other protested that she had been a fine lady of the same country, with long ears; but they displayed so much impertinence that the Indian mice lost all patience. A civil war commenced, and no quarter was given to the two newcomers, who pretended to impose laws on the

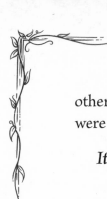

others; when, instead of being eaten up by cats, they were strangled by their own brethren.

It is useless to go far in search of safety; if we are not modest and wise, we only go to danger.

◁ 408 ▷

THE TONGUES

X anthus invited a large company to dinner, and Aesop was ordered to furnish the feast with the choicest dainties that money could procure. The first course consisted of Tongues, cooked in different ways, and served with appropriate sauces. This gave rise to a deal of mirth and witty remarks among the assembled guests. The second course, however, like the first, was also nothing but Tongues, and so the third, and the fourth. The matter seemed to all to have gone beyond a jest, and Xanthus angrily demanded of Aesop, "Did I not tell you, sirrah, to provide the choicest dainties that money could procure?" "And what excels the Tongue?" replied Aesop. "It is the great channel of learning and philosophy. By this noble organ addresses and eulogies are made, and commerce, contracts, and marriages completely established. Nothing is equal to the Tongue." The company applauded Aesop's wit, and good-humor was restored. "Well," said Xanthus to the guests, "pray do me the favor of dining with me again tomorrow. And if this is your best," continued he, turning to Aesop, "pray, tomorrow let us have some of the worst meat you can find." The next day, when dinnertime came, the guests were assembled. Great was their astonishment, and great the anger of Xanthus, at finding that again nothing but Tongues was put upon the table. "How, sir," said Xanthus, "should Tongues be the best of meat one day and the worst another?" "What," replied Aesop, "can be worse than the Tongue? What wickedness is there under the sun that it has not a part in? Treasons, violence, injustice, and fraud are debated, resolved upon, and communicated by the Tongue. It is the ruin of empires, cities, and of private friendships." The company were more than ever struck by Aesop's ingenuity, and successfully interceded for him with his master.

A wise answer saves a city.

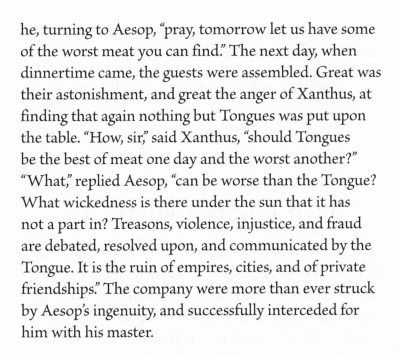

⚜ 409 ⚜

A BOAR CHALLENGES AN ASS

S ome hard words passed between a Boar and an Ass, and a challenge followed upon them. The Boar, priding himself upon his tusks, and comparing his head with the Ass's head, looked forward to the fight with confidence. The time for the battle came. The combatants approached one another. The Boar rushed upon the Ass, who, suddenly turning round, let his hoofs fly with all his might right in the jaws of the Boar,

so that the latter staggered and fell back. "Well," said he, "who could have expected an attack from that end?"

Attacks come from unexpected quarters.

⚜ 410 ⚜
THE FORTUNE-TELLER

A Man who gave himself out as a Wizard and Fortune-Teller, used to stand in the marketplace and pretend to foretell the future, give information as to missing property, and other matters of the like kind. One day, while he was busily plying his trade, a waggish fellow broke through the crowd, and gasping as if for want of breath, told him that his house was in flames, and must shortly be burnt to the ground. Off ran the Wizard at the news as fast as his legs could carry him, while the Wag and a crowd of other people followed at his heels. But the house was not on fire at all; and the Wag asked him, amid the jeers of the people, how it was that he, who was so clever at telling other people's fortunes, should know so little of his own.

'Tis a poor baker who will not eat his own wares.

◁ 411 ▷

THE ANT AND THE COCOON

An Ant, nimbly running about in the sunshine in search of food, came across a Cocoon that was very near its time of change. The Cocoon moved its tail, and thus attracted the attention of the Ant, who then saw for the first time that it was alive. "Poor creature!" cried the Ant disdainfully; "what a sad fate is yours! While I can run hither and thither, at my pleasure, and, if I wish, ascend the tallest tree, you lie imprisoned here in your shell, with power only to move a joint or two of your scaly tail." The Cocoon heard all this, but did not try to make any reply. A few days after, when the Ant passed that way again, nothing but the shell remained. Wondering what had become of its contents, he felt himself suddenly shaded and fanned by the gorgeous wings of a beautiful Butterfly. "Behold in me," said the Butterfly, "your much-pitied friend! Boast now of your powers to run and climb as long as you can get me to listen." So saying, the Butterfly rose in the air, and, borne along on the summer breeze, was soon lost to the sight of the Ant forever.

Judge not alone by the present.

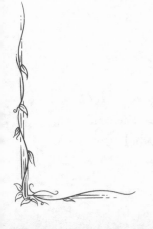

◁ 412 ▷

THE DEER AND THE LION

A Deer, being hard pressed by the Hounds, found a cave into which he rushed for safety. An immense Lion, couched at the farther end of the cave, sprang upon him in an instant. "Unhappy creature that I am!" exclaimed the Stag, in his dying moments. "I entered this cave to escape the pursuit of Men and Dogs, and I have fallen into the jaws of the most terrible of wild Beasts."

In avoiding one evil, plunge not into a worse.

◁ 413 ▷

MINERVA'S OLIVE

The gods, say the heathen mythologists, have each of them their favorite tree. Jupiter preferred the oak, Venus the myrtle, and Phoebus the laurel; Cybele the pine, and Hercules the poplar. Minerva, continues the mythologist, surprised that they should choose barren trees, asked Jupiter the reason. It is, said he, to prevent any suspicion that we confer the honor we do them, for the sake of their fruit. Let folly suspect what it pleases, returned Minerva; I shall not scruple to acknowledge that I make choice of the olive for the usefulness of its fruit. O daughter, replied the father of the gods, it is with justice that men esteem thee wise; for nothing is truly valuable that is not useful.

Whatever fancy may determine, the standing value of all things is in proportion to their use.

⚜ 414 ⚜
THE TWO SPRINGS

Two Springs which issued from the same mountain, began their course together; one of them took her way in a silent and gentle stream, while the other rushed along with a sounding and rapid current. Sister, said the latter, at the rate you move, you will probably be dried up before you advance much farther; whereas, for myself, I will venture a wager, that within two or three hundred furlongs I shall become navigable, and after distributing commerce and wealth wherever I flow, I shall majestically proceed to pay my tribute to the ocean: so farewell, dear sister, and patiently submit to your fate. Her sister made no reply; but calmly descending to the meadows below, increased her stream by numberless little rills, which she collected in her progress, till at length she was enabled to rise into a considerable river; while the proud stream, which had the vanity to depend solely upon her own sufficiency, continued a shallow brook, and was glad at last to be helped forward, by throwing herself into the arms of her despised sister.

There is more to be expected from sedate
and silent, than from noisy, turbulent
and ostentatious beginnings.

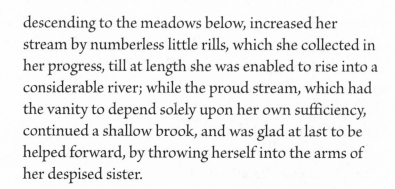

৺ 415 ৶

THE HERMIT AND THE BEAR

A certain Hermit having done a good office to a Bear, the grateful creature was so sensible of his obligation, that he begged to be admitted as the guardian and companion of his solitude. The Hermit willingly accepted his offer; and conducting him to his cell, they passed their time together in an amicable manner. One very hot day, the Hermit having laid him down to sleep, the officious Bear employed himself in driving away the flies from his friend's face. But in spite of all his care, one of the flies perpetually returned to the attack, and at last settled upon the Hermit's nose. Now I shall have you, most certainly, said the Bear;

and with the best intentions imaginable, gave him a violent blow on the face, which very effectually indeed demolished the fly, but at the same time mangled in a most shocking manner his benefactor's face.

The random zeal of inconsiderate friends is often as hurtful as the wrath of enemies.

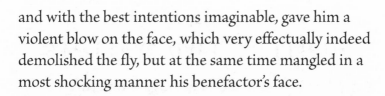

416

THE PEACOCK

The Peacock, who at first was distinguished only by a crest of feathers, preferred a petition to Juno that he might be honored also with a train. As the bird was a particular favorite, Juno readily enough assented; and his train was ordered to surpass that of every fowl in the creation. The Minion, conscious of his superb appearance, thought it requisite to assume a proportionable dignity of gait and manners. The common poultry of the farmyard were quite astonished at his magnificence; and even the pheasants themselves beheld him with an eye of envy.—But when he attempted to fly, he perceived himself to have sacrificed all his activity to ostentation; and that he was encumbered by the pomp in which he placed his glory.

The parade and ceremony belonging to the great are often a restraint upon their freedom and activity.

⚜ 417 ⚜
JUPITER'S TWO WALLETS

When Jupiter made Man, he gave him two wallets—one for his neighbor's faults, the other for his own. He threw them over the Man's shoulder, so that one hung in front and the other behind. The Man kept the one in front for his neighbor's faults, and the one behind for his own; so that while the first was always under his nose, it took some pains to see the latter. This custom, which began thus early, is not quite unknown at the present day.

One can always see his neighbor's
faults more easily than his own.

⚜ 418 ⚜
THE COCK AND THE HORSES

A Cock once got into a stable, and went about nestling and scratching in the straw among the Horses, who every now and then would stamp and fling out their heels. So the Cock gravely set to work to admonish them. "Pray, my good friends, let us have a care," said he, "that we don't tread on one another."

Disinterested counsel is rare.

419

THE GOURD AND THE PINE

A Gourd was planted close beside a large, well-spread Pine. The season was kindly, and the Gourd shot itself up in a short time, climbing by the boughs and twining about them, till it topped and covered the tree itself. The leaves were large, and the flowers and fruit fair, insomuch that the Gourd, comparing itself with the Pine, had the assurance to value itself above it. "Why," said the Gourd, "you have been more years growing to this stature than I have been days." "Well," replied the Pine, "but after the many winters and summers that I have endured, the many blasting colds and parching heats, you see me the very same thing that I was so long ago. But when you once come to the proof, the first blight or frost shall bring down that pride of yours, and strip you of all your glory."

Time tests merit.

420

THE WOLF IN SHEEP'S CLOTHING

A Wolf, wrapping himself in the skin of a Sheep, by that means got admission into a sheepfold, where he devoured several of the young Lambs. The Shepherd, however, soon found him out and hung him up to a tree, still in his disguise. Some other Shepherds passing that way thought it was a Sheep hanging, and cried to their friend, "What, brother! is that the way you serve Sheep in this part of the country?" "No, friends," cried he, turning the hanging body around so that they might see what it was; "but it is the way to serve Wolves, even though they be dressed in Sheep's clothing."

The credit got by a lie lasts only
till the truth comes out.

❧ 421 ☙

THE PORCUPINE
AND THE SNAKES

A Porcupine, seeking for shelter, desired some Snakes to give him admittance into their cave. They accordingly let him in, but were afterwards so annoyed by his sharp, prickly quills, that they repented of their hospitality, and asked him to withdraw and leave them their hole to themselves. "No," said he, "you may quit the place if you don't like it; for my part, I am very well satisfied where I am."

Be cautious in your choice of friends.

⚘ 422 ⚘
THE TRAVELERS
AND THE OYSTER

As two Men were walking by the seaside at low water, they saw an Oyster, and both stooped at the same time to pick it up. One pushed the other away, and a dispute ensued. A third Traveler coming along at the time, they determined to refer the matter to him, which of the two had the better right to the Oyster. While each was telling his story, the Arbitrator gravely took out his knife, opened the Shell, and loosened the Oyster. When they had finished, and were listening for his decision, he just as gravely swallowed the Oyster, and offered them each a Shell. "The Court," said he, "awards you each a Shell. The Oyster will cover the costs."

Those who seek justice must pay for it.

⚘ 423 ⚘
THE FOX AND THE COCK

A Fox, passing early one summer's morning near a farmyard, was caught in a trap which the farmer had planted there for that purpose. A Cock saw at a distance what had happened, and hardly daring to trust himself too near so dangerous a foe, approached him cautiously and peeped at him, not without considerable fear. Reynard saw him, and in his most bewitching manner addressed him as follows: "See, dear cousin," said he, "what an unfortunate accident has befallen me here! and, believe me, it is all on your account. I was creeping through yonder hedge, on my way homeward, when I heard you crow, and resolved, before I went any farther, to come and ask after your health. On the way I met with this disaster. Now if you would but run to the house and bring me a pointed stick, I think I could force it into this trap and free myself from its grip. Such a service, believe me, I should not soon forget." The Cock ran off and soon came back, not without the stick. But it was carried in the hand of the sturdy farmer, to whom he had told the story, and who lost no time in putting it out of Master Fox's power to do any harm for the future.

Use discrimination in your charities.

◁ 424 ▷

MERCURY AND THE TRAVELER

A Man, about to depart upon a long journey, prayed to the god Mercury, who was anciently supposed to speed Travelers, to give him good voyage and a safe return. He promised Mercury that, if he would grant his request, he would give the god half of everything he might find on his road. Soon after he set forth, he found a bag of dates and almonds, which some passerby had

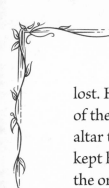

lost. He ate all but the stones of the dates and the shells of the almonds at once. These he laid upon a wayside altar to the god; praying him to take notice that he had kept his promise. "For," said he, "here are the insides of the one, and the outsides of the other, and that makes up your half of the booty."

A promise-breaker is never at a loss for an excuse.

❧ 425 ☙
THE APE AND THE BEE

An Ape, who, having a great desire to partake of the honey which was deposited in a rich Beehive, but was intimidated from meddling with it by having felt the smart of the sting, made the following reflection: "How strange, that a Bee, while producing a delicacy so passing sweet and tempting, should also carry with him a sting so dreadfully bitter!" "Yes," answered the Bee, "equal to the sweetness of my better work is the bitterness of my sting when my anger is provoked."

Beware how you arouse the patient man.

❦ 426 ❧

THE SPANISH CAVALIER

One day a quarrel happened about a lady, between a Spanish Cavalier and a Dutchman. Satisfaction was the word, and they met to decide the dispute: the contest was fierce and bloody, for they closed at the first encounter; and the Don, being mortally wounded, fell down; and cried out to an intimate of his who was running to his assistance, but too late: "My dear friend! for the love of Heaven, be so good as to bury me before anybody strips me." Having said this, so great a quantity of blood flowed from his wound, that he died immediately. Now this odd request of the Spaniard to his friend raised everybody's curiosity (as it generally happens in things prohibited) to see him naked, especially since it was the dying request and entreaty of a worthy hero of that wise nation, who never speak at random, nor drop a word that is not full of mysteries, and each mystery full of sense; so that everyone had a great desire to know the meaning of it; and, in spite of all his friend could do to prevent it, he was stripped immediately; and upon search, this spruce blade, who was completely dressed *a la Cavalier*, and with a curious ruff about his neck worth more than all the rest of his finery, was found—to have never a shirt to his back: at which the spectators could not help smiling, although the event was so pitiable.

Vanity prefers honor to life.

⊰ 427 ⊱

THE PLAYFUL ASS

An Ass climbed up to the roof of a building, and, frisking about there, broke in the tiling. The owner went up after him, and quickly drove him down, beating him severely with a thick wooden cudgel. The Ass said, "Why, I saw the Monkey do this very thing yesterday, and you all laughed heartily, as if it afforded you very great amusement."

Those who do not know their right
place must be taught it.

⊰ 428 ⊱

THE MASTIFF AND
THE CURS

A noble Mastiff, that guarded the village where he lived against robbers, was one day walking with one of his Puppies by his side, when all the little Dogs in the street gathered about him and barked at him. The Puppy was so enraged at this insult, that he asked his father why he did not fall upon them and tear them to pieces. To which the Mastiff answered, with great composure of mind, "If there were no Curs, I should be no Mastiff."

Nobility is its own defense.

⚜ 429 ⚜
THE LION AND THE FROG

The Lion hearing an odd kind of a hollow voice, and seeing nobody, started up. He listened again; the voice continued, and he shook with fear. At last seeing a Frog crawl out of the lake, and finding that the noise proceeded from that little creature, he crushed it to pieces with his feet.

Braggarts come to ill ends.

⚜ 430 ⚜
THE THRUSH AND THE FOWLER

A Thrush was feeding on a myrtle tree, and did not move from it, on account of the deliciousness of its berries. A Fowler observing her staying so long in one spot, having well birdlimed his reeds, caught her. The Thrush, being at the point of death, exclaimed, "O foolish creature that I am! For the sake of a little pleasant food I have deprived myself of my life."

Do not lose sight of the future in the present.

◁ 431 ▷
THE TRAVELERS
AND THE CROW

S ome Travelers setting out on a journey had not proceeded far, when a one-eyed Crow flew across their path. This they took for a bad omen, and it was proposed that they should give up their plan for that day, at least, and turn back again. "What nonsense!" said one of the Travelers, who was of a mocking and merry disposition. "If this Crow could foresee what is to happen to us, he would be equally knowing on his own account; and in that case, do you think he would have been silly enough to go where his eye was to be knocked out of his head?"

Common sense is better than auguries.

ᘓ 432 ᘔ

THE GOAT AND THE LION

The Lion seeing a Goat skipping about in high glee upon a steep craggy rock, called to him to come down upon the green pasture where he would be able to feed in much greater comfort. The Goat, who saw through the design of the Lion, replied, "Many thanks for your advice, dear Lion, but I wonder whether you are thinking more of my comfort, or how you would relish a nice morsel of Goat's flesh."

Interested advice is dangerous.

ᘓ 433 ᘔ

THE FLEA AND THE WRESTLER

A Flea settled upon the bare foot of a Wrestler, and bit him; on which he called loudly upon Hercules for help. The Flea a second time hopped upon his foot, when he groaned and said, "O Hercules! if you will not help me against a Flea, how can I hope for your assistance against greater antagonists?"

Help yourself in the little things, and
Fortune will help you in the greater.

⚜ 434 ⚜
THE HEN AND THE FOX

A Fox, having crept into a henhouse, looked up and down for something to eat, and at last spied a Hen sitting upon a perch so high, that he could by no means reach her. He therefore had recourse to an old stratagem. "Dear cousin," said he to her, "how do you do? I heard that you were ill, and kept at home; I could not rest, therefore, till I had come to see you. Pray let me feel your pulse. Indeed, you do not look well at all." He was running on in this impudent manner, when the Hen answered him from the roost, "Truly, dear Reynard, you are in the right. I was seldom in more danger than I am now. Pray excuse my coming down; I am sure I should catch my death if I were to." The Fox, finding himself foiled, made off and tried his luck elsewhere.

Craft can be answered with craft.

◁ 435 ▷

THE HUNGRY CAT AND THE PIGEONS

A certain Man brought up a Cat, which he fed but sparingly, and the poor animal, being very ravenous and not contented with her ordinary food, was wont to hunt about in every corner for more. One day, passing by a dovecote, she saw some young Pigeons that were scarcely fledged, and her mouth watered for a taste of them. To gratify her taste at once she climbed up into the dovecote, never caring to find out whether the master was in the way or not. But no sooner did the owner of the Birds see the Cat enter than he shut the doors and stopped up all the holes where she might get out again; and having caught the thieving Puss red-handed he hanged her up at the corner of the pigeon-house. Soon after the Cat's Master passed that way, and seeing his Cat, exclaimed, "Unfortunate creature, hadst thou been contented with thy meaner food, thou hadst not now been in this condition!"

Insatiable gluttons are the procurers
of their own untimely ends.

⚜ 436 ⚜
THE ANGLER AND THE SALMON

An Angler, on the margin of a river, was fishing for a smaller kind of fish, and therefore had furnished himself with such delicate tackle, that his hook was fixed to one single hair. Now it chanced that he hooked a large Salmon, which he concluded would have proved the destruction of his slender apparatus: however, by a judicious management, he so gently played with his prey in giving it way, and avoiding any act of violence, that at last he fairly conquered this huge fish, and drew it safely to the shore, exhausted by its own ineffectual efforts to get free. Thus the large Salmon had not strength enough to resist the power of a single hair.

Much may be done by a patient and prudent conduct where violence or strength would fail.

⚜ 437 ⚜
THE NIGHTINGALE AND HIS CAGE

A Nightingale, which belonged to a person of quality, was fed every day with plenty of choice dainties, and kept in a stately cage. Yet, notwithstanding this happy condition, he was uneasy, and envied the condition of those birds who lived free in the woods, and hopped up and down, unconfined, from bough to bough. He earnestly longed to lead the same life, and secretly pined because his wishes were denied him. After some time, however, it happened that the door of his cage was left unfastened, and the long-wished-for opportunity was given him of making his escape. Accordingly, out he flew, and hid himself among the shades of a neighboring wood, where he thought to spend the remainder of his days in contentment. But, alas! the poor bird was mistaken; a thousand evils which he never dreamed of attended this elopement of his, and he was now really that miserable creature which before he had been only in imagination. The delicate food which he used to eat was no more; he did not even know how to provide for himself, and was even ready to die with hunger. A storm of rain, thunder, and lightning filled all the air, and he had no place of safety; his feathers were wetted with the heavy shower, and he was almost blinded with the flashes of lightning. His tender nature could not withstand the severe shock; he even died under it. But just before he breathed his last he is said to have made this reflection: "Ah, were I but in my cage again, I would never wander more."

The grass is not always greener on the other side of the fence.

❧ 438 ☙

THE WOLVES AND THE SICK ASS

An Ass being sick, the report of it was spread abroad in the country, and some did not hesitate to say that she would die before the night was over. Upon this, several Wolves came to the stable where she lay, and rapping at the door inquired how she did. The young Ass thrust her head out the window, and told them that her mother was much better than they desired.

Words reveal wishes.

❧ 439 ☙

THE SNIPE SHOOTER

As a Sportsman ranged the fields with his gun, attended by an experienced old Spaniel, he happened to spring a Snipe; and, nearly at the same instant, a covey of Partridges. Surprised at the accident, and divided in his aim, he fired too indiscriminately, and by this means missed them both. Ah, my good Master, said the Spaniel, you should never have two aims at once. Had you not been dazzled and seduced by the extravagant hope of bringing down a Partridge, you would most probably have secured your Snipe.

We often miss our point by dividing our attention.

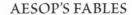

❧ 440 ❧
THE GEESE AND THE CRANES

A flock of Geese and a covey of Cranes used to feed together in a wheat field, where the grain was just ripening for harvest. One day the owner of the field came up and surprised them. The Cranes were thin and light, and easily flew away. But the Geese were heavy and fat, and many of them were caught.

Many criminals go unpunished.

⚜ 441 ⚜

THE SHEPHERD
AND THE SHEEP

A Shepherd, driving his Sheep to a wood, saw an oak of unusual size, full of acorns, and spreading his cloak under the branches, he climbed up into the tree, and shook down the acorns. The Sheep eating them carelessly tore the cloak. The Shepherd coming down, and seeing what was done, said: "O you ungrateful creatures! You provide wool to make garments for all other men, but you destroy the clothes of him who feeds you."

Carelessness is a form of ingratitude.

⚜ 442 ⚜

THE MASTER AND
HIS SCHOLAR

As a Schoolmaster was walking upon the bank of a river, not far from his School, he heard a cry, as of someone in distress. Running to the side of the river, he saw one of his Scholars in the water, hanging by the bough of a willow. The boy, it seems, had been learning to swim with corks, and fancying that he could now do without them, had thrown them aside. The force of the stream hurried him out of his depth, and he would certainly have been drowned, had not the friendly branch of a willow hung in his way. The Master took up the corks, which were lying upon the bank, and threw them to his Scholar. "Let this be a warning to you," said he, "and in your future life never throw away your corks until you are quite sure you have strength and experience enough to swim without them."

Too great assurance is folly.

⚜ 443 ⚜

THE SORCERESS

Night and silence had now given repose to the whole world; when an old, ill-natured Sorceress, in order to exercise her infernal arts, entered into a gloomy wood, that trembled at her approach. The scene of her horrid incantations was within the circumference of a large circle; in the center of which an altar was raised, where the hallowed vervain blazed in triangular flames, while the mischievous hag pronounced the dreadful words, which bound all hell in obedience to her charms. She blows a raging pestilence from her lips into the neighboring folds; the innocent cattle die, to afford a fit sacrifice to the infernal deities. The moon, by powerful spells drawn down from her orbs, enters the wood; legions of spirits from Pluto's realms appear before the altar, and demand her pleasure. Tell me, said she, where I shall find what I have lost, my favorite little dog.

How!—cried they all, enraged—Impertinent Beldame! must the order of nature be inverted, and the repose of every creature disturbed, for the sake of thy little dog?

There are numbers of people who would unhinge the world to ease themselves of the smallest inconvenience.

◁ 444 ▷
THE FOX AND THE WOLF

A Wolf who lived in a cave, having laid in a good store of food, kept himself very close, and set to work to enjoy it. A Fox, who missed the Wolf from his usual haunts, at last found out where he was, and, under pretense of asking after his health, came to the mouth of the cave and peeped in. He expected to be asked inside to dinner, but the Wolf gruffly said that he was far too ill to see anybody. So the Fox trotted off again, in anything but a charitable state of mind. Away he went to a Shepherd, and told the Man to get a good stick and come with him, and he would show him where to find a Wolf. The Shepherd came accordingly, and killed the Wolf. The Fox took possession of the cave and its stores. But he did not long enjoy the fruits of his treachery, for the Man, passing by that way a few days after, looked into the cave, and seeing the Fox there, killed him too.

He who brings mischief invites mischief.

◁ 445 ▷
THE BEAR AND THE BEEHIVES

A Bear that had found his way into a garden where Bees were kept, began to turn over the Hives and devour the honey. He paid no attention to the first Bees which came to attack him; or to the threats from others. But finally the Bees settled in swarms about his head, and stung his eyes and nose so much, that, maddened with pain, he tore the skin from his head with his own claws.

Despise not little things.

◁ 446 ▷
THE HARE AFRAID OF HIS EARS

The Lion being once badly hurt by the horns of a Goat, went into a great rage, and swore that every animal with horns should be banished from his kingdom. Goats, Bulls, Rams, Deer, and every living thing with horns had quickly to be off on pain of death. A Hare, seeing from his shadow how long his ears were, was in great fear lest they should be taken for horns. "Good-bye, my friend," said he to a Cricket who, for many a long summer evening, had chirped to him where he lay dozing: "I must be off from here. My ears are too much like horns to allow me to be comfortable." "Horns!" exclaimed the Cricket, "do you take me for a fool? You no more have horns than I have." "Say what you please," replied the Hare, "were my ears only half as long as they are, they would be quite long enough for any one to lay hold of who wished to make them out to be horns."

Avoid the appearance of evil.

◁ 447 ▷

THE EAGLE, THE JACKDAW, AND THE MAGPIE

The kingly Eagle kept his court with all the formalities of state, which was duly attended by all his plumed subjects in their highest feathers. But these solemn assemblies were frequently disturbed by the impertinent conduct of two, who assumed the importance of highfliers, and these were none other than the Jackdaw and the Magpie, who were forever contending for precedence which neither of them would give up to the other. The contest ran so high that at

length they mutually agreed to appeal to the sovereign
Eagle for his decision in this momentous affair.
The Eagle gravely announced that he did not wish
to make any invidious distinction by deciding to the
advantage of either party, but would give them a rule by
which they might determine it between themselves. "In
the future," said he, "the greater fool shall always take the
lead; but which of you it may be, I leave you to settle."

Be not great in your own eyes, lest
someone else deem you a fool.

◁ 448 ▷

THE TAIL OF THE SERPENT

The Tail of a Serpent once rebelled against the Head,
and said that it was a great shame that one end
of any animal should always have its way, and drag
the other after it, whether it was willing or no. It was
in vain that the Head urged that the Tail had neither
brains nor eyes, and that it was in no way made to lead.
Wearied by the Tail's importunity, the Head one day
let him have his will. The Serpent now went backwards
for a long time, quite gaily, until he came to the edge of
a high cliff, over which both Head and Tail went flying,
and came with a heavy thump on the shore beneath.
The Head was never again troubled by the Tail with a
word about leading.

Let those lead who are best fitted to lead.

❧ 449 ☙

THE WOLF AND THE MASTIFF

A Wolf who was almost skin and bone—so well did the Dogs of the neighborhood keep guard—met, one moonshiny night, a sleek Mastiff, who was, moreover, as strong as he was fat. The Wolf would gladly have supped off him, but saw there would first be a great fight, for which, in his condition, he was not prepared; so, bidding the Dog good night very humbly, he praised his good looks. "It would be easy for you," replied the Mastiff, "to get as fat as I am, if you liked. Quit this forest, where you and your fellows live so wretchedly, and often die with hunger. Follow me, and you shall fare much better." "What shall I have to do?" asked the Wolf. "Almost nothing," answered the Dog; "only chase away the beggars, and fawn upon the folks of the house. You will, in return, be paid with all sorts of nice things—bones of fowls and pigeons—to say nothing of many a friendly pat on the head." The Wolf, at the picture of so much comfort, nearly shed tears of joy. They trotted off together, but, as they went along, the Wolf noticed a bare spot on the Dog's neck. "What is that mark?" said he. "Oh, nothing," said the Dog. "How nothing?" urged the Wolf. "Just the merest trifle," answered the Dog; "the collar which I wear when I am tied up is the cause of it." "Tied up!" exclaimed the Wolf, with a sudden stop; "tied up! Can you not always, then, run where you please?" "Well, not quite always," said the Mastiff; "but what can that matter?" "It

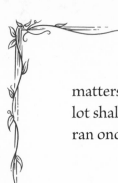

matters so much to me," rejoined the Wolf, "that your lot shall not be mine at any price;" and leaping away, he ran once more to his native forest.

Liberty is priceless.

⚜ 450 ⚜

THE RED-BREAST AND THE SPARROW

As a Red-breast was singing on a tree by the side of a rural cottage, a Sparrow perched upon the thatch took occasion thus to reprimand him: And dost thou, said he, with thy dull autumnal note, presume to emulate the Birds of Spring? Can thy weak warblings pretend to vie with the sprightly accents of the Thrush and Blackbird? with the various melodies of the Lark or Nightingale? whom other birds far thy superiors, have long been content to admire in silence? Judge with candor at least, replied the Robin; nor impute those efforts to ambition solely, which may sometimes flow from the love of art. I reverence, indeed, but by no means envy, the birds whose fame has stood the test of ages. Their songs have charmed both hill and dale, but their season is past, and their throats are silent. I feel not, however, the ambition to surpass or equal them; my efforts are of a much humbler nature, and I may surely hope for pardon, while I endeavor to

cheer these forsaken valleys, by an attempt to imitate the strains I love.

*Imitation may be pardonable, where
emulation would be presumptuous.*

◁ 451 ▷
THE LOBSTERS

I t chanced on a time that the shell of a boiled Lobster was thrown on the seashore, where it was quickly espied by one of the same tribe, who, young, ignorant, and vain, viewed it with admiration and delight. "See," said she, addressing her mother, who was at her side; "behold the beauty of one of our family, thus decked out in noble scarlet, so rich in color that no coral can surpass it in brilliancy! I shall have no rest till I am equally as fine, and have ceased to see myself the dingy object I am at present." "Vain creature!" replied the mother; "know that this same tawdry finery which you so earnestly covet was only acquired by death. And learn from this terrible example to be humble and content, obscure and safe."

*Fine feathers are a sign neither of
wealth nor of happiness.*

⚜ 452 ⚜
THE KID ON THE HOUSETOP

A kid climbed up onto the roof of an outhouse, attracted by the grass and other things that grew in the thatch; and as he stood there browsing away, he caught sight of a wolf passing below, and jeered at him because he couldn't reach him. The wolf only looked up and said, "I hear you, my young friend; but it is not you who mock me, but the roof on which you are standing."

⚜ 453 ⚜
THE FOX WITHOUT A TAIL

A fox once fell into a trap, and after a struggle managed to get free, but with the loss of his brush. He was then so much ashamed of his appearance that he thought life was not worth living unless he could persuade the other foxes to part with their tails

also, and thus divert attention from his own loss. So he called a meeting of all the foxes, and advised them to cut off their tails. "They're ugly things anyhow," he said, "and besides they're heavy, and it's tiresome to be always carrying them about with you." But one of the other foxes said, "My friend, if you hadn't lost your own tail, you wouldn't be so keen on getting us to cut off ours."

Misery loves company.

❧ 454 ❧
THE EAGLE AND THE OWL

The Eagle and the Owl, after many quarrels, swore that they would be friends forever, and that they would never harm each other's young ones. "But do you know my little ones?" said the Owl. "If you do not, I fear it will go hard with them when you find them." "No, I have never seen them," replied the Eagle. "The greater your loss," said the Owl; "they are the sweetest, prettiest things in the world. Such dear eyes! such charming plumage! such winning little ways! You'll know them, now, from my description." A short time after, the Eagle found the little Owls in a hollow tree. "These hideous, staring frights, at any rate, cannot be neighbor Owl's fine brood," said he; "so I may make away with them without the least misgiving." So saying he made a meal of them. The Owl, finding her young ones gone, loaded the Eagle with reproaches. "Nay," answered the Eagle, "blame yourself rather than me. If you paint with such flattering colors, it is not my fault if I do not recognize your portraits."

Love should not blind truth.

❧ 455 ❧
THE OAK AND THE WILLOW

A conceited Willow had once the vanity to challenge his mighty neighbor the Oak, to a trial of strength.

It was to be determined by the next storm, and Aeolus was addressed by both parties, to exert his most powerful efforts. This was no sooner asked than granted; and a violent hurricane arose: when the pliant Willow, bending from the blast, or shrinking under it, evaded all its force; while the generous Oak, disdaining to give way, opposed its fury, and was torn up by the roots. Immediately the Willow began to exult, and to claim victory: when thus the fallen Oak interrupted his exultation: "Callest thou this a trial of strength? Poor wretch! not to thy strength, but weakness; not to thy boldly facing danger, but meanly skulking from it, thou owest thy present safety. I am an oak, though fallen; thou still a willow, though unhurt; but who, except so mean a wretch as thyself, would prefer an ignominious life, preserved by craft or cowardice, to the glory of meeting death in a brave contention?"

The courage of meeting death in an honorable cause is more commendable than any address or artifice we can make use of to evade it.

◁ 456 ▷
THE BEE AND THE SPIDER

The Bee and the Spider once entered into a warm debate which was the better artist. The Spider urged her skill in the mathematics; and asserted that no one was half so well acquainted as herself with the

construction of lines, angles, squares, and circles; that
the web she daily wove was a specimen of art inimitable
by any other creature in the universe; and besides,
that her works were derived from herself alone, the
product of her own bowels; whereas the boasted honey
of the Bee was stolen from every herb and flower of the
field; nay, that she had obligations even to the meanest
weeds. To this the Bee replied, that she was in hopes
the art of extracting honey from the meanest weeds,
would at least have been allowed her as an excellence;
and that as to her stealing sweets from the herbs and
flowers of the field, her skill was there so conspicuous,
that no flower ever suffered the least diminution of its
fragrance from so delicate an operation. Then, as to the
Spider's vaunted knowledge in the construction of lines
and angles, she believed she might safely rest the merits
of her cause on the regularity alone of her combs; but
since she could add to this the sweetness and excellence
of her honey, and the various purposes for which her
wax was employed, she had nothing to fear from a
comparison of her skill with that of the weaver of a
flimsy cobweb; for the value of every art, she observed,
is chiefly to be estimated by its use.

Neither ingenuity nor learning is entitled
to regard but in proportion as they
contribute to the happiness of life.

❧ 457 ❧

THE CROW AND THE SHEEP

A troublesome Crow seated herself on the back of a Sheep. The Sheep, much against his will, carried her backward and forward for a long time, and at last said, "If you had treated a Dog in this way, you would have had your deserts from his sharp teeth." To this the Crow replied, "I despise the weak, and yield to the strong. I know whom I may bully, and whom I must flatter; and I thus prolong my life to a good old age."

The contemptible will ever be imposed upon.

❧ 458 ❧

THE MONSTER IN THE SUN

An Astronomer was observing the Sun through a telescope, in order to take an exact draught of the several spots, which appear upon the face of it. While he was intent upon his observations, he was on a sudden surprised with a new and astonishing appearance; a large portion of the surface of the Sun was at once covered by a monster of enormous size and horrible form; it had an immense pair of wings, a great number of legs, and a long and vast proboscis; and that it was alive was very apparent, from his quick and violent motions, which the observer could from time to time plainly perceive. Being sure of the fact (for

how could he be mistaken in what he saw so clearly?)
our Philosopher began to draw many surprising
conclusions from premises so well established. He
calculated the magnitude of this extraordinary animal,
and found that he covered about two square degrees
of the Sun's surface; that placed upon the earth he
would spread over half one hemisphere of it; and
that he was seven or eight times as big as the moon.
But what was most astonishing, was the prodigious
heat that he must endure; it was plain, that he was
something of the nature of the salamander, but of a far
more fiery temperament; for it was demonstrable from
the clearest principles, that in his present situation
he must have acquired a degree of heat two thousand
times exceeding that of red hot iron. It was a problem
worth considering, whether he subsisted upon the
gross vapors of the Sun, and so from time to time
cleared away those spots which they are perpetually
forming, and which would otherwise wholly obscure
and incrustate its face; or whether it might not feed
on the solid substance of the orb itself, which by this
means, together with the constant expense of light,
must soon be exhausted and consumed; or whether he
was not now and then supplied by the falling of some
eccentric Comet into the Sun. However this might be,
he found by computation that the earth would be but
short allowance for him for a few months; and farther,
it was no improbable conjecture, that, as the earth
was destined to be destroyed by fire, this fiery flying
Monster would remove hither at the appointed time,
and might much more easily and conveniently effect a
conflagration, than any Comet, hitherto provided for

that service. In the earnest pursuit of these, and many the like deep and curious speculations, the Astronomer was engaged, and was preparing to communicate them to the public. In the meantime, the discovery began to be much talked of, and all the virtuosi gathered together to see so strange a sight. They were equally convinced of the accuracy of the observation, and of the conclusions so clearly deduced from it. At last, one, more cautious than the rest, was resolved, before he gave a full assent to the report of his senses, to examine the whole process of the affair, and all the parts of the instrument; he opened the Telescope, and behold! a small Fly was enclosed in it, which having settled on the center of the object-glass had given occasion to all this marvelous Theory. How often do men, through prejudice and passion, through envy and malice, fix upon the brightest and most exalted characters the grossest and most improbable imputations. It behooves us upon such occasions to be upon our guard, and to suspend our judgments; the fault perhaps is not in the object, but in the mind of the observer.

The fault we sometimes impute to a character is only to be found in the observer.

৬ 459 ৬

THE CONCEITED OWL

A young Owl having accidentally seen himself in a crystal fountain, conceived the highest opinion of his personal perfections. It is time, said he, that Hymen should give me children as beautiful as myself, to be the glory of the night, and the ornament of our groves. What pity would it be, if the race of the most accomplished of birds should be extinct for my want of a mate! Happy the female who is destined to spend her life with me! Full of these self-approving thoughts, he entreated the Crow to propose a match between him and the royal daughter of the Eagle. Do you imagine, said the Crow, that the noble Eagle, whose pride it is to gaze on the brightest of the heavenly luminaries, will consent to marry his daughter to you, who cannot so much as open your eyes whilst it is daylight? But the self-conceited Owl was deaf to all that his friend could urge; who after much persuasion, was at length prevailed upon to undertake the commission. His proposal was received in the manner that might be expected: the king of birds laughed him to scorn. However, being a monarch of some humor, he ordered him to acquaint the Owl, that if he would meet him the next morning at sunrise in the middle of the sky, he would consent to give him his daughter in marriage. The presumptuous Owl undertook to perform the condition; but being dazzled with the sun, and his head growing giddy, he fell from his height upon a rock; from whence being pursued by a flight of birds, he was glad at last to make his escape into the hollow of an old oak, where he passed the remainder of his days in that obscurity for which nature designed him.

Schemes of ambition, without proper talent, always terminate in disgrace.

❦ 460 ❧

THE CROW AND THE MUSSEL

A Crow, having found a Mussel on the seashore, took it in his beak, and tried for a long time to break the shell by hammering it upon a stone. Another Crow—a sly old fellow—came and watched him for some time in silence. "Friend," said he at last, "you'll never break it in that way. Listen to me. This is the way to do it: Fly up as high as you can, and let the thing fall upon a rock. It will be smashed then, sure enough, and you can eat it at your leisure." The simpleminded Crow did as he was told, flew up and let the Mussel fall. Before he could descend to eat it, however, the other Bird had pounced upon it and carried it away.

Beware of interested advisers.

❦ 461 ❧

THE MASTIFF AND THE GOOSE

A Goose once upon a time took up her abode by a pond, which she immediately laid claim to. If any other animal, without the least design to offend, happened to pass that way, the Goose immediately flew at it. The pond, she said, was hers, and she would

maintain her right to it, and support her honor
while she had a bill to hiss, or a wing to flutter. In this
manner she drove away Ducks, Pigs, and Chickens, nay,
even the insidious Cat was seen to scamper. A Mastiff,
however, happened to pass by, and thought it no harm
if he should lap a little of the water, as he was thirsty.
"Get away!" hissed our valiant Keeper of the pond, as
soon as she saw him approaching. "Get away I tell you!
it's mine!" and she flew at him like a Fury, pecked at
him with her beak, and slapped him with her feathers.
The Mastiff grew angry, and had twenty times a mind
to give her a sly snap, but controlled his wrath, because
his Master was nigh. "You fool!" cried he. "Those who
have neither strength nor weapons to fight should at
least be civil." So saying, he quenched his thirst in spite
of the Goose, and followed his Master.

Arrogance inspires contempt.

❧ 462 ☙

THE MOTHER, THE NURSE, AND THE FAIRY

Give me a son!" The blessing sent, were ever parents
more content? How partial are their closing
eyes; no child is half so fair and wise. Waked to the
morning's pleasing care, the Mother rose, and sought
her heir. She saw the Nurse, like one possessed, with
wringing hands and sobbing breast. "Sure some disaster

has befell: speak, Nurse, I hope the boy is well." "Dear Madam, think me not to blame, invisible the Fairy came: your precious babe is hence conveyed, and in its place a changeling laid. Where are the father's mouth and nose, the mother's eyes, as black as sloes? See here, a shocking, awkward creature, that speaks a fool in every feature." "The woman's blind," the Mother cries, "I see wit sparkle in his eyes." "Lord, Madam, what a squinting leer! No doubt the Fairy has been here." Just as she spoke, a pigmy Sprite pops through the keyhole, swift as light; perched on the cradle's top he stands and thus her folly reprimands: "Whence sprung the vain, conceited lie, that we the world with fools supply? What! give our sprightly race away, for the dull, helpless sons of clay! Besides, by partial fondness shown, like you, we dote upon our own. Where yet was ever found a mother who'd give her baby for another? And should we change for human breed, well might we pass for fools indeed."

A mother's love is blind.

⊰ 463 ⊱
THE ENVIOUS GLOWWORM

A humble Glowworm lying in a garden was moved with envy on seeing the effect of lights from a brilliant chandelier in a neighboring palace, and in a melancholy mood complained of the comparative feebleness of his own splendor. When his companion, who was more sagacious than himself, checked his murmurs by saying, "Wait a little, have patience, and observe the event": when, after a short time, the light was seen no more, and the palace was left in total darkness. "Now," continued his mate, "you see we have outlasted those many glaring lights, which, though brighter for a time, yet hasten the more quickly to nothing."

The meteors of Fashion rise and fall.

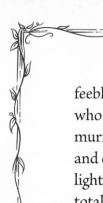

◁ 464 ▷
THE MICE AND THE TRAP

Once upon a time some Mice saw a bit of toasted bacon hanging up in a very little room, the door of which, being open, enticed them to fall to work on the dainty morsel with greedy appetites. But two or three of them took particular notice that there was but one way into the room, and, therefore, but one way to get out of it; so that if the door by misfortune or art should chance to be shut, they would all inevitably be taken. They could not, therefore, bring themselves to enter, but said that they would rather content themselves with homely fare in plenty, than for the sake of a dainty bit run the risk of being taken and lost forever. The other Mice, however, declared that they saw no danger, and ran into the room and began to eat the bacon with great delight. But they soon heard the door fall down, and saw that they were all taken. Then the fear of approaching death so seized them, that they found no relish for the delicious food, but stood shivering and fasting until the Cook who had set the Trap came and put an end to them. The wise Mice, who had contented themselves with their usual food, fled into their holes, and by that means preserved their lives.

He who enters a business should see his way out of it.

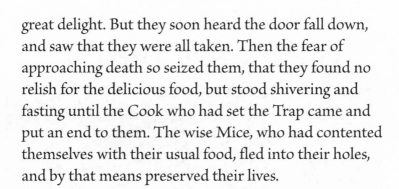

⁕ 465 ⁕

THE LION AND THE SNAKE

A lordly Lion, who was seeking for his prey, by chance saw a Snake basking in the sun, when, being rather sharp-set by hunger, and disappointed in his object, he, with a haughty air, spurned the reptile with his paw, as not being agreeable to his stomach. But the enraged Snake turned on him, and gave him a mortal sting, and said: "Die, imperious tyrant! and let thy example show that no power can always save a despot, and that even reptiles have rights."

The tyrant lays himself open to attack.

❧ 466 ❧

THE CAT AND THE FOX

The Cat and the Fox were once talking together in the middle of a forest. "Let things be never so bad," said Reynard, "I don't care; I have a hundred tricks to escape my enemies, if one should fail." "I," replied the Cat, "have but one; if that fails me, I am undone." "I am sorry for you," said the Fox. "You are truly to be pitied; and if you were not such a helpless creature, I'd give you one or two of my tricks. As it is, I suppose each must shift for himself." Just then a pack of Hounds burst into view. The Cat, having recourse to her one means of defense, flew up a tree, and sat securely among the branches, from whence she saw the Fox, after trying his hundred tricks in vain, overtaken by the Dogs and torn in pieces.

One thing well learned brings safety.

◁ 467 ▷

THE SPANIEL AND
THE MASTIFF

A good-natured Spaniel overtook a surly Mastiff
as he was traveling upon the high road. Tray,
although a complete stranger to Tiger, very civilly
accosted him; and if it would be no intrusion, he
said, he should be glad to bear him company on his
way. Tiger, who happened not to be altogether in so
growling a mood as usual, accepted the proposal, and
they very amicably pursued their journey together.
In the midst of their conversation they arrived at the
next village, where Tiger began to display his ugly
temper by an unprovoked attack upon every Dog he
met. The villagers immediately sallied forth with great
indignation to rescue their pets; and falling upon our
two friends without distinction or mercy, poor Tray
was most cruelly treated for no other reason but his
being found in bad company.

*Much of every man's good or ill fortune
depends upon his choice of friends.*

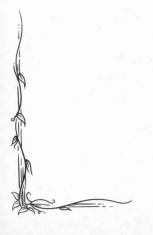

❦ 468 ❧
THE ELEPHANT AND THE ASSEMBLY OF ANIMALS

The wise Elephant, whose efforts were always directed towards the benefit of his society, saw with much concern the many abuses among the Beasts, which called loudly for reform. He therefore assembled them, and, with all due respect and humility, began a long sermon, wherein he spoke plainly to them about their vices and bad habits. He called their attention especially to their idle ways; their greed, cruelty, envy, hatred, treachery, and deceit. To many of his auditors this speech was excellent and they listened with open-mouthed attention, especially such as the innocent Dove, the faithful Dog, the obedient Camel, the harmless Sheep, and the industrious Ant; the busy Bee also approved much of this lecture. Another part of the audience were extremely offended, and could scarcely endure so long an oration; the Tiger, for instance, and the Wolf were exceedingly tired, and the Serpent hissed with all his might, while a murmur of disapprobation burst from the Wasp, the Drone, the Hornet, and the Fly. The Grasshopper hopped disdainfully away from the assembly, the Sloth was indignant, and the insolent Ape mimicked the orator. The Elephant, seeing the tumult, concluded his discourse with these words: "My advice is addressed equally to all, but remember

that those who feel hurt by any remarks of mine acknowledge their guilt. The innocent are unmoved."

It is the bit dog that howls.

✤ 469 ✤

THE PARROT

A certain Widower, in order to amuse his solitary hours, and in some measure supply the conversation of his departed helpmate of loquacious memory, determined to purchase a Parrot. With this view he applied to a dealer in birds, who showed him a large collection of Parrots of various kinds. While they were exercising their talkative talents before him, one repeating the cries of the town, another asking for a cup of sack, and a third bawling out for a coach, he observed a green Parrot, perched in a thoughtful manner at a distance upon the foot of a table. And so you, my grave gentleman, said he, are quite silent. To which the Parrot replied, like a philosophical bird, I think the more. Pleased with this sensible answer, our Widower immediately paid down his price, and took home the bird; conceiving great things from a creature, who had given so striking a specimen of his parts. But after having instructed him during a whole month, he found to his great disappointment, that he could get nothing more from him than the fatiguing repetition of the same dull sentence, I think the more. I find, said

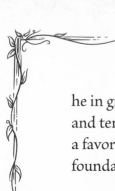

he in great wrath, that thou art a most invincible fool, and ten times more a fool was I, for having formed a favorable opinion of thy abilities upon no better foundation than an affected solemnity.

Gravity, though sometimes the mien of wisdom, is often found to be the mask of ignorance.

◁ 470 ▷
THE TWO FOXES

Two Foxes once found their way into a hen-roost, where they killed the Cock, the Hens, and the Chickens, and began to feed upon them. One of the Foxes, who was young and inconsiderate, was for devouring them all upon the spot; the other, who was old and covetous, proposed to reserve some of them for another time. "For experience, child," said he, "has made me wise, and I have seen many unexpected events since I came into the world. Let us provide therefore, against what may happen, and not consume all our stores at one meal." "All this is wondrous wise," replied the young Fox, "but for my part I am resolved not to stir until I have eaten as much as will serve me a whole week; for who would be mad enough to return hither, where it is certain the owner of these fowls will watch for us, and if he catch us, will put us to death?" After this short discourse, each pursued his own scheme. The young Fox ate till he burst himself, and had scarcely strength enough to reach his hole before he died. The old one who thought it much better to deny his appetite for the present, and lay up provision for the future, returned the next day, and was killed by the farmer. Thus the young one came to grief through greed, and the old one through avarice.

Every age has its peculiar vice.

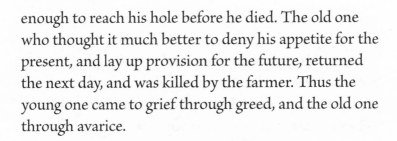

⚜ 471 ⚜

THE OSTRICH AND THE PELICAN

The Ostrich one day met the Pelican, and observing her breast all bloody, Good, God! says she to her, what is the matter? What accident has befallen you? You certainly have been seized by some savage beast of prey, and have with difficulty escaped from his merciless claws. Do not be surprised, friend, replied the Pelican; no such accident, nor indeed anything more than common, hath happened to me. I have only been engaged in my ordinary employment of tending my nest, of feeding my dear little ones, and nourishing them with the vital blood from my bosom. Your answer, returned the Ostrich, astonishes me still more than the horrid figure you make. What, is this your practice, to tear your own flesh, to spill your own blood, and to sacrifice yourself in this cruel manner to the importunate cravings of your young ones? I know not which to pity most, your misery or your folly. Be advised by me: have some regard for yourself, and leave off this barbarous custom of mangling your own body; as for your children, commit them to the care of providence, and make yourself quite easy about them. My example may be of use to you. I lay my eggs upon the ground, and just cover them lightly over with sand; if they have the good luck to escape being crushed by the tread of man or beast, the warmth of the sun broods upon, and hatches them, and in due time my young ones come forth; I leave them to be nursed by nature, and fostered by the elements; I give myself no trouble about them, and I neither know nor care what becomes of them. Unhappy wretch, says the Pelican, who hardenest thyself against thy own offspring, and through want of natural affection renderest thy travail fruitless to thyself! who knowest not the sweets of a parent's anxiety; the tender delights of a mother's sufferings! It is not I, but thou, that art cruel to thy own flesh. Thy insensibility may exempt thee from a temporary inconvenience, and an inconsiderable pain, but at the same time it makes thee inattentive to a most necessary duty, and incapable of relishing the pleasure that attends it; a pleasure, the most exquisite that nature hath indulged to us; in which pain itself is swallowed up and lost, or only serves to heighten the enjoyment.

The pleasures of parental fondness make large amends for all its anxieties.

◁ 472 ▷

SOCRATES AND HIS FRIENDS

S ocrates once built a house, and everybody who saw it had something or other to say against it. "What a front!" said one. "What an inside!" said another. "What rooms! not big enough to turn round in," said a third. "Small as it is," answered Socrates, "I wish I had true Friends enough to fill it."

Houses are easier to get than friends.

◁ 473 ▷

THE FARMER AND HIS THREE ENEMIES

A Wolf, a Fox, and a Hare happened to be foraging, one evening, in different parts of a farm. Their first effort was pretty successful, and they returned in safety to their several quarters; however, not so happy as to be unperceived by the Farmer's watchful eye, who, placing several kinds of snares, made each of them his prisoner in the next attempt. He first took the Hare to task, who confessed she had eaten a few turnip-tops, merely to satisfy her hunger; besought him piteously to spare her life, and promised never to enter his grounds again. He then accosted the Fox, who, in a fawning, obsequious tone, protested that he came into his premises through no other motive than pure good nature, to restrain the Hares and other vermin from the plunder of his corn; and that, whatever evil tongues might say, he had too great a regard both for him and justice to be in the least capable of any dishonest action. He last of all examined the Wolf, as to the business that brought him. The Wolf boldly declared that it was with a view of destroying his Lambs, to which he had an undoubted right; that the Farmer himself was the only felon, who robbed the community of Wolves of what was meant to be their proper food. That this, at least, was his opinion; and whatever fate attended him, he should not scruple to risk his life in the pursuit of his lawful prey. The Farmer, having heard their pleas, determined the cause in the following manner: "The Hare," said he, "deserves compassion for the penitence she shows, and the humble confession she has made. As for the Fox and the Wolf, let them be hanged together; their crimes deserve it, and are heightened by their hypocrisy and impudence."

The wrongdoer can obtain forgiveness most easily by confessing his sin.

◁ 474 ▷

THE FOX, THE WOLF, AND THE HORSE

A Fox seeing a Horse for the first time, grazing in a field, at once ran to a Wolf of his acquaintance, and described the animal that he had found. "It is, perhaps," said the Fox, "some delicious prey that fortune has put in our path. Come with me, and judge for yourself." Off they ran, and soon came to the Horse, who, scarcely lifting his head, seemed little anxious to be on speaking terms with such suspicious-looking characters. "Sir," said the Fox, "your humble servants wish to learn the name by which you are known to your illustrious friends." The Horse, who was not without a ready wit, replied that his name had been curiously written upon his hoofs for the information of those who cared to read it. "Gladly would I," replied the sly Fox, suspecting in an instant something wrong, "but my parents were poor, and could not pay for my education: hence, I never learned to read. The family of my companion here, on the contrary, are great folk, and he can both read and write, and has a thousand other accomplishments." The Wolf, pleased with the flattery, at once went up, with a knowing air, to examine one of the hoofs which the Horse raised for his convenience; and when he had come near enough, the Horse gave a sudden and vigorous kick, and back to earth fell the Wolf, his jaw broken and bleeding. "Well, cousin," cried the Fox, with a grin, "you need never ask for the name a second time, now that you have it written so plainly just below your eyes."

Curiosity and conceit come to grief.

◁ 475 ▷

THE OLD TROUT, THE YOUNG TROUT, AND THE SALMON

A Fisherman, in the month of May, stood angling on the bank of a river with an artificial fly. He threw his bait with so much art that a Young Trout was rushing towards it, when she was prevented by her mother. "Stop, child!" said she, "never be too hasty where there is a possibility of danger. Take due time to consider, before you risk an action that may be fatal. How do you know whether that is indeed a fly, or the snare of an enemy? Let someone else make the experiment before you. If it be a fly, he will very probably elude the first attack, and then the second may be made, if not with success, at least with safety." She had no sooner uttered this caution than a Salmon seized upon the pretended fly, and was captured.

Do not rush into a strange position.

❧ 476 ❧

THE WOLF TEACHING
THE FOX

Said the Fox to the Wolf, one day, "My friend, you have no idea how badly I often fare. A horribly tough old Cock, or a lean and shriveled Hen, is a kind of food of which it is quite possible in time to get tired. Now, it seems to me that you live a good deal better than I do, and don't run into so much danger either. I have to go prowling about the houses: you get your prey in the fields. Teach me your business. Let me be the first of my race to have a fat Sheep whenever I wish. Teach me, there's a good fellow, and you shall find yourself no loser in the end." "I will," said the Wolf; "and, by-the-by, I have just lost a brother. You will find his body over yonder. Slip into his skin, and come to me again." The Fox did as he was told, and the Wolf gave him many a lesson in growling, biting, fighting, and deportment, which the Fox executed first badly, then fairly, and in the end quite as well as his master. Just then a flock of Sheep came in sight, and into the midst of them rushed the new-made Wolf, with such fury and noise that Shepherd Boy, Dog, and Sheep fled in terror to gain their home, leaving only one poor Sheep behind, that had been seized by the throat. Just at that instant a Cock in the nearest farm crowed loud and shrill. There was no resisting the familiar sound. Out of the Wolf's skin slipped the Fox, and made towards the Cock as fast as he could, forgetting in a moment his lessons, the Sheep, the Professor, and everything

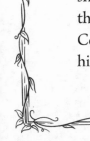

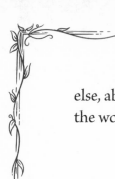

else, about which he had just been making all the fuss in the world.

Training cannot overcome nature.

◁ 477 ▷

THE CORMORANT
AND THE FISHES

A Cormorant whose eyes were become so dim with age, that he could not discern his prey at the bottom of the waters, bethought himself of a stratagem to supply his wants. Hark you, friend, said he, to a Gudgeon whom he observed swimming near the surface of a certain canal, if you have any regard for yourself or your brethren, go this moment and tell them from me, that the owner of this piece of water is determined to drag it a week hence. The Gudgeon immediately swam away, and made his report of this terrible news to a general assembly of the fish: who unanimously agreed to send him back as their ambassador to the Cormorant. The purport of his commission was to return him their thanks for the intelligence; and to add their entreaties, that, as he had been so good as to inform them of their danger, he would be graciously pleased to put them into a method of escaping it. That I will, most readily, returned the artful Cormorant, and assist you with my best services into the bargain. You have only to collect yourselves

together at the top of the water, and I will undertake to transport you safely one by one to my own residence, by the side of a solitary pool, to which no creature but myself ever found the way. The project was perfectly well approved by the unwary fish, and with great expedition executed by the deceitful Cormorant; who having placed them in a shallow water, the bottom of which his eye could easily discern, they were all devoured by him in their turns, as his hunger or his luxury required.

It is extreme folly to ask advice of an interested adviser.

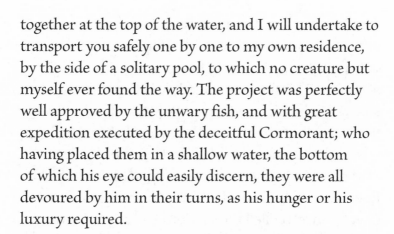

⪦ 478 ⪧

THE LION, THE BEAR, THE MONKEY, AND THE FOX

The tyrant of the forest issued a proclamation, commanding all his subjects to repair immediately to his royal den. Among the rest, the Bear made his appearance; but pretending to be offended with the steams which issued from the monarch's apartments, he was imprudent enough to hold his nose in his majesty's presence. This insolence was so highly resented, that the Lion in a rage laid him dead at his feet. The Monkey, observing what had passed, trembled for his carcass, and attempted to conciliate favor by the most abject flattery. He began with protesting, that for his part, he thought the apartments were perfumed with

Arabian spices, and exclaiming against the rudeness
of the Bear, admired the beauty of his majesty's paws,
so happily formed, he said, to correct the insolence
of clowns. This fulsome adulation, instead of being
received as he expected, proved no less offensive than
the rudeness of the Bear, and the courtly Monkey
was in like manner extended by the side of Sir Bruin.
And now his majesty cast his eye upon the Fox. Well,
Reynard, said he, and what scent do you discover here?
Great prince, replied the cautious Fox, my nose was
never esteemed my most distinguishing sense, and
at present I would by no means venture to give my
opinion, as I have unfortunately got a terrible cold.

*It is often more prudent to suppress our
sentiments than either to flatter, or to rail.*

⚜ 479 ⚜

MINERVA AND THE OWL

My most solemn and wise bird, said Minerva one
day to her Owl, having hitherto admired you
for your profound taciturnity, I have now a mind for
variety, to hear you display your parts in discourse;
for silence is only admirable in one who can, when he
pleases, triumph by his eloquence, and charm with
graceful conversation. The Owl replied by solemn
grimace, and made dumb signs. Minerva bid him lay
aside that affectation, and begin; but he only shook his

wise head, and remained silent. Whereupon Minerva, provoked with this mimicry of wisdom, commanded him to speak immediately on pain of her displeasure. When the Owl, seeing no remedy, draws up close to Minerva, and whispers very softly in the ear this sage remark: "That since the world has grown so depraved, they ought to be esteemed most wise who have eyes to see, and wit to hold their tongues."

A busy tongue makes the mind repent at leisure, but silence is a gift without peril.

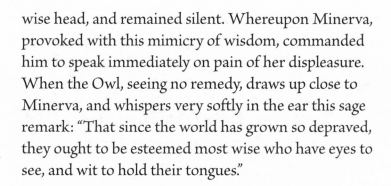

480

THE SNAIL AND THE STATUE

A Statue of the Medicean Venus was erected in a grove sacred to beauty and the fine arts. Its modest attitude, its elegant proportions, assisted by the situation in which it was placed, attracted the regard of every delicate observer. A Snail, who had fixed himself beneath the molding of the pedestal, beheld with an evil eye the admiration it excited. Wherefore, watching his opportunity, he strove, by trailing his filthy slime over every limb and feature, to obliterate those beauties which he could not endure to hear so much applauded. An honest linnet, however, who observed him at his dirty work, took the freedom to assure him that he would infallibly lose his labor: For although, said he, to an injudicious eye, thou mayst sully the

perfections of this finished piece; yet a more accurate and close inspector will admire its beauty, through all the blemishes with which thou hast endeavored to disguise it.

It is the fate of envy to attack even those characters which are superior to its malice.

⚜ 481 ⚜
THE MULES AND THE ROBBERS

Two Mules were being driven along a lonely road. One was laden with Corn and the other with Gold. The one that carried the Gold was so proud of his burden that, although it was very heavy, he would not for the world have the least bit of it taken away. He trotted along with stately step, his bells jingling as he went. By-and-by, some Robbers fell upon them. They let the Mule that carried the Corn go free; but they seized the Gold which the other carried, and, as he kicked and struggled to prevent their robbing him, they stabbed him to the heart. In dying, he said to the other Mule, "I see, brother, it is not always well to have grand duties to perform. If, like you, I had only served a Miller, this sad state would not now be mine."

Do not flatter yourself simply because you carry a little gold.

◁ 482 ▷

JUPITER AND THE ANIMALS

Jupiter one day, being in great good-humor, called upon all living things to come before him, and if, looking at themselves and at one another, there should be in the appearance of any one of them anything which admitted of improvement, they were to speak of it without fear. "Come, Master Ape," said he, "you shall speak first. Look around you, and then say, are you satisfied with your good looks?" "I should think so," answered the Ape; "and have I not reason? If I were clumsy like my brother the Bear, now, I might have something to say." "Nay," growled the Bear, "I don't see that there's much to find fault with in me; but if you could manage to lengthen the tail and trim the ears of our friend the Elephant, that might be an improvement." The Elephant, in his turn, said that he had always considered the Whale a great deal too big to be comely. The Ant thought the Mite so small as to be beneath notice. Jupiter became angry to witness so much conceit, and sent them all about their business.

Think not of yourself more highly
than of your neighbors.

⚜ 483 ⚜

THE TRUMPETER
TAKEN PRISONER

U pon the defeat of an army in battle, a Trumpeter
was taken prisoner. The Soldiers were about to
put him to death, when he cried, "Nay, gentlemen, why
should you kill me? This hand of mine is guiltless of
a single life." "Yes," replied the Soldiers; "but with that
braying instrument of yours you incite others, and you
must share the same fate as they."

Those who aid are as guilty as those who do evil.

⚜ 484 ⚜
The Miser and the Magpie

As a Miser sat at his desk counting over his heaps of gold, a Magpie, which had escaped from its cage, picked up a coin and hopped away with it. The Miser, who never failed to count his money over the second time, immediately missed the piece, and rising up from his seat in the utmost consternation, observed the thief hiding it in a crevice in the floor. "And are you," cried he, "that worst of thieves, who has robbed me of my gold, without the plea of necessity and without regard to its proper use? Your life shall atone for so great a villainy!" "Soft words, good master," replied the Magpie; "have I, then, injured you in any other sense than you defraud the public? And am I not using your money in the same way that you do? If I must lose my life for hiding a single coin, pray what do you deserve, who secrete so many thousands?"

Remember your own infirmities when correcting those of others.

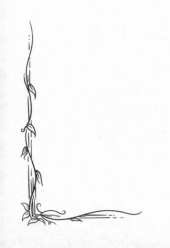

◁ 485 ▷

THE FLY IN ST. PAUL'S CUPOLA

As a Fly was crawling leisurely up one of the columns of St. Paul's Cupola, she often stopped, surveyed, examined, and at last broke forth into the following exclamation. Strange! that anyone who pretended to be an artist, should ever leave so superb a structure, with so many roughnesses unpolished! Ah, my friend! said a very learned architect, who hung in his web under one of the capitals, you should never decide of things beyond the extent of your capacity. This lofty building was not erected for such diminutive animals as you or me; but for a certain sort of creatures, who are at least ten thousand times as large; to their eyes, it is very possible, these columns may seem as smooth, as to you appear the wings of your favorite Mistress.

We should never estimate things beyond our reach
by the narrow standards of our own capacities.

◁ 486 ▷

THE TOAD AND THE MAYFLY

As some workmen were digging marble in a mountain of Scythia, they discerned a toad of an enormous size in the midst of a solid rock. They were very much surprised at so uncommon an appearance, and the more they considered the circumstances of

it, the more their wonder increased. It was hard to
conceive by what means this creature had preserved
life and nourishment in so narrow a prison; and still
more difficult to account for his birth and existence in
a place so totally inaccessible to all of his species. They
could conclude no other, than that he was formed
together with the rock in which he had been bred,
and was coeval with the mountain itself. While they
were pursuing these speculations the Toad sat swelling
and bloating, till he was ready to burst with pride and
self-importance; to which at last he thus gave vent:
—Yes, says he, you behold in me a specimen of the
Antediluvian race of animals. I was begotten before
the flood; and who is there among the present upstart
race of mortals, that shall dare to contend with me in
nobility of birth or dignity of character? A Mayfly,
sprung that morning from the river Hypanis, as he was
flying about from place to place, chanced to be present,
and observed all that passed with great attention and
curiosity. Vain boaster, says he, what foundation hast
thou for pride, either in thy descent, merely because it
is ancient; or thy life, because it hath been long? What
good qualities hast thou received from thy ancestors?
Insignificant even to thyself, as well as useless to others,
thou art almost as insensible as the block in which thou
wast bred. Even I, that had my birth only from the
scum of the neighboring river, at the rising of this
day's sun, and who shall die at its setting, have more
reason to applaud my condition, than thou hast to
be proud of thine. I have enjoyed the warmth of the
sun, the light of the day, and the purity of the air; I
have flown from stream to stream, from tree to tree,

and from the plain to the mountain; I have provided for posterity, and shall leave behind me a numerous offspring to people the next age of tomorrow; in short, I have fulfilled all the ends of my being, and I have been happy. My whole life, it is true, is but of twelve hours; but even one hour of it is to be preferred to a thousand years of mere existence; or that have been spent, like thine, in sloth, ignorance, and stupidity.

A lazy reliance on the antiquity of a family is, by far, less honorable than an honest industry.

⚜ 487 ⚜

THE TRAVELERS AND THE CHAMELEON

Two Travelers happened on their journey to be engaged in a warm dispute about the Chameleon, which, as you know, changes its color. One of them affirmed it was blue, that he had seen it with his own eyes upon the naked branch of a tree, feeding on the air in a very clear day. The other strongly asserted it was green, and that he had viewed it very closely and minutely upon the broad leaf of a fig tree. Both of them were positive, and the dispute was rising to a quarrel; but a third person luckily coming by, they agreed to refer the question to his decision. "Gentlemen," said the arbitrator, with a smile of great self-satisfaction, "you could not have been more lucky in your reference,

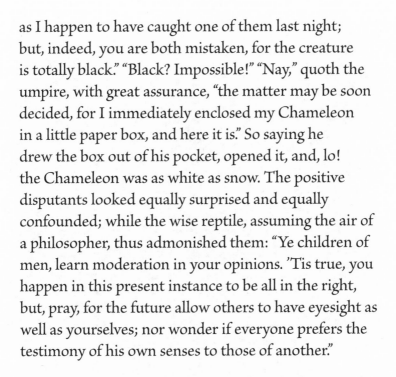

as I happen to have caught one of them last night; but, indeed, you are both mistaken, for the creature is totally black." "Black? Impossible!" "Nay," quoth the umpire, with great assurance, "the matter may be soon decided, for I immediately enclosed my Chameleon in a little paper box, and here it is." So saying he drew the box out of his pocket, opened it, and, lo! the Chameleon was as white as snow. The positive disputants looked equally surprised and equally confounded; while the wise reptile, assuming the air of a philosopher, thus admonished them: "Ye children of men, learn moderation in your opinions. 'Tis true, you happen in this present instance to be all in the right, but, pray, for the future allow others to have eyesight as well as yourselves; nor wonder if everyone prefers the testimony of his own senses to those of another."

Have respect for the opinions of others.